WITCH ON THIRD

A Jinx Hamilton Mystery

Book Six

Also by Juliette Harper

WITCH ON THIRD

A Jinx Hamilton Mystery

BOOK SIX

JULIETTE HARPER

Skye House Publishing, LLC
4517 Ranch View Road
Fort Worth, TX 76109

Edited by Patricia Pauletti

Print ISBN: 978-1-943516-77-3

First Edition: December 2016

DEDICATION

"And above all, watch with glittering eyes the whole world around you because the greatest secrets are always hidden in the most unlikely places. Those who don't believe in magic will never find it."

Roald Dahl, *The Minpins*

PROLOGUE

The storm boiled up out of the north at dusk, splitting the skies over Briar Hollow, North Carolina with crackling tendrils of lightning. Seemingly oblivious to the fury raging over their heads, four women stood in the center of the town square with hands clasped. As one, they sent their magic skyward, finding and harnessing a single bolt to do their bidding.

In the intensity of that moment, they didn't know that smaller bolts also answered the call, crashing to earth on the slopes of the neighboring mountains. One of those strikes angled toward a lonely corner of the local cemetery. It sought out the weathervane crowning a forgotten crypt. At impact, the electricity engulfed the crumbling structure in a static web that found and flowed through even the tiniest cracks.

As quickly as the crescendo built, the weather stilled. The clouds parted revealing a full moon. A single beam of light falling through the high, round window atop the crypt wall illuminated a chessboard sitting on the floor.

The pieces carved to represent musical notations, cast long, distorted shadows in the dust. One by one, they fell to the side until only the white king stood upright. Then, as if lifted by an unseen hand, the lone chessman rose six inches in the air, hanging suspended for several seconds

1

before descending with a resounding thud.

Miles away in Raleigh, a man looked up from the pages of his book and smiled. "Well," he said, "there you are."

ONE

Six weeks ago I made a promise to a dying man. I kept my word, even though he had no right to ask anything of me. Anton Ionescu cursed my mother, forced my infant brother into exile, and hired a hitman to go after me and everyone I love. Most folks would argue that I didn't owe the man a blessed thing.

They'd be wrong.

Earlier that summer, thanks to an irresponsible bit of magic, I raised Anton's daughter and niece from their graves—as vampires. Anton died thinking they'd been freed from that curse. I thought the same thing until the next night at the Halloween carnival when they came strolling by my table on the courthouse lawn.

That appearance in itself created an obvious problem, but there's more. The two girls were arm in arm with a Creavit wizard named Irenaeus Chesterfield who has been working against my family for thirty years.

At the time, all I saw was a man in white tie and tails and two women dressed as Victorian hookers. I thought they were going for a kind of Jack the Ripper/*Phantom of the Opera* costume vibe.

Then my costume had a violent reaction to the sighting.

It may not have been the most creative decision, but I

went to the carnival as a witch. My Barbie-sized friend, Glory Green, came with me the only way she could without being obvious—plastered flat on the crown of my pointy hat. That, and the ability to fly on her broom, are Glory's only real powers.

So, to be perfectly accurate, Glory was the one who reacted violently. She began to shake so hard I had to put my hand on the hat to keep it from tumbling to the ground.

Chesterfield cursed Glory to live a miniature existence as a stereotypical green-faced witch. Then he sent her into the store I run with my best friend, Tori Andrews, to act as a spy. Glory is on our side now, but she lives in constant terror that Chesterfield will capture and punish her.

That night, however, the wizard and the two women with him didn't threaten Glory or me in any way. They were already past us when Glory told me the man was Chesterfield.

As I watched, the trio crossed the street and paused long enough to look at me and remove their masks. That's when I recognized Seraphina and Ioana. Before I could do much more than stare, the three of them disappeared into thin air.

Speaking in a low, soothing tone, I said, "They're gone, Glory. He's not going to hurt us."

"Not now," she croaked, "but he'll be back."

"Yes," I said, behind my hand. "He will."

For the record, if people catch you talking to your hat in public, they tend to believe you've lost your mind.

"But after everything that happened yesterday, don't you think we can let the others enjoy the rest of the carnival? Don't we owe them that?"

Who are "the others?"

That's quite a shopping list—my parents, Tori's mother, a couple of agents with the Division for Grid Integrity, my ex-boyfriend/werecat protector, his father, a mostly solid ghost, a brownie, and a rat. Just stick with me here. If you don't know them already, you'll meet them pretty soon.

As Glory considered my words, the witch's hat grew still. "I owe you all everything," Glory said in a calmer voice. "I'm okay now."

Neither one of us believed that. I certainly wasn't "okay." Before Chesterfield and the girls showed up, I'd been lost in thought trying to assimilate the events of the last 24 hours. The point was to *act* okay.

From where I was sitting, I could see Mom and Gemma Andrews laughing together at the cake walk. Tori was volunteering in the face painting booth, and that ghost I mentioned, Colonel Beauregard T. Longworth, stood in the shadow of the Confederate monument talking to a group of tourists.

I can't even begin to tell you what a long week we'd had. Our most recent magic-related crisis coincided with the town's first annual paranormal festival. The event proved to be a huge success. The carnival amounted to a victory lap for the organizing committee and offered up some badly needed relaxation for my people. I didn't shatter that illusion until we all walked across the street to the store.

As I locked the front door, I glanced at my watch—just past midnight.

Dad yawned and stretched, announcing his attention to head straight to bed. I hated to do it, but I shook my head. "You can't," I said. "We all need to get down to the lair. Glory and I saw Chesterfield and the Strigoi Sisters this evening."

That's our nickname for Seraphina and Ioana. The Ionescu are a clan of transplanted Romanian Strigoi viu or, as I like to think of them, Vampires Lite. They feed on electricity, not blood. What happened to turn the girls into bloodsuckers? They weren't buried correctly after dying in a car crash—and I'm the one who woke them up. Go me.

My words froze everyone in place. All the air seemed to leave the room. Mom ultimately broke the silence. "Are you sure?" she asked.

"Totally," I said. "Glory recognized Chesterfield, and I saw Seraphina and Ioana."

"So what do we do now?" Gemma asked.

"You all head downstairs," I said, taking out my phone. "I'm going to call Chase and Festus. I'll be down in a minute."

Even though he's my ex, Chase McGregor and I don't actually get to be completely "off." We still have to work together. He and his father, Festus, are werecats pledged to protect the witches in my family.

Chase answered on the first ring. "What is it?" he asked. "Did something happen tonight?"

When Chase told me he intended to skip the carnival, I understood. Attending the same function in a small town when we were no longer together was still too awkward for him. Honestly, the last few months had been hard on Chase. When he guarded my Aunt Fiona, the work amounted to eating chocolate chip cookies and lending a hand with minor repairs around the shop. Then I took over—without a clue how to be part of the magical world—and everything became much more complicated.

Chase knows the hierarchy of things as well as anyone. Technically, he works for me, but in the first few months of my new life, I let him call a lot of the shots. As my confidence grew and I began to exercise my role as a leader, Chase wasn't ready for the change. Frankly, he acted like a jerk.

Finally, Festus set his son straight in front of everyone, a scene that made me feel genuinely bad for Chase. I know his heart is in the right place, and I know he's in love with me.

Unfortunately, there's a taboo against werecats and witches getting together. The magics are incompatible, and during our short relationship, we even had to face a crazy werecat half-breed, Malcolm Ferguson, who tried to kill us. Granted, he was a claw for hire in the employ of Anton Ionescu, but Malcolm brought loads of personal enthusiasm to the assignment.

Chase had been grappling with frustration, a wounded ego, and a hurting heart. But *he* made the decision about the breakup without even talking to me. I wanted to tackle those hurdles. He couldn't take the pressure.

The relationship drama coincided with major events that left me no time to sit around and moon over a broken heart, although there were plenty of crying nights. For whatever sympathy I might feel for him, Chase had to live with the consequences of his choices the same way I did and get on with life.

Truthfully, I hadn't even considered for me that might include another guy. Then Lucas Grayson showed up. And get this—he's assigned to protect me, too. He and Chase were bound to butt heads anyway, but there is a pre-existing tension between them I still don't understand.

Lucas works for the Division of Grid Integrity, an agency which serves the network of Mother Trees. (Don't worry if you don't know what that means. At the time, my understanding about the Grid was pretty sketchy, too. Just keep reading, and you'll learn at the same pace I did.)

Along with his partner, Greer MacVicar, Lucas has been running primary interference for me of late—and it doesn't take radar to see that the man is interested in me. If you'd asked me the night of the carnival, I would have said I *thought* I was interested in him, too, but that feeling came with a hearty dose of confusion.

At the same time that I was intrigued and flattered, I still missed Chase. But there's no sense in lying about it now. There is a real spark between Lucas and me.

But none of that changed the bottom line. We all had to function as a single team. I made it clear to Chase that my personal life was none of his business. Chesterfield and the Strigoi Sisters, however, *were* his business, which is why I called. Chase and Festus joined us in the lair in less than 5 minutes.

Chase's cobbler shop next door connects to our basement via a small passageway. The whole store sits atop a fairy mound that appears to be endless. When we go to Shevington, the Fae community that is Briar Hollow's direct counterpart in the magical Otherworld, the hike to the portal takes an hour. We've started using bikes to cut down on the travel time.

I think there's a similar passageway that runs next door to Amity Prescott's pottery shop and art gallery. We need to take a second here and talk about Amity.

She's also a witch and one of the few survivors of the now-defunct Briar Hollow coven. Oddly enough, however, Amity absented herself by choice from everything that happened around the paranormal festival and its aftermath.

At first her refusal to do more than help organize the event put me off. We needed all hands on deck. I said as much to Barnaby Shevington, the founder of the city that bears his name and its current (and only) lord high mayor. I recently discovered Barnaby is also my several times great-grandfather, but that's not something we'd discussed yet.

In response to my annoyance over Amity's absence, Barnaby said, "When her participation is needed, she will be there. Trust Amity's wisdom in this, and trust mine."

The answer didn't leave me much room to complain, but I will say for now that Barnaby was right. He usually is.

When Chase and Festus arrived in the lair, we all settled around the fire. The space, which serves as equal parts family room and command center, lies in a layer of reality known as the In Between that separates the realm of the humans and the Otherworld.

Festus headed straight for his favorite spot on the hearth, which also happened to be right by Greer's chair. Because he has a lame hip, Festus lives his life primarily as a yellow house cat, but that doesn't dim his appreciation for a beautiful red-haired Scotswoman.

As we watched, Festus turned in three tight circles, put his back to the fire, cleared his throat, and proceeded to drop a bombshell. Earlier that evening, from his perch in the cobbler shop window, Festus watched everything that happened with Chesterfield and the Strigoi Sisters.

"Dad!" Chase protested. "Did it ever enter your mind to call me?"

Festus fixed his son with a perfectly impassive feline glare. "No, it did not," he said. "The Creavit scum didn't do anything. After the week we've had, I thought it could wait, and apparently so did Jinx."

"Hold on," I said, "you *recognized* Chesterfield?"

Festus turned his eyes toward me. An old anger stirred in their amber depths. "Of course, I recognized him," he growled. "It's because of him I've been limping since 1936."

From one of the couches across the room, Gemma said, "You're certain you saw Seraphina and Ioana with Chesterfield?" She managed to stay calm, but the strained quality of the words and the pallor of her skin betrayed the depths of her fear.

"Yes," I said. "It was them."

"What if they go after Scrap again?" she asked.

A few days earlier Greer showed up at Andrews Lumber in neighboring Cotterville just in time to keep the

Strigoi Sisters from snacking on Tori's father, Howard "Scrap" Andrews.

Beside me, Tori started to her feet. "We have to find out if Dad is okay," she said, fighting to keep from sounding as panicked as she must have felt.

"Slow down," Greer said. "The GNATS drone is still watching your father. We would have known by now if anything had happened."

GNATS stands for "Group Network Aerial Transmission System." The tiny drones, each powered by a single grain of fairy dust, create the perfect juncture of magic and technology. No larger than the insect they're named after, the drones, under the command of Major Aspid "Ironweed" Istra of the Brown Mountain Fairy Guard, are our remote eyes.

"Can you show us?" Gemma asked, sounding a little steadier. "I'd be happier if I could see with my own eyes that Scrap is safe."

"Sure," Chase said, hitting the button to lower the big screen TV from its recessed niche in the ceiling above the fireplace. As the set came into place, he punched commands into his iPad to transfer the drone's video feed to the larger display.

Gemma instantly sat up. "That's not our house," she said. "There must be some mistake."

Chase studied the tablet in his hands. "There's no mistake," he said gently. "Scrap moved his things out of your house this afternoon. He's staying at Mrs. Llewellyn's Boarding House on Oak Street in Cotterville."

No one said anything. Gemma deflated, sinking back into the sofa. Mom put an arm around her shoulder. They'd gone to the carnival dressed as Lucy and Ethel. Mom wore a blue dress with big white polka dots and colored her dark hair flaming red with washout dye. Gemma engineered a credible imitation of Ethel's blonde permanent with my curling iron. Like their television idols, the two women had been best friends for as long as I could remember

"At least he's safe, Gem," Mom said. "You two will get this all sorted out."

The "all this" she referred to was the state of the Andrews' marriage. Mom had the good sense to tell my Dad about the magical world before they married. Even though Fae politics forced them to send their only son into exile as an infant, Dad accepted that part of my mother's identity because he loves her. For years she turned her back on magic, but now that she's back in the game—largely because of me—he supports that choice, too.

Gemma, on the other hand, never told her husband about her life as a witch and alchemist. When he found out, he didn't take the news well—and then pretty much lost his mind after a face-to-face counter with the Strigoi Sisters. Scrap's rejection extended to his daughter, which had left Tori, a true Southern daddy's girl, devastated. Mother and daughter were holding it together in the name of taking care of business, but barely.

Blinking back tears, Gemma said, "I'd still like to see for myself that Scrap is safe. Can the drone do that?"

Chase typed in a request to GNATS Ops Command. As we watched, the image of the boarding house grew larger. When the porch loomed into view, the pilot maneuvered along the left side of the house. He reached a cracked window, slipped through, and brought the surveillance craft near the ceiling.

The camera trained on Scrap sound asleep in bed. From the way his mouth opened and closed rhythmically, we could tell he was snoring. That put a tremulous smile on Gemma's face.

"I don't even need sound to know he's raising the roof," she said in a choked voice. "I've been listening to that man snore for 35 years. Will the drone keep watching him?"

"For as long as we need it to," Chase assured her. "We'll clear it with Barnaby, but I know he'll say yes."

"I appreciate that," Gemma said, still staring at the screen. "I'm mad enough at that man to wring his damned neck, but that doesn't mean I want anything to happen to him."

Thank God my mother laughed first, which gave the rest of us permission to do the same. "He's your husband," Mom said, "if he's going to get killed, you definitely get first dibs on doing the murder."

That's when Dad chimed in. He's been playing straight man for them forever. "Can I point out that as the only married man in the room, this conversation is starting to make me a little nervous?" he said.

Beau chortled. "I, too, once had a wife and I feared her wrath far more than any horror of the battlefield."

"Ditto," Festus said, raising his paw in agreement. "My Jenny knew how to put her claws out. She had a damned good aim, and I've got the scars on my backside to prove it."

He was sitting on the hearth between Lucas and Greer. Since I didn't know a lot about Lucas, I noticed that he grinned at the banter, but didn't say anything. I took that to mean he'd never been married. Even though we'd just met, I already understood that sometimes Lucas gives away a great deal more about himself when he says nothing.

"Quit your bellyaching, you scoundrels," Greer teased, making her eyes flash. "You're all lucky those good women agreed to marry the likes of any of you in the first place."

"Here, here," Beau agreed. "You could not be more correct, dear lady."

Dad caught Mom's free hand. "I never said I wasn't

lucky," he grinned, "just that I want to stay on your good side."

"You don't have anything to worry about," Mom said, pausing for the perfect amount of time before adding, "for now."

At that, all the men in the room roared with laughter. "She's got you there, Jeff," Festus said, looking fondly at my mother. "That's a Ryan woman for you."

In his long career, Festus has guarded both my mother, and my grandmother, Kathleen Allen Ryan. And honestly? I think he fell in love with both of them.

The good-natured teasing at the expense of the men present helped Gemma to regain her composure. When she asked the next, and perhaps most important question yet, her voice sounded strong and confidant.

"Let's get back to business," she said. "How did Seraphina and Ioana survive us dropping a lightning bolt on their heads?"

When we confronted the Strigoi Sisters the night before under the boiling clouds of a gathering storm, Anton temporarily distracted the girls with a taser. His gaze met mine and he told me what we needed to do to kill them. "Call down the lightning," he said. "It's the only way."

Apparently not.

Chase answered Gemma. "Good question," he said. "We kept the drones in place over the square tonight for good measure. First, let's all take a look at what Jinx and Dad saw."

He started to change the display, but Gemma stopped him. She had a strange look on her face.

"Before you switch the video," she said, "could you ask the drone pilot to zoom in on the dresser by Scrap's bed?"

"Sure," Chase said, tapping on the screen.

As we watched, the camera panned over the top of the

piece of furniture revealing a set of keys, a wristwatch, a wallet, and a bottle of *Obsession* perfume.

"Thank you," Gemma said briskly. "That's all I wanted to see."

I looked at Tori and raised an eyebrow in question. She shook her head. It wasn't until later, when we had a moment alone, that she told me Gemma doesn't wear *Obsession*. In fact, she hates the stuff.

Two

The drone's perspective gave us new insights into the evil trio's movements, in particular, the fact that they entered and exited from the same spot on the corner.

"Do you think there's a portal there?" Tori asked.

Greer held out her hand to Chase, who relinquished the tablet. She played the video frame-by-frame. When Chesterfield and the Strigoi Sisters became visible, the wizard appeared to be slipping a pocket watch into his white waistcoat.

Greer froze the screen. "There," she said. "Do you see that?"

"What?" I said. "The pocket watch?"

"Yes," Greer said. "Now, observe his behavior in this frame."

She fast-forwarded to the end of the video, slowing the speed again as Chesterfield and the Strigoi Sisters approached the corner to leave. This time, the wizard took the watch out of his pocket and paused long enough to fiddle with it.

"Is he setting the time?" Chase asked, squinting at the screen.

Greer zoomed in. The high-resolution camera yielded amazing detail. Chesterfield's watch had not one, but three winding crowns.

"That looks more like a stopwatch," Tori said. "Maybe he timed how long they stayed at the festival?"

From her perch on the arm of the sofa beside me, Glory spoke up. "It's not a stopwatch," she said. "Mr. Chesterfield built that pocket watch himself. I watched him do it. He's obsessed with clocks. They were all over his shop. At night, the ticking almost drove me crazy."

Greer pulled one of the chairs out from under the work table and turned it around. That put her more or less at eye level with Glory. "Can you tell us anything else about the watch?" she asked.

Closing her eyes as if she were trying to picture the timepiece, Glory said, "The case is gold, and there's a big, shiny diamond on the face up at the top where the number 12 should be. Then down on the right, these little windows cover up the place for the 3."

"How many little windows?" Greer prodded.

Glory counted on her fingers. "One, two, three, four . . . five," she said. "There are five."

It wasn't hard to imagine a watch showing month, day, and year, but what were the other two?

"When did Chesterfield begin to work on the watch?" Greer asked.

The little witch opened her eyes. "He had already started when I . . . when I, uh, moved in," Glory said. "But when he sent me over here, the watch wasn't finished. It was still sitting in this clamp thingy on his desk. You know, holding it steady while he worked."

"How often did he tinker with it?" Greer wanted to know.

"Oh, every night," Glory said, "but especially after he bought some new kind of clock. It was like he'd study the one he bought to get ideas for the pocket watch. Then, sometimes he'd be at his workbench until the sun came up."

Tori frowned. "You mean he sat there in the middle of his shop and played with the pocket watch where everyone could see him?"

"Oh, no," Glory said. "Nobody was ever allowed to go in Mr. Chesterfield's workroom. He didn't know that I could see through the little window up on top of the door."

"The transom?" Lucas said.

Glory nodded. "Yes, that's it. I knew it had a name. I could see right through the corner where the hinge opened up. The top of his workbench was just clear as day. Since I couldn't watch movies or TV, it was something to do." She glanced around uncertainly. "Did I do something good? Does what I saw help?"

The tiny woman's spare, but eloquent description of her lonely imprisonment on the side of the cup, coupled with her eagerness to contribute almost broke my heart. Don't be fooled by the way Glory talks, or her obsession with decades-old popular culture. She's plenty smart, but she's also guileless. Chesterfield would never hurt her again if I had anything to say about it.

Greer smiled at Glory, who couldn't help but flinch at the sharp canines studding the corners of the woman's dental work. Greer is baobhan sith, a form of Scottish vampire. She's every bit as much a bloodsucker as the Strigoi Sisters, but Greer long ago threw in her hand with the forces of order in the Fae world. She's one of the good guys.

"What you've told us is extremely important, Miss Green," Greer said. "I suspect we will be relying on you for more insights into Mr. Chesterfield's machinations."

Glory's face turned a deeper shade of emerald, which meant she was blushing. "You can call me Glory," she said shyly.

Greer extended one slender hand. "Thank you, Glory," she said. "I do hope we will become friends."

Hesitating for a second, Glory reached out and took

hold of Greer's index finger, giving it a delicate shake. "I'm sure we will," she said, looking up at the tall vampire with eyes gone round and wide. "You're just the most glamorous person I've ever met who wasn't on a movie screen or a magazine cover," Glory blurted out.

Greer rewarded the words with a radiant smile. "Thank you," she said. Then, leaning in conspiratorially, she added, "Perhaps, dear, we can work together on your wardrobe. This Barbara doll person with whose clothes they've burdened you may be quite popular, but her sense of style lacks a certain *je ne sais quoi.*"

"Barbie," Glory said earnestly. "Her name is Barbie. And not all her stuff is bad. Would you really help me pick things out that would make me look better?"

"Of course," Greer said. "We girls must stick together. We'll talk later."

For the rest of the meeting, Glory stared at Greer with rapt adoration. Before long, the rest of us would be staring at the baobhan sith, too, but for completely different reasons.

Greer stood up from her conversation with Glory, sliding the chair back under the table. Then she turned her attention to the room. "I cannot yet be certain," she said, "but I believe Chesterfield used that bespoke watch to activate a means of travel for himself and the Strigoi Sisters."

Tori frowned. "Be-what?" she asked.

"Bespoke," Beau supplied helpfully. "It means an item made to order for the customer."

"Correct, Colonel Longworth," Greer said. "A bespoke item is, in your vernacular, 'one of a kind.' If I am correct, this concept applies ten fold to Chesterfield's watch."

Lucas had been listening to his partner with a thoughtful expression. "You've put together a theory based on what he's been buying since 1936, haven't you?" he asked.

"I have," Greer said.

Oh, geez. Here we go again. I thought I had made my

feelings about being left out of the loop totally clear—several times.

"Hold on," I said. "You two are leaving some things out. Big things from the sound of it. How do you know what Chesterfield has been buying all these years?"

Shoving his fedora back on his head as if he knew I wasn't going to like what he was about to tell me, Lucas answered my question. "Okay," he said. "Confession time. After Brenna Sinclair used that miner's cap to break into your basement and had the Amulet of the Phoenix in her hot little hands, Barnaby asked the DGI to reassign us. We've spent the last few months trying to figure out why so many magical artifact trails seem to lead straight back to Irenaeus Chesterfield."

Out of the corner of my eye, I saw Chase smirk. He seemed to be enjoying the prospect of another man getting his ears pinned back for withholding information from me. I hated to disappoint him, but I didn't plan to fuel their little game of schoolyard tit for tat.

Still, I couldn't keep my voice from sounding terse when I said, "And you were going to share this with the class when?"

Lucas shot me a disarming grin. "Sorry, Teach," he said, "we weren't done with the unit on vampires yet."

That was a fair answer, and the grin didn't hurt his case. With his hat pushed up at a silly angle and a shock of unruly, dark bangs falling over his forehead, Lucas looked like one of those lovable scoundrels Clark Gable played in the 1930s. I know. Ancient reference, but I was raised by a classic film nut.

It's worth adding that for all I knew then, Lucas might have looked the same in the 1930s as he did now. So far, Lucas had denied being a wizard, alchemist, and werecat, but he wouldn't tell me anything else. Why did it matter, you ask?

Chase doesn't look a day over 35, but, thanks to his enhanced werecat metabolism, he's 85 years young. Festus will be 110 on his next birthday. Depending on his Fae race, Lucas might be as old or older. Definitely information I wanted to know if there was a chance we might get involved.

"It's more my fault than his," Greer said, loyally throwing herself under the bus for her partner. "I didn't have my thoughts in order, and Grayson here doesn't know enough about time to set his own watch, much less form a theory about someone else's."

"Hey!" Lucas cried with mock indignation. "I'm just too spontaneous to be forced into a rigid schedule."

"Sell it to someone who's buying, laddie," Greer grinned.

"Okay, fine," I conceded, "we were preoccupied with vampires, a subject that now seems to involve Chesterfield's pocket watch. So, what's the theory?"

"That Chesterfield time shifted himself in and out of the square this evening," Greer said, "he likely used the same ability to snatch Seraphina and Ioana from beneath the lightning bolt before it struck."

"But I heard them scream," I protested.

"Yes," Greer said, "but we don't know *why* they screamed. Was it from the fear of certain death falling from the sky or because an unseen hand was pulling them away?"

Those were questions I couldn't answer. It wasn't the first time Greer mentioned the idea of Chesterfield time shifting. The subject came up before the encounter with the Strigoi Sisters, as did the notion that he had used that power against us before. More on that in a minute.

"Okay," I sighed, "I guess we have to deal with this now. You told us Chesterfield has time shifting powers, but you didn't tell us he could use them on other people."

Greer fixed me with a bemused expression. "You watched *me* stop time on the courthouse square last night to protect a whole crowd of humans," she said.

She had me there.

"Stopping time and moving through it with other people in tow are different things," Gemma pointed out.

"Ah, that's true," Greer said, "but every time you step through a portal to Shevington, you're moving through time, and often in groups."

"Yes, but the portals occupy a fixed point," Gemma countered. "That's how they work. The gateways are anchored in time and space, so they don't disrupt the natural flow of the temporal streams they connect."

"Spoken like an alchemist," Greer said, "but you know as well as I do that where science and magic meet, many things that seem impossible within the laws of nature suddenly become possible."

Festus, who had been listening to the whole conversation behind closed eyelids, spoke up. "You aren't talking about moving forward and backward in time, are you?" he asked. "You think Chesterfield is making lateral jumps."

Well, score one for the yellow tomcat.

"Precisely," Greer said, "and that would be what makes Chesterfield's ability stand out. If he has, indeed, learned to navigate time in that fashion, it's a use of temporal magic unlike any we've seen before."

"You've lost me now," I said, shaking my head.

"Try to follow my line of reasoning," Greer said. "Can we agree that the same increments of time occur simultaneously in a given reality regardless of the corresponding physical space?"

I could already tell that temporal magic was going to give me a major headache, but so far I was keeping up. "I think so," I said, "but break that down for me a little more."

"A second, a minute, an hour—they're all experienced

concurrently by everyone within the stream of time," Greer explained, "but at different geographic locations."

That actually did make sense. "Okay, I'm with you," I said.

"Good," she said. "Now, consider this. What if the extra windows on Chesterfield's watch are designed to hold coordinates?"

Lucas whistled appreciatively. "Well, I'll be damned, Red," he said. "You've figured out how to connect the dots in the inventory."

"What inventory?" I asked impatiently. "You're leaving stuff out again."

"Sorry," Lucas said. "My bad. I'm talking about the other stuff Chesterfield has been collecting for the past 79 years. It's not only clocks. He's been buying up famous navigational instruments going all the way back to the Age of Exploration."

Navigation. Geographic coordinates.

I was starting to see where Greer was headed with her theory.

"How did you find all of this out?" I asked.

Lucas and Greer described their research in detail, a narrative that included an interesting revelation. Thirty years ago, Chesterfield faked his death. Since the Creavit are immortal, the strategy made sense and was certainly something I'd seen done in science fiction movies.

In fact, during the whole conversation, my mind worked overtime—pardon the pun—to access any understanding I had about time travel. That extended to reading H.G. Wells in high school and watching *Star Trek*.

Tori neatly summed up my thoughts when she said, "Okay, all I know about time travel is the basic rule. You go back and change something, you probably just killed everyone you know and maybe yourself."

Greer laughed. She has a good laugh, by the way. Deep

and throaty. Greer doesn't need her vampire charms to turn men's heads. Even my father, who is as faithful as one of his six "fishing" dogs, grinned appreciatively as he watched the baobhan sith—and he was sitting right beside my mother when he did it.

"A nicely succinct take on temporal paradoxes," Greer said. "Without complicating the matter any further, your understanding is reasonably correct. Traveling backward in time and altering events rarely turns out well, which is why, in general, time travel is avoided except in cases of absolute necessity."

"A rule that wouldn't bother Chesterfield in the slightest," Chase pointed out.

"Correct," Greer agreed. "However, we are discussing something unique, the plotting of time jumps like a course on a map."

"Is this a power Chesterfield gained when he became Creavit?" I asked.

Greer shook her head. "No, based on what Grayson and I learned in our research, coupled with what Glory has shared with us, Chesterfield has gone to some lengths to cultivate his temporal magic," she said. "The DGI's files on the man are sketchy at best before 1936, but what we do have indicates that he was once a human who dabbled in alchemy. I believe that is the skill set upon which he has drawn to craft this new ability."

"What a minute," I said, "don't all alchemists have magical powers?"

"No," Greer said. "The alchemists you know are all descended from Fae lineage, which is the source of their magic. We have every reason to believe that Chesterfield was purely human before he bargained for his powers."

"Who was he" Mom asked, "before he became Creavit?"

"Rather an ordinary man for his station in the 12th century," Greer said. "He was associated with a wealthy family, which afforded him the opportunity to develop his alchemical interests. We also believe he went to the Crusades."

I ran the math in my head. "You can't be serious," I said. "That would make him more than 800 years old."

"True," Lucas said, "but he only lived 50 years as a human before gaining Creavit immortality. We've verified his birth in Derbyshire in 1130."

"Where?" Tori asked.

"The East Midlands," Lucas said. "Think the middle of England, a little better than half way up on the map."

The DGI seemed to know a fair amount about the start of Chesterfield's life and what he had been doing for the last 80 years or so. Beyond that, huge gaps riddled the wizard's biography. Their best guess had him leaving Europe in the early 1930s, possibly to escape the political unrest on the continent preceding World War II.

Then, in the mid-Eighties, he created a new identity for himself, posing as his nephew—conveniently with the same name. We all agreed that he'd probably reinvented himself many times over the centuries.

"Given all that," Greer said, "coupled with Chesterfield's rather meek acceptance of his punishment following the incident in which Festus was injured, things do not paint the picture of a penitent Creavit minding his own business."

"I tried to tell Barnaby that slimy Creavit was up to no good," Festus grumbled, edging closer toward the warmth of the fire. "For the life of me, I have never understood why Barnaby let Chesterfield off with probation."

Festus was right. Barnaby's leniency made no sense under the circumstance. We were going to have to take up that very subject with him. Everything Greer and Lucas said convinced me that my grandfather had seriously underestimated Chesterfield. We couldn't afford to let that happen again.

We couldn't afford to underestimate *anybody*.

I knew Chase wasn't going to like what I had to say next, but I said it anyway. "Does it bother anyone else that Chesterfield and the Strigoi Sisters popped in and out of sight right outside the Stone Hearth Pizzeria?"

Ex-boyfriend or not, I know my man. Chase chimed in right on cue with a note of exasperation in his voice that set my teeth on edge.

"Oh for God's sake!" he said. "Let it go, Jinx! There isn't a shred of evidence that Pete is somehow in collusion with Irenaeus Chesterfield!"

I didn't have to reply, Greer did it for me with that deadly, arched eyebrow of hers. "Is that so?" she said coolly. "Perhaps you should let us be the judge of that. Is there some issue with the owner of this eatery?"

In my opinion, there certainly was.

I believe Pete told Malcolm Ferguson that Chase and I intended to visit an isolated waterfall outside of town to speak with the ghost of Knasgowa.

The genealogy would make your head swim, so let's keep this brief. Knasgowa is the founder of our magical line. We're all her descendants by blood—me, Mom, Gemma, and Tori. Collectively, we're called the Daughters of Knasgowa.

Chase and I talked about going to the waterfall over lunch at the pizzeria. Pete was the only person outside our immediate circle who could have possibly known about our plans.

We came back to our car after seeing Knasgowa to ripped up upholstery and a threatening note from Ferguson.

Chase thought I was being paranoid, but when I finished telling the story, the others didn't agree with him.

"You're sure that no one else outside the group here could have known you were heading out there?" Lucas asked, leaning forward with his elbows on his knees.

"I'm sure," I said. "But Pete had the perfect opportunity to hear us discussing the visit when we were in the pizzeria. I'm positive he's the one who gave Ferguson the information."

Chase made a dismissive sound in his throat. "Pete is no more Fae than George and Irma at the corner grocery."

"No one suggested he's Fae," Lucas said, leveling his gaze at Chase, "but someone or something could be manipulating him. Did you ever think about that, McGregor?"

Was it *ever* going to be possible for these two to be in the same room without verbal sparring?

Chase started to bristle but caught himself when both Festus and I looked daggers in his direction. "I suppose that could be possible," he admitted grudgingly, "but if that's the case, Pete is a victim who needs our help, not some villain."

"And help him we will," Greer said, "as soon as we determine what, if any, association he has with Chesterfield. Now, let's have a look at the drone video of the confrontation with the Strigoi Sisters. If I'm right, we may be able to discern the instant when Chesterfield rescued them."

THREE

When we watched the encounter with Seraphina and Ioana on the big screen, I tried to pretend the chilling events were scenes from a movie. Oddly enough, however, the longer I watched, the more empowered I became.

Even as the storm's fury built to its peak, cruelly buffeting the microscopic drone, the camera caught everything that happened.

The moment when I stepped out of the store with Tori, Mom, and Gemma.

Our walk across the street.

The face-to-face with the Strigoi Sisters.

Anton Ionescu appearing out of nowhere and tasering Ioana.

My mother rushing past me to snatch a child out of harm's way.

Gemma tackling Seraphina.

And then the four of us clasped hands and called to the lightning.

I was standing behind the couch with my hands resting on my mother's shoulders as we watched the video. The bolt of electricity falling from the sky made the screen flare white. When the picture cleared, the girls were gone and Anton lay dying on the grass.

As I watched myself comfort the fallen man, Mom

rested her right hand over my left. Fighting to swallow the lump that instantly rose in my throat, I looked at Greer.

"It all happened too fast," I said. "The video doesn't tell us anything."

"To the contrary," Greer said, "I think the video tells us a great deal."

The look of compassion from the baobhan sith comforted me as much as the weight of my mother's hand, but the admiration and empathy in her gaze startled me.

"Am I missing something here?" I asked awkwardly.

"Only that last night we witnessed four of the Daughters of Knasgowa standing together for the first time," Greer said. "The moment is worthy of recognition."

"It is, indeed," Festus agreed. "Chesterfield may not know it yet, but he's taking on more than he can handle this time."

I started to squirm away, but to my surprise, Mom's hand tightened on mine. "Own your power, Jinx," she said. "Own your ability to unite *our* powers."

Through the thick knot in my throat, I said, "Thank you. Thank you all."

I couldn't manage more than that. I shot Greer an imploring look, and she gracefully picked up the beat.

"Let's examine this sequence in greater detail," she said.

So, we watched it again. One painful image at a time. That's when we saw what really happened. A fraction of a second before the screen flashed to white, Seraphina and Ioana disappeared.

Greer moved to shut off the video, but to my surprise, Dad stopped her. "Would you let the rest of the tape play?" he asked.

"Of course," Greer said, "but may I ask why?"

Dad sat up straight. "Because I've never seen my wife and daughter in action," he said, "and when you did your thing with time, you froze the Colonel and me along with everyone else. I want to see all of it."

My heart swelled with love for him. Dad may have to be a bystander in our magical world, but he's cheering from the sidelines.

Even though I had been right in the middle of the events, I saw things on the screen that surprised me. Greer held time still until Anton's people removed his body from the square. As the human carnival goers began to wake up, Greer and Lucas moved among them, talking.

"What were you saying to them?" I asked.

Lucas grinned. "We were using a little bit of psychology," he said. "When humans are confronted with the unexplained, they're highly receptive to the first likely story they hear. So we told them a likely story."

"Which was?" Tori asked.

"That the entire crowd was experiencing disorientation from the static electricity generated by the lightning strike," Lucas said. "Mixed in with some healthy exhortations to be grateful for their good luck."

"Exhortations, huh?" I said, grinning back at him in spite of myself.

"Yeah," Lucas said. "You can't sell a story without the right degree of enthusiasm, salted with a little embellishment for flavor."

"I'll remember that the next time you're trying to sell *me* a story," I said mischievously.

Let me tell you something about flirting. There's more than one way to do it, but the basic forms are intentional and unintentional. I had just flirted with Lucas Grayson in front of Chase McGregor as naturally as I would have taken a breath. One man liked my answer a lot, and the other one didn't. If I have to tell you which one was which, you haven't been keeping up.

Several things happened next. Chase stiffened. Festus

said something sharp in Gaelic. Greer laughed, and Chase blushed to the roots of his hair. The rest of us wisely decided to let it go.

Beau got us back on track. "Miss Greer," he said, "do you also have an ability to travel through time?"

Greer shook her head. "No," she said. "I only possess the ability to halt time. Temporal magic is rare. It's unique to the practitioner and only works in the realm of the humans."

"Why is that the case?" Beau asked.

"The Fae accept the fluidity of time," Greer said. "We work with that flexibility naturally. Humans, and consequently their reality, depend more on the concrete and the known. That is why we can so easily explain away any time anomalies they experience. Humans possess a willingness—a need—to accept pat explanations."

Beau considered the information. "If Miss Tori is correct in her assessment of the dangers of creating a temporal paradox," he said, "and your supposition that Chesterfield executes lateral movements is true, does that preclude an attempt on his part to go back in time?"

"It does not," Greer said. "I believe, in fact, that he did precisely that, and that Jinx and Tori saw him do it."

"We did?" Tori said. "When?"

"When you and Jinx psychometrically experienced the car accident in which Seraphina and Ioana were first killed," Greer answered.

Short explanation. I touch things and get visions. When I tried to use my power to derive information from the girls' mangled car, I inadvertently pulled Tori into the vision with me. We relived the whole accident as if we were there—and we saw a figure standing at the top of the cliff looking over the wreckage.

That's when it hit me. I knew Chesterfield looked vaguely familiar. Greer read my expression.

"Was Chesterfield the man you saw in your vision?" she asked.

When Greer first mentioned Chesterfield's temporal magic to us, she said she believed he was present the day of the accident itself and in the psychometric vision of the wreck Tori and I experienced.

Now that I knew more about her theory, those two possibilities confused me even more. *When* did we see him? At the moment of the accident? When he spied on our vision? Both?

"I think it was him," I said helplessly, "but I can't be sure, and I don't know *when* he was there."

Glory piped up with a completely unexpected, but brilliant idea. "I can be sure," she said. "At least about whether it was him or not. Is there some way you can show me the man on top of the cliff? You know, like the way they do instant replays at football games?"

"I don't know that either," I admitted.

Mom patted my hand. "I do," she said. "My mother had the gift of psychometry, too. She replayed visions for me many times. Come around here and sit with me."

I did as I was told, taking the seat beside my mother when Gemma scooted over. Mom held out her hand to Glory, who immediately settled on the edge of her palm. She brought the little witch up to eye level with me.

"What do I do?" I asked uncertainly. "I don't want to hurt Glory."

"You won't," Mom assured me. "Put your hand out. Glory, take hold of one of Jinx's fingers."

Glory's hands rested as light as a whisper on my skin. The look of complete trust on her face only made me more nervous.

"Both of you close your eyes," Mom ordered. "Jinx, find the part of your power where your psychometry lives. Imagine your visions like cards in a file. Riffle through them, just like the old card catalog at the library. Remember? Look for the vision of the wreck and when you find it, bring it out. Let the scene rise in your mind's eye."

Her voice took on an almost hypnotic, sing-song quality. My psychometry stirred, sending me flashes of Glory's life. Her apartment filled with Elvis memorabilia. Her desk at work. The park where she liked to feed the squirrels. Her fears and uncertainties.

Before my mind could probe further, I pulled back. I had no intention of using my powers to invade the privacy of Glory's thoughts and memories. Mom saw me tense.

"I know," she said. "Your power will go first to the thing or the person you're touching. Don't let it. You are in control of the ability. It does not control you. Focus. Look for the visions that live in your memory."

Drawing in a deep breath, I tried again, imagining an antiquated card catalog, seeing myself open the long, narrow drawer, feeling my fingers sorting through the cards. I sensed my power smoothing into a steady stream rather than thrumming against my awareness.

Intuiting, rather than understanding what I needed to do next, I touched the imaginary card in my mind, and I was once again in the car with Seraphina and Ioana—and with recorded images of myself and Tori.

The thought crossed my mind that there was no room for me in the backseat. That's all it took for my perception of myself to shrink down to something close to Glory's size. I saw myself perched on the headrest behind Ioana, a vantage point that let me survey the entire interior of the car.

"I'm there," I whispered.

"Good," Mom said. "Now give the vision to Glory."

"Don't be scared, Glory," I said softly. "I won't let anything happen to you. Join me."

And like that, she was in the car, too, sitting beside me.

"Whoa!" she said, swiveling her head back and forth before stopping to stare at me. "We're the same size!"

"There wouldn't be room for us in here any other way," I said, nodding toward the reflections of Tori and me in the backseat.

"What happens now?" Glory asked.

"In a few seconds the car is going to go over the cliff," I said. "Maybe we should find something to hang on to."

The suggestion came too late. As the car went over the edge, I caught hold of Glory to try to shield her, but instead of experiencing the rough and tumble of the crash, we hung perfectly suspended in air while the vehicle rolled around us.

"This is like being inside a Mixmaster," Glory said. "But without all the eggs and the gooey stuff."

I started to ask her if she'd ever actually been in a bowl of batter and then thought better of it. I'd learned the hard way to roll with the flow of Glory's metaphors rather than try to apply logic to the garbled imagery.

This time, I used an intentional thought rather than a random one. "We need to get out of this car."

That's all it took to put us outside the crumpled wreckage, where we waited until my image and Tori's appeared beside us.

"Okay," I told Glory. "This is it. Wait until they—we—look up. Then the man will be at the top of the cliff."

Even without looking myself, I knew Glory recognized the figure. The waves of tremors wracking her body said everything. Realizing I couldn't let her be the only one to face her fears, I let my gaze furtively track toward the looming figure in the black hat and raincoat. I couldn't see his face, but I knew he was looking right at me. The knowledge flooded me with a cold wave of panic. I broke the connection fast.

It wasn't my most graceful exit from a psychometric

vision. I gasped as the lair came into focus around me. Glory was breathing hard, too, and she was still shaking.

"It's okay," I assured her. "It wasn't real."

That may or may not have been the truth. I still don't know, but Glory needed it to be true, so she nodded in agreement.

"It was him," she said shakily. "That man on the cliff was Mr. Chesterfield."

Greer knelt beside the couch and rested her hand on my knee. "Think," she said. "The rain in your vision, did it strike the man on the cliff or did it fall around him?"

"It fell around him," I said. "The same way it fell around us. Why?"

"If Chesterfield has found a way to insulate himself," she said, "he could move through the stream of time as an observer without altering events, much in the manner of a submersible moving through the water."

"But how did he know Tori and I were going to be there in a vision?" I said, watching as my mother delicately returned Glory to the arm of the sofa.

"By placing an alarm of some sort to announce your presence," Greer said. "Remember that he is navigating through time. I believe he essentially put a pin on the map."

"But why would he do that?" I asked.

Mom answered. "Because he *was* there the first time," she said. "Chesterfield caused the wreck. He bookmarked the time so he would know if anyone—if we—ever accessed that point in the temporal stream again and figured out his scheme. He really has orchestrated everything that has happened in our lives."

Greer, who was still kneeling beside me, turned toward my mother. "I believe so," she said. "The girls, Anton, you and your husband, your child. All we've learned suggests you've been Chesterfield's victims for more than 30 years."

"But why?" Mom asked. "What does he want?"

"I don't know," Greer said, "but I assure you, we are going to find out."

FOUR

Between the video evidence and Greer's time theory, we had a lot to process—and we were all exhausted. I admit it. I yawned first.

"Forgive me," Greer said. "It's quite late. I forget that others have need of sleep."

"You don't . . . ," Tori started and then clamped her mouth shut.

"Climb into a casket and turn into a well-rested corpse for a few hours?" Greer grinned. "No, I do not."

"Sorry," Tori said, grinning back. "Too many bad vampire movies."

"They're all bad, dear," Greer replied pleasantly. Then, with a shooing motion of her hand, she said, "Go to bed. All of you. We can take this up in the morning."

For a second no one knew how to respond. We weren't used to getting orders from the Mother Superior of Vampires, but no one seemed inclined to argue. There were some mumbled thanks from around the room as people started to get up from their seats. That's when Glory put two fingers in her mouth and let out with a shrill whistle.

Festus's ears immediately went flat. "What the hell?" he said. "You have something to say, Dill Pickle?"

A few days earlier that remark would have reduced

Glory to wailing tears. This time she said, "Yes, Old Yeller, I do."

"Old Yeller," Festus hissed, "was a *dog*. I am a cat."

"Same diff," Glory shot back.

Sensing a deluge of cross-species trash talk in the works, I stepped in. "What is it, Glory?"

"Before you all go to bed," she said, "I was wondering if maybe one of you could use your magic to get my broom up to size? If you do, I'll be able to get around easier by myself and . . . well . . . escape if I need to."

I had been so confident in our ability to protect Glory, it never occurred to me that without her broom, Glory had no way to hide from Chesterfield on her own. The store and fairy mound are heavily warded, but with the revelations about the wizard's time shifting powers, we could no longer assume those protections would keep him out. Glory's request was both reasonable and obvious—so obvious, I found myself apologizing for not thinking of it myself.

"You've had a lot on your mind," she said generously. "I didn't want to bother you, but it looks like you're never going to not have something to worry about."

I was pretty sure there might be a double negative in that statement somewhere, but her point was still well taken.

Plucking the tiny boom from the corner of the shelf where we'd leaned it after Glory's growth spurt, I used the same spell Barnaby had employed to Barbie-size Glory.

Holding my hand over the broom, I said, "*Amplifico!*"

On cue, the broom lengthened from cocktail skewer to pencil length. I handed it to Glory, who hopped on and rocketed across the lair with more enthusiasm than precision. Lucas had to duck to avoid getting stabbed in the forehead.

"Sorry!" Glory called over her shoulder. "I'm a little rusty."

With that, she made a hard left, aimed low over the hearth and buzzed Festus. At the last minute, the old cat reared on his hind legs and took a swipe at the passing witch. Executing a perfect barrel roll, Glory flew right through his paws.

"Try that again, Green Hornet," Festus growled, "and you are going *down*."

Still laughing, Glory came to a hovering stop in front of me. "Thank you *so* much!" she gushed.

"You're welcome," I said, "but maybe you should save the acrobatic stuff for the stacks before you put somebody's eye out. And seriously, don't do that fly-by thing with Festus again. I've seen him take down moths and it's not pretty."

"Exactly," Festus said, curling his lips in a feral smile. "And I'm dying to know if you taste like pistachio crunch ice cream."

That was enough to make Glory blanch a little. "Of course," she agreed hastily, "safety first. Night, all."

With that, she flew up to Graceland East, the dollhouse replica of the King's house that is her home, parked her broom by the front door and quickly disappeared inside.

"Put somebody's eye out?" Tori said. "Why didn't you tell her not to run with sparklers, too?"

Both moms stopped half-way up the stairs and gave us "the look" in tandem. "Laughing about running with sparklers is all well and good until you *do* put someone's eye out," Gemma said.

Right on cue, Tori bristled and started to back talk her mother.

"Stop," I ordered. "There are no sparklers. No running and no sparklers. Do what Greer said. Go to bed."

Festus jumped off the hearth, still muttering under his breath, and fell in beside Chase, who was already headed for the passageway leading to the cobbler shop.

Beau excused himself for the night. Lucas snagged one of the now vacant couches, stretched out, and put his hat over his face. Greer reclaimed both her chair by the fire and her book.

Tori and I followed the Moms and my father up the steps. When we reached the first floor, Mom drew Gemma toward the front of the store to have a word in private.

Dad, sensing that Tori and I would like to do the same, disappeared up to my place where my four cats were no doubt waiting impatiently for him. Since my parents had been staying over, Zeke, Yule, Xavier, and Winston had gotten used to three times the attention. Dad's a softy for any kind of critter and my guys adore him—so much, in fact, that the cats had been sleeping with my parents in my bedroom leaving me alone on the couch.

As soon as Dad was out of earshot, Tori explained about the *Obsession* perfume.

"Maybe Scrap didn't realize your mom hates *Obsession* and got it for her as a peace offering," I suggested hopefully.

"Nice try, Jinksy," Tori said, a little flicker of anger edging the words. "He may have bought that stuff for a woman alright, but it wasn't my mother."

"Don't jump to conclusions," I said, but the platitude sounded flat.

"Tell *her* that," Tori said, nodding toward the front of the store.

I turned to see Gemma standing in the light thrown from the streetlamp outside the window. She had her arms crossed defensively over her chest and was shaking her head while my Mom talked.

"What are you going to do?" I asked.

"Whatever Mom says to do," Tori replied. "Right now we have too many other things to be worried about, but if my dad wasn't already on her 'list,' he's definitely on it now."

Tori was right about all those "other things." We had made some group decisions before tending to Glory's flight status. First thing in the morning, the two of us, the Moms, and Greer planned to head up into the mountains to visit the site of the wreck. Greer hoped we'd be able to detect lingering traces of Chesterfield's temporal magic.

Chase and Festus would be leaving for Raleigh to check out Chesterfield's shop, Anton Ionescu's office, and the "divinatory emporium" owned by Miss Shania Moonbeam—the fortune teller who put Glory in touch with Chesterfield in the first place.

Miss Shania sounded like a total flake, but she apparently knew Chesterfield in some way. Like I said—no more underestimating anyone. Every lead, no matter how whacky, would get checked out.

The next morning when I came downstairs—which was all of five hours later—I found the coffee made and Beau waiting for me at one of the tables in the espresso bar with Duke, the ghostly coonhound, lying at his feet. When the dog saw me, he sat up and wagged his tail.

"Good morning," Beau said. "I procured bear claws for breakfast."

"How did you do that?" I yawned. "George and Irma aren't open on Sunday."

I sat down and reached to scratch Duke's ears before I remembered my hand would pass right through him unless we were downstairs. In the lair, any ghosts who joined us took on a greater degree of solidity thanks to energy radiated by the fairy mound.

Duke, who had been one of Beau's ghostly companions at the cemetery, recently moved in with us and refused to leave. He had been so devoted in life, he'd been buried with his master whose spirit, inexplicably, was not present at the graveyard. The old dog transferred his affection to Beau and rarely left his side.

Now, apparently in appreciation for my attempts to pet him, Duke positioned himself beside my chair and grinned at me. Together we watched as Beau poured me the coffee, placing the cup and a heaping blob of iced-pastry goodness in front of me.

"Master Darby rushed into the breach to provide the pastries," Beau said. "I must say that had we had brownies working with us in the Army of Northern Virginia our supply problems would have been solved."

He pointed toward a silver platter on the counter. Darby had indeed made enough bear claws to feed an army. The brownie, once in the employ of Knasgowa's husband, Alexander Skea, became part of our odd little family when we freed him from his duty of guarding Knasgowa's grave.

Not one to sit around and twiddle his magical thumbs, Darby promptly began to organize the stacks in the basement and took over all our housekeeping duties.

Since the basement is a working repository for Fae artifacts and documents, and he was helping Myrtle at that time, that part of Darby's work didn't bother me, but having him cooking and cleaning made me a little uncomfortable at first. It felt like we were exploiting house elf labor like in the Harry Potter books.

That feeling lasted until I tried to wash my dishes and Darby had a fit when I didn't dry after I rinsed and left spots on the glasses. He's such a fussy housekeeper; he'd make Martha Stewart look like a slacker.

"There must be three dozen bear claws there," I said.

"At least," Beau agreed. "I fear he was, as usual, somewhat overly enthusiastic."

Right on cue, my stomach grumbled.

"Or perhaps his consumption estimate was better targeted than I surmised," Beau deadpanned.

Half asleep or not, that got a laugh out of me. I bit into the bear claw, savoring that first bite before washing it down with coffee brewed to perfection and sweetened exactly the way I like it.

"You," I said, "are getting seriously good at the barista thing."

"Thank you," Beau said, inclining his head. "I do subscribe to the Napoleonic theory that an army marches on its stomach."

That stopped me in mid-chew. "What army?" I mumbled, completely breaking my mother's rule about not talking with your mouth full.

"You do not see yourself as the commander of a force combating an enemy?" Beau asked with a smile.

"I see myself as a half-awake woman who is going to need three more cups of this coffee to get her brain jump started," I said. Then something occurred to me. "You're like Greer, aren't you? You don't sleep either."

Beau sighed. "Sadly, no," he admitted, "but it is not the sleep I miss. For me, the loss is in being unable to dream. At best, I lie down, close my eyes, and spend quiet time in memory and reflection. That is not the same, however, as a mind unleashed by Morpheus."

"Did you dream when you were a ghost?"

He shook his head. "No, then there were simply periods of essential unawareness, generally when the sun was up. Even those times disappeared the longer I remained on this plain. I have not slept since the night before my demise 151 years ago."

When I met Beau, he was capable of appearing during the daylight hours, unlike his cemetery friends who only came out after dark.

"But you like the way you are now, right?" I asked uncertainly.

Beau smiled. "Very much so," he said. "Any deficits of

full corporeality that I might experience, such as the inability to sleep, are a most acceptable exchange for the privilege of participating, even in a small way, in the world of the living again."

"The rest of us don't see you as a small part of anything," I assured him. "You're a big deal to us."

"A fact quite dear to my heart," Beau said, inclining his head to approximate a bow. "As are you, which is why I have lain in wait with coffee and pastries this morning."

"I'm not turning down the food or the concern," I said, "but really, I'm fine."

Beau looked at me and said nothing.

"What?" I protested.

Facing down looks like that was getting to be a regular thing for me.

"Having held the hands of men as they died," Beau said softly, "I know well the affecting nature of the experience. No matter what Anton Ionescu may have done, it was with you that he spent the last seconds of his life."

Blinking back sudden tears, I said, "No one deserves to be alone when they die."

"My dear friend," Beau replied, "we are all alone when we die, but the hand of a companion in that moment is still most welcome."

I suddenly realized I had never asked. "Did you have anyone with you when . . . ?"

"When I died?" Beau finished for me. "No, I did not. I recall striking the ground on my back and watching the clouds floating overhead. I drifted with them while a great sense of fatigue washed over me. When next I had self-awareness, I was standing over my body."

Toying with the edge of the cup, I asked softly, "Were you afraid?"

He shook his head. "No, my death occurred very quickly."

"Ionescu told me he was afraid," I said, my voice breaking. "I didn't want him to be afraid."

Beau reached across the table and took my hand in both of his. He may not technically be alive, but the touch was still warm and reassuring.

"You are a very good person, Miss Jinx," he said. "You afforded Mr. Ionescu the gift of your presence as he passed to the next stage of his journey. I assure you he was aware of that generosity."

The next words tumbled out of my mouth before I even realized what I was going to say. "I don't want to see anyone else die."

"You mean," Beau corrected me, "that you do not want to see anyone whom you love die. Is that not the case?"

I nodded.

"You must not let that fear cripple your abilities or weaken your resolve," he said. "You are experiencing the great terror of every leader. The people who follow you, myself included, do so by choice, Miss Jinx. You must trust us to do our part in all of this, but moreover, you must trust yourself. Doubt is a dangerous thing. Irenaeus Chesterfield would most certainly use hesitation against you. Do you understand?"

"Yes," I said, "I do, but it's hard. Four months ago I was just a waitress."

"Young lady," Beau said firmly, "you were never *just* anything."

FIVE

Kelly Hamilton walked tentatively to the edge of the cliff and looked into the rocky gorge where Seraphina and Ioana's car landed so many years before. A wave of dizziness passed through her. She swayed slightly but then a strong arm encircled her waist.

"You okay?" Gemma asked.

"I'm never prepared for how high it is," Kelly said, leaning slightly into her friend. "No matter what they've done now, those last seconds must have been terrifying for them. We have to help them, Gem."

Gemma sighed. "There's no question where Jinx gets her good heart from," she said. "You two are the only people I know who could feel sorry for a couple of undead bloodsuckers."

"Hush," Kelly said, "Greer will hear you."

"That woman hears everything we say anyway and you know it," Gemma said, nodding at Greer who was standing several yards away talking with Jinx and Tori. On cue, Greer smiled and nodded back.

"See?" Gemma said. "She's listening right now and just waiting for one of us to make that bad joke about bat's ears."

At that, the sound of the baobhan sith's husky laughter floated toward them.

"Greer," Kelly said, "Gemma and I need to talk in private. Tune us out, okay?"

Greer graciously inclined her head and turned back to Jinx and Tori.

"I like her," Kelly said. "It will do Jinx good to have the example of a woman like that."

"Your daughter already has a fine example in you," Gemma said, returning to studying the rocky gorge.

"You're biased," Kelly said, giving Gemma a little hip bump.

"I'm right," Gemma retorted, bumping back.

"Maybe I'm a good example now," Kelly said wistfully, "but for most of Jinx's life she's only known the woman crippled by guilt over what happened on this spot."

Gemma shook her head. "That's not all that crippled you, honey. What happened here is why you had to give up Connor."

"That won't be the case much longer," Kelly said. "We're going to get him back. Jinx is going to know her brother."

"Yes," Gemma agreed, "she will, but first we have to make sure it's safe for him to come home. That means putting an end to Seraphina and Ioana, and doing something about Irenaeus Chesterfield.'

Kelly looked up at her taller friend. "Doing all of that isn't only for us," she said seriously. "Anton was right. The girls are monsters now. He wanted to free them and couldn't. We have to do it for him, Gemma. We may not have been responsible for their first deaths, but we have to see them truly dead, once and for all."

Gemma made a sour face. "Can I let them eat Scrap first?" she asked.

Kelly couldn't help giggling. "You don't know that he's seeing someone. Scrap is perfectly capable of being clueless enough to buy perfume for you that you hate."

"Okay, fine," Gemma said grudgingly. "My husband is as thick as one of his two-by-fours, but he better come up with some damned convincing answers or Seraphina and Ioana won't be the only ones winding up at the bottom of this cliff."

Tori and I stood on the side of the road over the wreck site with Greer while the Moms moved off to one side. I knew the experience of visiting the scene had to be emotional for them both in a way only they could share.

For years they believed—or at least Mom believed—Seraphina and Ioana died from a spell cast to make the girls late for cheerleader tryouts. It wasn't true, but the ramifications of the car crash were still far reaching and tragic.

Greer was talking to us about realigning our conception of time, suggesting that we not see it as a linear progression but rather as a data stream that could be accessed at given points. Suddenly, and without warning, she laughed. Tori and I exchanged a "look" of our own.

"What's so funny?" Tori asked.

"Your mother," Greer replied, "having a bit of sport with my vampiric senses at a distance. She and Jinx's mother will be joining us shortly. I believe they are processing being on this spot for the first time with an awareness of their innocence involving the automobile crash."

She was right. We didn't have to wait long for the Moms to join us. As they walked up, I looked at Greer and said, "Okay, now what?"

"We already know the four of you can merge your powers," she said. "None of you possess temporal magic. I suggest you meld as you did night before last and then bring me into the joining. When we are united, you should be able to use the essence of your psychometric power to see how, and when, Irenaeus Chesterfield was here."

Gemma nodded. "Coven magic," she said simply.

"Yes," Greer replied, "a standard matter of course for witches."

Yeah. Maybe other witches. Back at the beginning of the summer, Aunt Fiona told me that one of my jobs was to rebuild the Briar Hollow coven. Thankfully, that task had been shoved on the back burner because I had no idea how to round up additional witches to swell our numbers to thirteen.

"Tori and I have never worked with a coven," I admitted.

Mom reached for my hand. "Gemma and I have," she said. "You know how to do this, honey. Coven magic is what we used to call the lightning. Open your heart and mind. Your power will find the right conduit."

With that, she reached for Gemma's hand, and I reached for Tori. The instant we all made contact, our combined magic began to hum distantly at the edge of my consciousness. I let the tone rise. With the growing volume came the sense of a wavering light. Dropping all my barriers, I allowed both fully formed into the heart of my perception. When I did, the sound and the light merged, flowing over and through us until we stood at the center of perfect clarity.

When I turned to say something to Greer, iridescent green flames lit her pupils and the large ruby ring on her left hand pulsated with a carmine rhythm. At the same moment, Tori and I released each other and drew Greer toward us. When her fingers entwined with ours, an alien energy entered the circle. Something warm and chained, equal parts passion and hunger.

"Open your mind's eye, Jinx Hamilton," Greer said, the burr of her native Scotland thick on her tongue. "Show us the passing of time in this place."

I had foolishly expected my vision to go instantly to

Chesterfield. Instead, we saw the changing of the seasons on the side of the mountain. The falling of the snow and the warm thaw of spring. Flowers bloomed, only to die and give way to the golden leaves of fall.

The mountain changed around us, pristine in one moment, shaped by the hand of man in another. First, there was only a dirt track fit for wagons snaking out of the slopes. Then came the dynamite, the movement of earth, and the laying of pavement.

Model T trucks passed us, then semis with rocking loads of lumber. And then, a red 1975 Toyota Corolla carrying Seraphina and Ioana.

The magic afforded us a view better than a GNATS drone. We saw everything all at once, from every angle—including Irenaeus Chesterfield standing hidden in the woods opposite the cliff.

In the sliver of time before Seraphina lost control of the car, his arm shot out sending a rippling wave of transparent energy across the road and into the car. The force drove the vehicle over the cliff as a light, misty rain began to fall.

Chesterfield drew out a black silk handkerchief and delicately mopped at his brow, taking the time to fold the cloth before putting it away. Then he leisurely walked to the edge of the cliff and surveyed the wreckage, admiring his handiwork.

Reaching under his raincoat, presumably into the breast pocket of his suit, the wizard extracted a small brass pin that he tossed skyward. The pin caught in mid-air and began to spin slowly.

"*Memores estote, et vigilate,*" Chesterfield commanded, sending the pin plunging deep into the earth at his feet.

"Remember and alert."

We had our beacon.

Greer let go of our hands and stepped out of the circle, the envelope of our shared magic reforming in the space she left behind. I took Tori's hand again. We slowly let the joining fade until once again we stood in the sunlight of a cool fall morning.

"Does he know we're here now?" Mom asked.

Greer shook her head. "No," she said, "the marker was for a point in time, not the present. He doesn't know."

It wasn't a huge advantage, but it was something.

———◦◦◦———

We managed to catch Chase and Festus before they left for Raleigh. Greer wanted to talk to Festus about the day he faced off against Chesterfield.

The Creavit wizard had been attempting to engineer a land grab in the area around Briar Hollow prior to the passage of the legislation that created the Blue Ridge Parkway. When it looked as if Congress would pass the bill and snatch the land out from under him, Chesterfield headed for Washington with a bag full of bribe money. Festus and Moira, the resident alchemist in Shevington, stopped his train.

With no regard for the humans present, Chesterfield fired off an energy bolt at Moira who had to defend herself. In the running magical duel that ensued, Festus took a shot to the hip that melted the joint. Shapeshifters can heal from almost anything by changing forms, but in this instance, the damage was too great. Now Festus has only one option; a human hip replacement. But if he does that, he'll never be able to shift again because the device wouldn't change with him.

That's why Festus lives in his house cat form. He limps, but when he needs to, he picks up the bad leg and lets the other three do the work. If you've never seen a three-legged cat get around, trust me, the old boy still has mad moves. He is, however, troubled by arthritis, which explains the long hours spent sunning or snoozing in front of the fire. Well, that and the fact that when he's not working, Festus raises all definitional standards for the phrase "lazy tomcat."

Even though Festus was hurt, he and Moira managed to capture Chesterfield. She clouded the minds of the human witnesses, implanting false memories of the incident. Since she had stopped the train by blocking the tracks with a landslide, extrapolating on that scenario in a way the people there would accept was simple. Greer wanted to go over the events with Festus to see if Chesterfield had shown any evidence of working temporal magic that day, or of implanting one of his beacons on the scene.

Since I knew the backstory, I declined Greer's invitation to join them. "If you learn anything new," I said, "you can fill me in later. I want to have a cup of tea with my mother now."

The tall redhead regarded me curiously. "Is there something amiss?" she asked.

"No," I said. "I just want to spend some time with her. The last 48 hours have been pretty intense."

"Without a doubt," Greer agreed, "but Kelly has acquitted herself more than admirably."

I looked toward my mother who was standing behind the counter in the espresso bar preparing the tea with Rodney perched on her shoulder.

Rodney, a handsome (and scary smart) black-and-white domestic rat, was left at the door of the shop in a cage shortly before Mom's sister, my Aunt Fiona, faked her death to move to Shevington. When I inherited the store, my powers awakened.

"Mom's been pretty amazing, hasn't she?" I said. The words came out undeniably proud and slightly baffled.

The mixed tone of my response wasn't lost on Greer. "You don't know this side of her, do you?" she asked.

Behold the understatement of the century.

"The mother I know puts plastic on the good sofa to protect the upholstery," I admitted. "That woman over there? She's incredible—and I have no idea who the hell she is."

Greer chuckled. "I reacted the same way to my Mum the first time I saw her in action."

"You had a . . ."

Greer's grin broadened when I blushed with embarrassment. "Oh, God, Greer," I stammered. "We just keep saying stupid stuff to you. I am so sorry."

"Not stupid," she said. "You know nothing of my kind save Hollywood drivel. You believe vampires are created from living humans, but I was born as I am. My mother is also baobhan sith."

Well, okay, if she was willing to talk, I figured I might as well try to learn something.

"And your father?" I asked.

"Shall we say he was a dinner date gone wrong and leave it at that?" Greer suggested.

Dinner date?

Oh!

Yeah. We could leave it. *Totally.*

When I clearly had no come back for her statement, Greer graciously explained anyway. "Baobhan sith magic dominates any union in which we engage. All children born to us are female. My mother shaped every aspect of who I am now from the moment of my conception."

"Are you immortal like the Creavit?" I asked.

"By your reckoning, yes," Greer said. "We are among the oldest of the Fae beings. Because of that, it is rare for a baobhan sith to choose to bear a child. Although she would kill you, literally, before she would admit it, Mum has a bit of a sentimental streak, or I would not be here."

"Are the two of you close?" I asked.

Greer continued to smile, but I saw something in her

eyes, like a crack spreading through stone. "We were," she said, "but she does not share my affinity for the people you would refer to as the 'good guys.' She disowned me when I began to work with the DGI."

The inescapable conclusion to be drawn from that statement? Greer's mother was one of the bad guys. I decided not to ask and Greer didn't offer any more information. Still, something told me to pray that we never had to tangle with Mama MacVicar.

SIX

After Greer had gone down to the lair, Gemma and Tori opted to go for a walk. They had things to talk about as well, but I could tell they were both too keyed up to sit still. That left me, my mother, Rodney, and a pot of tea in the deserted espresso bar.

Normally we'd open for a few hours on a Sunday afternoon, but since no one was in a mood to deal with customers we left the "closed" sign firmly in place on the front door.

Mom went the full nine yards with the tea, using the good, loose leaf stuff and covering the pot with a cozy I didn't even know we owned.

The delicate porcelain cup she handed me felt incredibly fragile, but elegant and soothing at the same time. When I drink coffee, I prefer a cup roughly the size of a gallon jug.

"Where did you find these cups?" I asked, sipping the steaming liquid. I then added, "And what kind of tea is this?" The smoky, full-bodied taste surprised me. This was not the kind of tea that comes in little bags at the grocery store.

"These were mother's," Mom said, lovingly running her finger around the gold rim of the cup. "Fiona had them upstairs in one of the cabinets. The tea is lapsang souchong, mother's favorite."

At that, Rodney tapped Mom on the shoulder and pointed at her cup.

"Want to try some, Rodney?" she asked.

He nodded enthusiastically.

Mom put her cup down and picked up her spoon, which she half-filled with tea. "Come down on the table so we don't slosh any," she said.

Obediently, Rodney trotted down her arm and sat up on his haunches. Mom held the spoon out, warning, "Be careful, it's hot."

I swear to you, he blew on the tea before he took a sip, then worked the liquid around in his mouth.

"Well?" Mom said. "What do you think?"

Rodney gave her the thumbs up.

"You want some more?"

When he nodded, Mom ladled several spoonfuls into her saucer and put it in front of the rat, who began to lap happily.

"What would Grandma say about that?" I asked her.

"She would say I should give him a proper cup," Mom chuckled.

My grandmother died seven years ago, in 2008. Festus described her to me once as a woman with so much power it would "curl your whiskers." I only knew her as a little old church lady, and I'm ashamed to say I didn't spend as much time with her as I should have.

"Grandma was 88 when she died, right?" I asked.

"Yes," Mom said, "almost 89. Why?"

It was my turn to toy with my cup.

"What do you want to ask me, Norma Jean?" Mom asked when it became clear I couldn't get the words out.

Have you ever kept a question inside so long the yearning to know the answer built up like steam in a kettle? That's how I felt when I blurted out, "Are we human?"

"Ah," Mom said, "I wondered when we'd get around to having this conversation. The magic in our family runs through the women; you understand that?"

I nodded.

"For the most part, all the Daughters of Knasgowa have married human men, but the Fae blood finds the girls in each generation," she explained. "My brothers are dead signals. They couldn't work magic to save their lives, but they know of our world and keep our secret. My sisters have varying degrees of ability, but none of them are strongly drawn to practice. Fiona and I were the most powerful."

There are nine Ryan children. Aunt Fiona is the oldest and mom is the baby. I tried to envision my aunts and uncles being part of the Fae world, but all the images in my mind were of Thanksgiving dinners and family reunion barbecues. That, coupled with the conversation I'd just had with Greer, led in part to my next question.

"So we're Fae, but we don't live as long as Barnaby or Moira?" I asked.

"We would if we spent as much time actually working magic and living in the Otherworld as they do," Mom said. "Since the days of Knasgowa herself, the women in our family have chosen to live primarily among humans. We opted for a degree of normalcy, but with trade offs. That's why Fiona decided to move to Shevington. She loves life too much to give it up anytime soon."

We both laughed at that. Aunt Fiona inherited a cottage in Shevington from her friend Endora Endicott, the woman who raised my brother, Connor. Now happily ensconced in the Fae community, Fiona trades gardening tips with her next door neighbor, Stan, who happens to be a Sasquatch. He also raises bunnies and grows roses.

Stan's taken the Shevington Rose Cup for the past five years running. Fiona has vowed to win it next year, and good natured rivals or not, they're both determined never to relinquish the title to Hester McElroy, the local inn-keeper and their arch nemesis.

A word of advice. Do not get any of these people started on the subject of the acidic qualities of unicorn manure—especially rainbow unicorn manure—as fertilizer for roses. They won't shut up for hours.

Mom reached over the table and took hold of my hand. "Honey," she said, "there's more to humanity than genet-ics. Look at Stan. In this realm, he's seen as a monster, but I've never known a more humane being. For a long time, I tried to deny my true nature. That's not the way to be happy. We're Fae witches. That's the journey we were meant to take."

"Are you happy now?" I asked.

"Happier than I've been in years," Mom said, "and my happiness will be complete when we bring your brother home."

"Since that night when you and Gemma faced Brenna, your powers have been growing by leaps and bounds," I said. "It's like I don't even know who you are anymore."

A cloud of doubt passed over Mom's face. "Are you sorry that my powers reawakened?"

"Are you *kidding* me?" I said. "Mom, you're a badass!"

For just an instant I thought she was going to lecture me about my language, but then she stopped and grinned. "Yeah," she said, a little shyly. "I kinda am, aren't I?"

Gemma and Tori stepped out the back door of the shop together and headed down the alley behind George and Irma's grocery store. They reached the street and turned left, passing through a mostly deserted residential neigh-borhood. At the edge of town, a well-worn path led mother and daughter into the cover of the woods.

The soft October air and the carpet of fallen leaves muffled their steps and soothed their hearts. When they came upon a tiny, meandering stream, Gemma gestured to a fallen tree. "Let's sit for a while," she suggested.

Tori joined her mother on the log. "Whenever I come out here," she said, "I know I have Druid blood. The trees make me feel better."

"You're about to learn more about trees than you ever imagined," Gemma said. "All these trees around us? They're connected to the Mother Trees, too, in a web of life that crosses the In Between and transcends the realms."

Twisting around to face her mother, Tori said, "I really don't want to talk about all that right now. I want to talk about you and Dad."

Gemma sighed, looking off into the woods as if to collect her thoughts. "Honey," she said slowly, "I don't know what to tell you. I don't think he's going to accept us for what we are. That may be my fault for lying to him all these years or he may just be using that as an excuse to cover up something else."

"The perfume?" Tori asked.

Nodding, Gemma said, "He knows I hate *Obsession*."

"That's pretty thin evidence to accuse a man of cheating," Tori said.

"Fair enough," Gemma agreed. "But how about this? In the 35 years I've lived with your father, he's never bought me perfume once. Do you remember what he gave me last year for my birthday?"

Tori looked uncomfortable. "A log splitter."

"Exactly," Gemma said. "Scrap and I certainly have had our good times. You're sitting right there to prove it, but I can honestly say he's never been romantic like that. That perfume bottle sitting on his dresser says a whole lot more than you realize."

"So what are you going to do?" Tori asked.

"I'm going to confront him," Gemma said. "Scrap may have been sneaking around behind my back, but if he lies to my face, I'll know it. Depending on what he has to say, I'll decide what to do next. For now, I'm needed here in Briar Hollow."

"Yes," Tori said, "you are. And Dad is a moron."

"I should tell you not to talk about your father that way," Gemma said.

"Yeah, but you're not going to, are you?" Tori grinned.

"No," Gemma said, "I'm not."

Festus sniffed appreciatively at the bowl of single malt whisky Greer sat on the hearth in front of him. "Oban?" he asked.

"Indeed," Greer said, sitting down across from him in one of the leather chairs. "I've been drinking their whisky since the day the distillery opened its doors in 1794."

"You don't look a day over a hundred," Festus said.

"Laddie," Greer said, "I'm twice your age and more and you know it. I remember you when you were a wet-behind-the-ears kitten."

"A *handsome* wet-behind-the-ears kitten," Festus said. "We had ourselves some good times back in the day, didn't we?"

"We did," Greer said, "and more to come. *Slàinte.*"

"*Do dheagh shlàinte,*" Festus said, acknowledging her raised glass with a nod of his head before delicately touching the tip of his tongue to the Scotch and lapping at the whisky. His eyes widened in appreciation. "Is this the 1969?"

"It is," Greer said. "Thirty-two years old straight out of the cask and into the bottle. I have a few put aside."

"What's the occasion?" Festus asked, bending to take another drink.

"A wee bit of a celebration," Greer said. "It pleases me to be working with Clan MacGregor again. And I like the girl, Jinx. She has no idea how special she is, does she?"

"Not an inkling," Festus said, licking his whiskers, "but she's getting there. My God, what the four of them did on the town square. I felt like I was watching Kathleen risen from the grave."

"Herself was a fine woman," Greer said. "I've missed her."

"We've all missed her," Festus said. "Jinx never knew her the way we did, and more's the pity. So, are we just drinking our whisky and talking over old times or is there something you want to know?"

Greer described the morning's excursion to the wreck site and explained how Chesterfield embedded the temporal marker at the site. "Did he do anything like that the day you fought him?"

"Not that I saw," Festus said. "He came out of that train blasting energy bolts. Everything happened pretty fast, and as soon as I managed to get him to the ground, Moira bound him with magic. I don't think he had an opportunity to do the sort of thing you just described. Is it important?"

"It puts a frame of reference on his temporal magic," she said. "Based on his purchases and what you're telling me, he began to hone his powers in that regard after 1936 and while he was, in theory, on probation."

Festus made a low sound of disapproval. "Barnaby was a fool to do that," he said. "Moira and I both begged him to lock Chesterfield up for good."

"Why wouldn't he?" Greer asked. "Chesterfield used magic in front of the humans. He risked exposing the Otherworld to them."

"You're singing to the choir," Festus said, flicking his tail in annoyance. "Barnaby said he'd given in to the urge to seek revenge once in his life and he wouldn't do it again. He wanted to give Chesterfield a chance to live in peace."

Greer shook her head. "Barnaby never got over Adeline's death," she said, "or the things his grief drove him to do."

"I've been thinking about that," Festus said.

"Have you now?" Greer said, finishing her drink and setting the glass down on the end table. "And what have you been thinking?"

"That a lot of roads seem to lead back to Irenaeus Chesterfield," Festus said. "He was certainly there, during the Fae Reformation. What if he's the wizard who killed Adeline Shevington?"

"You cannot be suggesting that Barnaby knowingly allowed his wife's killer to go free," Greer said. "That would raise questions about Barnaby's loyalty to the Fae world."

"It would," Festus agreed.

"We don't have a shred of evidence to link Chesterfield to Adeline's death and more than enough to pin on him for other crimes," Greer said. "I'm not stirring that pot until I know what tempest I'm likely to create."

"Agreed," Festus said, "but I don't believe the idea is something we can dismiss out of hand."

"We keep every option open," Greer said, "but this notion remains between us, yes?"

"Yes," Festus said. "My boy's a little too off his game right now to bring him into the loop. Think you can get Lucas to quit taking shots at Chase's temper?"

"I've already had a word with him," Greer said, "but you know as well as I do that the two of them need to get off alone and settle the whole matter with their fists."

"If Lucas toys with Jinx's heart," Festus said, "I'll be taking my own fists to him."

"Don't concern yourself with that," Greer said, smiling

enough to reveal the tips of her fangs. "If Grayson does anything that stupid, he'll deal first with me, and I assure you, that is the last thing the dear boy wants to do."

Festus started to respond and then thought better of it. Messing with Greer wasn't on his "to do" list either.

SEVEN

As the lightning descended toward them, Ioana screamed and clutched at Seraphina. A strong hand clamped down on her arm before the world went white. When her vision cleared, she and her cousin stood in the middle of a pizzeria.

Beside them, a man dressed in a dark suit and matching black shirt fiddled with his pocket watch. When the setting satisfied him, he slipped the timepiece into his maroon silk vest.

"Where are we?" Seraphina demanded. "Who are you? What did you do to us?"

The man's expressionless eyes set deep on either side of a harsh, aquiline nose remained cool. "Tut, tut," he murmured. "Does not the act of saving you from incineration deserve even a token thank you? Manners, young lady, manners."

Exchanging an uneasy glance with Seraphina, Ioana said, "Thank you, mister . . . ?" Her voice went up in question, waiting for the stranger to fill in his name.

After several seconds, he heaved a weary sigh. "Chesterfield," he said. "Irenaeus Chesterfield. Anton was my attorney."

"Where is my father?" Seraphina asked. "What did those witches do to him?" Lingering traces of youthful confusion colored her words.

Chesterfield's lips curved into a sardonic smile. "Why they killed him, my dear," he said. "Or, rather, he is dying as we speak. Those are hardly questions a nascent vampire should be asking."

"I don't know what that means," Seraphina said defensively, "but I don't think I like it."

That elicited a dry chuckle from the man in black. "Well, at least your instinct for offense is well honed," he said. "Nascent means developing, showing potential. And you do, my dear—show potential—both of you, but asking after one's daddy is hardly the mark of an evil being."

Seraphina snarled. "Get out of my way, sorcerer," she said. "I'll get the answers I want on my own."

Chesterfield raised his hand. "Not so fast," he said coldly. "You didn't ask permission. Besides, we are no longer in the time stream occupied by the humans, and I assure you that your father is quite dead. The stake is already in his body and the beheading is not far behind."

Ioana glanced nervously at her cousin. "What is he talking about, Seraphina?" she whined.

"All he's doing is talking," Seraphina said. "There's a human man sitting right over there at the table."

"So there is," Chesterfield purred. "By all means, attempt to interact with him."

Ioana took a step and then hesitated. When Chesterfield made no move to stop her, she crossed the dining room and looked down at the man who was working with a set of figures in a ledger. "Hello," she said. "Are you the owner?"

When the man didn't look up, Ioana trailed a finger down his cheek, turning her razor-like nails inward to slice the skin. As she moved down toward the jaw, one after another crimson droplets appeared and were instantly absorbed by the healing tissue. After several seconds, the oblivious man absent-mindedly scratched his face but otherwise remained fixated on his accounts.

"You see," Chesterfield said, "Peter is completely unaware of your presence and your touch leaves but the faintest annoyance. He's in quite a hurry. He wants to finish his task and attend the remainder of the carnival across the street. The festivities have resumed now that your Uncle Cezar and his people have disposed of Anton's body."

"What trickery is this?" Seraphina hissed. "Tell us where we are."

Chesterfield drew out his watch again. "Come here," he said. "Both of you."

Reluctantly the girls complied.

"Look at the second hand on my watch," he ordered. "What do you see?"

The long thin hand ticked back and forth in place, repeating the same second over and over again.

"It's broken," Seraphina said. "So what?"

Shaking his head, Chesterfield ran his thumb lovingly over the pristine glass covering the watch's face. "It is not broken," he said. "It is functioning beautifully, holding us all suspended within a single second of time playing on an endless loop."

Seraphina narrowed her eyes. "Set us free this instant."

"Or what?" Chesterfield asked, snapping his fingers. A silver stake appeared in his hand. "Do not try my patience, vampire, or I will leave you suspended here for eternity, condemned to watch human food come and go in this little pedestrian eatery."

He paused as if savoring the words.

"Oh, I quite like that idea," he said. "Left to starve to death in a restaurant. It has poetry."

When neither girl spoke, Chesterfield said, "What? No more idle threats? Then we are making progress. We will have to work on this pathetically predictable streak you both exhibit. Your capture offered not even a hint of sport."

"You've been watching us?" Seraphina asked. "Why? What are we to you?"

"In answer to your first question, yes," Chesterfield said. "I knew you could not resist staging some sort of grandstanding scenario with the witches. Forgive me for pointing this out, but you were severely outclassed tonight."

"This time," Seraphina hissed. "But we're not done with the witches yet."

"Silence!" Chesterfield snapped. "I am not finished speaking. You asked two questions. I have already answered the second, but you were not paying attention. Your value to me lies in your potential to evolve beyond your current infantile state. Once you understand and accept that you belong to me, your training will commence."

"We belong to no man," Seraphina said. "Ioana, come. We're leaving."

With a backward motion of his hand, Chesterfield sent them both flying against the brick wall of the pizzeria. "No," he said. "You are not. Nor will you be fed until you develop a better attitude. The humans cannot see you and you cannot harm them. You are, my dears, nothing more than rocks in the stream. Succulent life flows around you, but you are powerless to draw sustenance from it."

Ioana cowered beside her cousin, burying her face in Seraphina's shoulder. "Make him stop," she whined. "I'm hungry."

"Now, now," Chesterfield clucked. "No woman likes to be on a diet, but I assure you that curbing your excessive appetites will benefit you enormously. You will eat when I say you eat, and when you do, there will be no vampiric tricks of enthrallment involved. No creation of acolytes."

Still shielding her cousin, Seraphina said, "Why are you doing this?"

"Because Anton disappointed me," Chesterfield said. "He allowed his sentiments to overwhelm his judgment in his desire to save you from what he saw as a hideous existence. He failed me, therefore, I have ensured that he failed you. Monsters you are and monsters you shall remain. But you are *my* monsters now. If you do not like the arrangement, I will be happy to return you to your relatives for staking and beheading."

For the first time, real fear showed on Seraphina's face. "What do you want us to do?" she asked.

"Whatever I tell you to do," Chesterfield replied. "So long as *you* do not fail me, you will live and you will eat. If you perform well, I will allow you the occasional human treat with whom you may toy. Consider this a rewards-based arrangement. Your first job will be to attend the carnival with me tomorrow evening. I have just the costumes in mind to suit your . . . forward manners."

Ioana raised her head. "I can't wait that long to eat," she whimpered. "Please."

"You will wait as long as I tell you to wait," Chesterfield replied, taking out his pocket watch and working the winding crowns. "I must be going now."

"You're just going to leave us here?" Seraphina said, her voice gone shrill with terror.

"For now," he replied. "You may observe your food, but not play with it. The circumstances may be mildly frustrating for you, but frustration can breed appreciation. Let me be quite clear about this. Your lack of discipline does not serve me. Prove to me that you have the capacity for self-control and this temporal cage will not be necessary. Now, if you will excuse me, I have a pressing errand."

With that, he was gone.

The watch in Chesterfield's hand began to tick normally the instant he arrived at his destination—a shadowed clearing at the edge of the local cemetery. Smiling in satisfaction, the wizard pocketed the timepiece. He stood silently for a moment surveying the scene before him.

At the far end of the graveyard, pale spirits milled about engaged in their various afterlife pastimes. An elderly man appeared to be throwing some sort of ball back and forth with a younger ghost wearing the kind of helmet used in the human sport of football.

While Chesterfield did not squander undo attention on such nonsense, he made himself aware of the avocations of the greater populace. Knowledge, even of the mundane, might represent advantages to be exploited.

He wanted nothing more than to retrieve his property and return with it to his new home base—an inaccessible cavern deep beneath the mountains near Briar Hollow. Almost a week had passed since the chessboard delivered its last intelligence report from within the Hamilton woman's store in Briar Hollow.

The board could not, however, transmit on its own. When it fell silent, Chesterfield knew his operative, that little fool Glory Green, had allowed herself to be discovered. Other priorities held precedence over dealing with Miss Green, but deal with her he would.

Chesterfield raised his index finger and drew a circle in the air. A cloud of pale smoke wrapped around his form, which disappeared only to materialize inside the deserted crypt. The chessboard rested mere inches from the toe of his polished evening shoes, all the pieces except the white king lying scattered in the dust.

Holding the palm of his hand flat over the board, Chesterfield scanned it with his senses. The cacophony of musical fragments chained for eternity within the board's cells swelled in his mind. He detected no enchantment designed to work against him.

With a sweeping gesture, Chesterfield returned all the pieces to their proper places and then levitated the board to his side. Just as he was prepared to leave, however, he paused, frowning slightly. Was there a voice missing? As if on cue, the high, keening wail rose from the board. He did not know the name of that screeching entity, but something in its mournful cries had always pleased him.

"Even the damned must pause for breath," Chesterfield said, the corners of his mouth turning upward at the thought. "If only you could tell me, does each gasp feel as if it is your last?"

Chuckling, Chesterfield summoned the transforming smoke and was gone.

When he materialized, he stood at the center of a space so like a cathedral, the notion turned his chuckle into a hollow laugh. The irony was simply too delicious for a Crusader turned Creavit wizard.

Though embittering, Chesterfield's ties to the church led him to his destiny. Nothing but that minor concession remained of his fealty to the God of the Israelites, however. Chesterfield long ago abandoned his pathetic faith. On the day he walked away from the living death of mortality, the wizard embraced a different power, the only God to whom he now pledged his allegiance.

Chesterfield floated the chessboard toward a low table sitting between two chairs that flanked a central fire pit. His baroque desk and massive bookcases were arranged under the arched cavern ceiling to create a makeshift "room." Overlapping Persian rugs disguised the dirt floor, helping the warmth of the blaze to hold the cave's dank chill at bay.

Farther back in the shadows, the artifacts collected over

his many lifetimes rested securely in heavy wooden cases. Their glass doors picked up and reflected the light from the fire pit, creating the illusion of flaming rows marching away into the darkening shadows.

But only one object truly dominated the scene—the translucent globe hanging suspended over Chesterfield's workbench. Held aloft by an unseen enchantment, the cartographic construct depicted the world of the humans contained within a larger sphere representing the Fae Otherworld.

At key locations on the outer shell, holographic models of two Mother Trees sent virtual roots downward, penetrating the In Between to connect the realms. The filaments pulsated with simulated energy, lighting up regions on the sphere marked "Shevington" and "Rosslyn."

Next to the map, the jumbled detritus of an evolving theory sprawled across a massive work board. There, Chesterfield had tacked scraps of paper covered in wandering handwriting to compete for space with illustrations pinned at odd angles, the torn pages of books, smaller maps, and even leaves and branches. Webs of multi-colored string plotted connections across the metaphysical chaos.

How many trees? — Nodes on a network?
Thirteen? A coven X 4? — 52 elements? Periodic table.
Chemical or metaphysical?
Thirteen — karmic — ground to be broken.
Selfish power — purpose — destruction/elevation of self?
Permutation of opposites?
The staffs — cut apart but not disconnected.
The amulets — embodiment of the elements?
The witches. — The blood.

And now a new resource to consider. The Strigoi.

Granted, the young ladies were unstable at best and unpredictably dictated by their hunger, but could they play a role in his larger purpose? He'd rescued them on an angry whim, incensed by Anton's useless sentimentalism. At the very least, Seraphina and Ioana would create a distracting aside with which the Daughters of Knasgowa must deal, but if the vampiric wenches could be used to greater advantage, Chesterfield would certainly bring them into play.

Striding toward the globe, the wizard surveyed the overlapping, winding ideas. Was the whole endeavor the mechanical shorthand of a genius or the living scrapbook of a depraved mind?

As he studied the board, Chesterfield himself pondered the potential dichotomy. Then, a phrase caught and held his attention, sending his eyes darting over the conceptual landscape. A coil of red string lay on the floor beneath the board. With an idle gesture, Chesterfield unwound a length of the crimson cord, which he sent snaking upward with an undulating rhythm.

Weaving across the vertical surface, the string stopped at Chesterfield's command. A brass pin lifted from a dish on the desk and impaled the twine, which now pulled against the anchor point to reach a new terminus.

With a snap of his fingers, Chesterfield pegged and clipped the now taunt crimson line. It ran with tight precision from a medieval sketch of a demonic *Strigoi mort blasfematoare* to a meticulously drawn ancestral chart bearing the title, "The Daughters of Knasgowa."

"*And there went out another horse that was red,*" Chesterfield muttered, "*and power was given to him that sat thereon to take peace from the earth, and that they should kill one another: and there was given unto him a great sword.*"

Perhaps there *was* a way to use the Strigoi to further his goals.

The sound of something falling broke the wizard's reverie. Turning, he saw the white king from the chess set scurrying across the table as if in flight.

With long strides, Chesterfield crossed the space and snatched up the chess piece, feeling instantly the vibration of life in his hand.

"Be still," he commanded, "or I will crush you into splinters."

The king quieted instantly.

"Who are you?" Chesterfield said. "Tell me your name."

Slowly, the king, carved in the shape of the musical bass clef elongated, the thick nob at the top of the symbol rising to look upward. Chesterfield saw the shadow of a face gazing out of the wood grain.

"Gareth," the king said in a frightened voice. "I am the Alchemist, Gareth."

Chesterfield considered the partially obscured visage. "Gareth," he said, rolling the name around on his tongue as if tasting the flavor of it. "And how, Master Gareth, have you come to infiltrate my chessboard?"

Seeming to gather his courage, the man said, "Truly, Great Wizard, I did not. I have lived many years trapped in this chess set."

"And no doubt spent your time spying on me as a result," Chesterfield said, tightening his fingers. "Tell me why I should not destroy you this instant."

"Please," Gareth begged. "Please don't hurt me. It was only the lightning that set me free. Before that, I heard nothing but the screaming. I saw nothing. Please, Great Wizard, I speak the truth."

Chesterfield said nothing. Still holding the king trapped in his fist, he turned to the fire pit and held Gareth suspended over the flames. "Do you feel the heat, alchemist?" he asked in a silky voice.

"Yes, Great Wizard," Gareth stammered.

"If you lie to me," Chesterfield said, "if I even so much

as believe you are lying to me, I will incinerate you without hesitation. Do you understand?"

"Yes, Great Wizard."

Withdrawing his hand, Chesterfield sat down in one of the high-backed chairs. He reclined leisurely and placed the chess piece upright on the table.

"Now," Chesterfield said, "let us begin again. How long have you been in my chessboard?"

"Since 1890, sir," Gareth answered.

"And given that," Chesterfield went on, glowering darkly, "you wish me to believe that you have not been gathering information on my activities?"

"Truly, Great Wizard, I have not," Gareth said desperately. "Not at all. Never. I speak the truth when I tell you that I could hear nothing in that madhouse. Nothing. I have had not one moment's peace until the lightning fell from the sky and . . . "

"Stop!" Chesterfield commanded. "Let us deal with each topic singly. What madhouse?"

"Inside the board," Gareth replied. "To live within its confines is to descend through the levels of hell. The music screams and wails to be free and a fearful presence stalks those chambers. For years I fled to stay beyond its grasp. I craved only the quiet. Nothing more."

"Do not weary me with your babbling," Chesterfield warned. "What did you mean when you said the lightning set you free?"

"Lightning came through the ceiling of the prison," Gareth explained, "through the edges of the boxes and down into the cells. I thought the power came from the angels because one by one the voices fell silent. Then I saw it, an open channel, a way out. I reached for it, pushing through an unseen barrier, and then I was here, inside the king. The screaming started up again beneath me, but far away, better, quieter, so I stayed here."

"And you did not think to make your presence known to me sooner?" Chesterfield said.

Gareth dropped his eyes. "Forgive me, Great Wizard, but I fear your power."

"You would do well to continue to fear me," Chesterfield said. "Tell me how you came to be in the chessboard in the first place."

"In 1890 I worked as a gardener at the home of Richard Wagner in Bayreuth, Bavaria," Gareth said. "I found the chessboard packed away in a box hidden in a shed. I confess, Great Wizard, I stole the set in hopes of selling it."

"Why?"

"To raise money for my alchemical experiments," he said. "But each time I tried to approach a buyer, the board itself stopped me. At night, I came to believe the set spoke to me. Foolishly, I attempted to make contact with that voice and allowed myself to become trapped in its depth."

Steepling his fingers, Chesterfield considered Gareth's story. As the silence in the room grew longer, the chess piece began to tremble slightly. Finally, the wizard spoke. "You will sit in your place, for now, Master Gareth, and utter not so much as a single word until I decide what to do with you. Do you understand?"

Gareth opened his mouth to speak, reconsidered and opted instead to bow his head in wordless contrition.

"Excellent," Chesterfield said. "You learn quickly. I recommend you cultivate that aptitude in the interest of your long-term survival. Otherwise, little chessman, you most assuredly will burn."

EIGHT

As crazy as it may sound, Lucas, Greer and I managed to find other things to talk about on the way to Shevington. When I explained to Greer that we used the bikes to cut down on the walk time to the portal, she regarded me with a raised eyebrow and a look of mock horror.

"I think not," she said, holding out one hand to me and one to Lucas.

When I hesitated, Lucas said, "Don't worry. It's no worse than a roller coaster ride."

As much as I was tempted to tell them I don't do roller coasters, it seemed like entirely the wrong time to even imply that I didn't trust either of them. I took Greer's hand.

One summer our church hosted a contest to memorize Bible verses. Mom made me enter, but I was determined not to be one of those kids who pulled out "Jesus wept" when the cards were down. I learned some pretty obscure verses including this one from the book of Hosea, "They that sow the wind, shall reap the whirlwind."

That's where Greer took us. The heart of the whirlwind. I saw it all. The endless rows of stacks. The dark places in the archives. The wavering lights in the sconces—and then we were standing in front of the portal.

The abrupt change made me stagger on my feet. Lucas caught my elbow. "Steady girl," he said. "You okay?"

When I nodded, Greer said, "I would have tried to prepare you, but I've found most people just have to experience the flight of the baobhan sith."

"No problem," I said. "Do we have to do that very often?"

Grinning, Greer pointed to her high-heeled stiletto boots. "When I'm wearing these, yes," she said.

"Do you even own sensible footwear?" I countered.

"Define 'sensible,'" Greer said, just as Lucas coughed into his hand to hide the words "not a chance."

Greer cuffed him solidly on the side of the head, knocking his fedora askew. Lucas yelped, "Hey, watch the hat!"

Leaving the two of them to their good-natured scuffle, I approached the portal, held out my hand, and softly chanted the opening spell. As the solid wall dematerialized, a shaft of sunlight from the Valley of Shevington flooded the basement. On the other side of the opening, a line of six dragonlets sat waiting.

"Welcoming party?" Greer asked, stepping up beside me.

"Always," I said. "And don't ask me how they know when I'm going to show up because I don't have a clue."

The three of us passed through the portal and into the big meadow below the city. The day was clear, but I turned the collar of my coat up against the cold wind blowing out of the north. We don't really get snow in Briar Hollow, but Mom already had me looking forward to a white Christmas in the Valley.

Minreith, the dragonlet flock leader, and the others bowed low before me, their beaks scraping the ground. When I last saw them a few days earlier, the mischievous creatures confessed to some pilfering of minor, shiny objects in and around the city out of envy for the "big dragons" in Europe who get to have treasure.

Since I wasn't supposed to be in the Valley at the time,

we'd made a deal to hide each other's transgressions. The dragonlets would get me into Shevington undetected, and I wouldn't tell Barnaby about their thievery.

They upheld their end of the bargain, but things didn't work out for me in the covert department. That was the day the Mother Tree sent Lucas to stop me from contacting my brother, Connor. Which, by the way, was a completely false charge. All I had wanted to do was see him, but the Mother Tree apparently didn't trust me not to go a step further.

When Minreith raised his head to stare at me with his alert, jewel-faceted eyes, I said, "Did you take care of the returns?"

That touched off an earnest stream of clicks and chirps. I speak dragonlet, so what I heard was, "Just the way we promised, but we didn't have anything to do with Lucas catching you."

Without thinking, I said, "You know Lucas?"

"They do," Lucas said, before Minreith could answer. "And just so you know, I speak dragonlet, too. What did they steal?"

"Nothing valuable," I said. "Just odds and ends."

"All of it shiny, I'm betting," Lucas said, pushing back the open sides of his duster and shoving his hands in his pockets. "Big dragon envy is going to be the end of you, Minreith."

The dragonlet glared at Lucas with barely concealed indignation and said something I didn't understand about Lucas being a boastful "Gwragedd Annwn."

Before I could ask what that meant, Lucas said sternly, "That will be quite enough out of you. We have business with Barnaby and Moira, and we need to get a move on."

With that, he started up the path with long, swinging strides. I looked at Greer, who said in a soft voice, "Leave it for now."

Since she knew Lucas far better than I did, I took her advice, falling in beside her as we set out after Lucas. The dragonlets rose in the air to fly escort.

Other than exchanging greetings with Bill Ruff at the bridge, the remainder of the walk passed in silence, but once inside the main gate of the city, the happy sounds of the busy citizenry surrounded us. Sunday in Shevington is a day of rest and socializing. The village green in the center of town plays host to picnicking families and romping children, all under the watchful eye of the Mother Tree.

Our destination was the Lord High Mayor's house on the far side of the square. Innis, Barnaby's matronly brownie housekeeper, welcomed us at the door.

When I immediately went to the fire in the front room to warm my hands, the round little woman exclaimed, "Where are my manners? You must be chilled to the bone. I'll be right back with tea and scones."

She bustled past Barnaby, almost knocking him down as he came through the parlor door. "Innis! What on earth!" he said, sidestepping to make way for the determined woman.

When Innis didn't slow down enough to answer him, Barnaby turned questioning eyes toward me.

"She thinks I'm cold," I explained. "Hi, by the way."

"Hello," Barnaby said. "I've sent for Moira as you asked me to. She will be joining us shortly. Lucas, Greer, a pleasure as always."

Once the alchemist arrived, we'd be all business, so this was my only chance.

"Would it be terribly rude of me if I asked to have a word with Barnaby in private before Moira gets here?" I asked.

Neither Greer nor Lucas seemed to think anything about my request, but Barnaby's brows arched in surprise before his native graciousness kicked in.

"Of course," he said, "shall we step into my private study?" He held his hand out to indicate a door at the back of the room.

"Excuse us," I said to Lucas and Greer. "This won't take long."

"Not a problem," Lucas said. "We need to check in with the DGI anyway."

Barnaby held the door open for me and I stepped into his small, cozy study. My grandfather is a scrupulously tidy man in every other part of his life, but in that one room, a kind of cheerful chaos reigns. Open books litter every available surface along with a profusion of loose notes and an odd detritus of curious objects that at that moment included what appeared to be a Viking helmet and what I could have sworn was Aladdin's lamp.

"So sorry," Barnaby said, scooping a stack of books off the chair beside his desk. "I'm in the middle of multiple research projects."

"About what?" I asked, sitting down.

"Principally human literature of the late 20th century," he said. "I endeavor to stay abreast of the things that interest our counterparts in the other realm, but I've allowed myself to become rather outdated."

"How outdated?"

"The last human novels I read were by three sisters living in Yorkshire," he said, sitting down behind the desk. "Their father was a clergyman . . . "

"The Bronte sisters," I said.

Barnaby's face brightened. "You know their works?" he asked.

"I had to read them for senior English in high school," I said.

"How intriguing," he said. "We must find time to discuss the human educational system. That is on my list of interest. But do tell me, did you find Charlotte's novel to be rather . . . sentimental?"

Well, that was a polite way to put it.

"I threw the book across the room when Mr. Rochester got his eyesight back," I grinned.

Barnaby laughed. "Thank you," he said. "I feared my reaction might have been a product of my gender rather than a solid literary analysis. It would seem we have somewhat similar tastes."

That was the opening I needed.

"Like, grandfather like granddaughter?" I asked as lightly as I could manage.

At first, Barnaby looked as if he had no idea what to say. When he did speak, his voice was so soft I almost couldn't hear him. "How did you find out?" he asked.

"The Mother Tree told me," I said. "Why didn't you?"

My bluntness seemed to make things easier for him.

"Moira asked me the same question," he admitted. "I honestly did not know how."

"How about just saying it?" I suggested.

Barnaby sighed. "Forgive me," he said, "but I did not find the task quite that easy."

"Did you find it easy to have a relationship with Connor all these years and not have one with me?" I asked.

The words came out much sharper than I intended and filled with a degree of hurt and anger that surprised even me.

Barnaby leaned forward and caught hold of my hand. "My dear child," he said, "I assure you that Connor knows me only as the Lord High Mayor. He has no more idea than you have had of our true relation."

That surprised me. "But why?" I asked in confusion. "Your grandson was right here in Shevington, and you didn't want to know him?"

"Quite to the contrary," Barnaby protested. "There was nothing I would have liked more than to have been a guiding presence in the boy's life, and in yours as well, but in my capacity as Lord High Mayor, I had a responsibility to guard his secret. I could hardly intrude in your life when you knew nothing of magic or the Otherworld."

I was willing to concede that point, but he wasn't completely off the hook with me yet. "And what about my mother?" I asked.

"Kelly does not know my true identity either," he said. "The last member of your family privy to the information was your grandmother, Kathleen."

That left me feeling considerably less left out, but still fairly exasperated.

"You know, Grandad," I said, "we have to do something about this whole family secret thing because it's just not working for me."

As I watched, Barnaby's face took on an element of something between astonishment and wonder. "You just called me Grandad," he said.

He looked so adorable I couldn't stay annoyed with him.

"Would you like 'Great Great Great Grampie' better?" I teased.

"I would not," he replied emphatically, squeezing my hand before he released it. "'Grandad' will be just fine."

"So can I tell everyone now?"

"Well," he hedged, obviously grappling with indecision and uncertainty, "if you think the news will be welcomed."

"I think it will be more than welcomed," I assured him.

From the other room, the sound of a woman's voice caught Barnaby's attention. His expression was unmistakable and since we were in "tell the truth" mode, I asked.

"You're in love with Moira, aren't you?"

He hesitated, seemed to think better of it, and then sighed. "Are you always this forthright?"

"Only about things that count," I said. "I watched you when you heard Moira's voice. I'd say this counts."

Something akin to pride filled his features. "You are correct," he said. "Moira does 'count.' In fact, I love her deeply."

A knock at the door interrupted us.

Barnaby sat back in his chair. "Come," he said.

The door opened and Moira stepped over the threshold. "Hello Jinx, Barnaby," she said, looking first at me and then at my grandfather. "Is everything alright?"

That's when I took pity on Barnaby and bailed him out. "Everything's great," I said. "Barnaby and I just had some things to talk about. He'll tell you all about it later. I think we better get back to business now."

Moira shot Barnaby a quizzical, questioning look. "It's alright, my dear," he said softly. "Jinx knows . . . everything . . . but she is quite right that we have pressing matters."

The alchemist couldn't have cared less about "pressing matters." All of her attention was focused on my grandfather. "Are you alright, Barnaby?" she asked.

"Very much so," he said. "Quite happy, in fact."

The love in Moira's answering smile put a lump in my throat. I quietly stepped out of the room to give them some privacy. There was a brief murmur of voices, and then Barnaby and Moira joined us all in the parlor.

Over the next hour and a half, Greer laid out all of her theories about Chesterfield's time shifting abilities. We reviewed the drone video again and related the details of our trip to the site of the wreck. At the end of the recitation, Barnaby's ashen face told me he'd already arrived at the same conclusion we'd reached about how dangerously he'd underestimated Chesterfield's powers in 1936.

Since Greer had more or less been running the meeting, I let her pursue the point.

"Why did you do it, Barnaby?" she said quietly. "What

motivated you to allow Chesterfield the clemency of probation?"

We all waited. Barnaby seemed to be trying to collect his thoughts. Finally, he said, "I suspect you are all aware that my first wife was murdered by a renegade Creavit wizard. My search to locate the brigand was motivated by a level of rage and revenge I hope never to revisit. Chesterfield expressed remorse for his actions and assured me he wished only to live quietly and pursue his interest in antiquities. I allowed myself to believe him. That was clearly an error."

There was no arguing with that, so I didn't even try. "I have to admit I feel like we're sitting ducks now that we know Seraphina and Ioana are still alive," I said. "We don't know where Chesterfield is, what he wants, or why he's been after my family for 30 years—which, by the way, seriously creeps me out. What do we do now?"

"We do not panic," Barnaby said firmly. "We are not without resources. I will speak with Major Istra and place GNATS command entirely at your disposal. We will not leave you exposed until we locate and apprehend Chesterfield and properly dispose of the vampires with whom he is clearly in league."

"The higher ups at DGI want us coordinating directly with you," Greer said. "Where do you want us?"

"In Briar Hollow," Barnaby said. "Chesterfield's focus appears to be on the fairy mound. Whatever he does next, I believe that will be his target."

I can't say that made me feel better, but at least we were getting organized. It was a start.

NINE

Barnaby stood at the parlor window watching Jinx, Lucas, and Greer. The two DGI agents headed for O'Hanson's Pub, but Jinx walked toward the Mother Tree. With a private pang of remorse, he hoped the great Oak would be able to offer her more reassurance than he had just managed with his platitudes and excuses.

"What are you thinking?" Moira asked.

"How much I hate lying to them," he said heavily.

She came up behind him, encircling his waist with her arms. "Lie is a strong word," she said. "You spoke the truth when you said you had no desire to be motivated by revenge."

Covering her hands with his own, Barnaby said, "I thought he was telling me the truth."

"I know."

"After everything that happened, I just wanted us to live peacefully. Did I want that so much I allowed myself to be duped?"

"You could not have known his true plans."

Barnaby turned to face her. "Couldn't I, Moira?" he said. "I, of all men, should know the lengths to which Irenaeus will go to get what he desires."

"And I, of all women," Moira said, "know the extent to which you will restrain yourself in the name of the

84

greater good. You decided to grant clemency to a man who did not deserve it. That is your only sin."

"A sin that has placed everyone I love, and this community we've worked so hard to build, in potential danger," he said.

Moira smiled at him, cupping his cheek in the palm of her hand. "My darling, we have been in danger since the day we pulled up stakes and quit Europe to protest the rising power of the Creavit," she said. "We have enjoyed more than four centuries of peaceful isolation. We both knew that could never last."

Barnaby rested his forehead against hers. "So now we must rejoin the fight," he said.

"We never left the fight, Barnaby," she said, kissing him softly. "We only took a long rest."

<hr>

As we came out of the Lord High Mayor's house, Lucas suggested getting a drink at O'Hanson's Pub. "The three of us are working together now," he said. "Wouldn't it be a good idea to get to know each other outside some life-or-death crisis?"

Postponing diving back into the crisis at hand sounded like a great idea, but first I had to speak with the Mother Tree. I had a branch to pick with the old girl.

"Order me a beer," I said. "I just want to pay my respects to the Great Oak."

Since they both worked for the Tree, neither of them seemed to think that was out of the ordinary. They struck out for the pub, and I crossed the street to the village green.

The late afternoon sun cast long shadows across the perfectly manicured lawn. Even with the coming cold months, the grass remained lush and verdant. As I stepped beneath the massive oak's spreading canopy, the sounds of the town faded away and the temperature warmed several degrees.

Taking a seat on one of the stone benches, I looked up. "We need to talk," I said, "and thanks for the heat, by the way."

The Mother Tree's voice rose in my mind, resonant and melodic. "You are welcome," she said. "Winter comes more quickly to our Valley than in your world."

"I hope so," I replied. "Mom promised me my first white Christmas up here."

"There will be snow," the Tree said, "long before the celebration of the Winter Solstice."

Okay, so now that we had the weather discussion out of the way.

"The last time we talked you told me to find out what really happened to Seraphina and Ioana," I said. "Now that we know our mothers weren't responsible for the accident and that the girls are still alive, can I meet my brother?"

"They live," the Tree agreed, "but in a greatly altered form."

"True," I said, "but that's all on Irenaeus Chesterfield. I answered the question you asked me."

Word to the wise. Never get too confident you've passed a test until the teacher actually puts a big, fat red "A" on the top of the page.

"Why did the Creavit wizard cause the accident?"

With a sinking heart, I said, "I don't know."

"Then you have not fulfilled the task I set before you."

To my credit, I didn't kick the dirt in frustration, but I came danged close.

"Come on!" I protested. "Does everything have to be some huge riddle? I want to meet my brother!"

The limbs over my head stirred with what I took to be a patient sigh.

"Those puzzles that return the most worthwhile prizes do not lend themselves to simplistic answers," the Oak said. "Complete your work, Jinx Hamilton. The thing you desire most will come to you at the end of your labor. Go now. Join your new friends. You have much to learn from them."

Once the Mother Tree finishes speaking, it's useless to try to get anything else out of her. And I was so disappointed in her answer, I needed that beer I'd asked Lucas to order for me. I didn't have to wait long. As soon as I walked in the front door of O'Hanson's, the DGI agent appeared by my side.

"Hi," Lucas said, handing me a glass of ale. "I've been watching for you. Follow me. We're in the back by the fire."

As we threaded our way through the mostly full tables, I fell instantly in love with the place. Heavy exposed beams criss-cross the low, dark ceiling. Antique brass fixtures cast pools of light throughout the room, and behind the mahogany bar, rows of liquor bottles glint warmly.

A low hum of conversation and laughter constantly animates the great room, but unlike the Dirty Claw, the werecat bar across town, O'Hanson's is a place to sit and talk, not get roaring drunk and start a fight.

Lucas led me to a scarred and worn plank table positioned in front of a massive, roaring fire. Greer occupied one of the four barrel-back chairs, talking with a bright-faced raccoon named Rube.

When he saw me, Rube cried, "Doll! Great to see you again! Red here tells me you tried to fry yourself a couple of vamps. Suh-wheet!"

The raccoon held up his paw for a high five, which I returned on cue. "Hey, Rube," I said. "How are things going down in the sewers?"

"Good, good," he said, waving me toward a chair. "Have I ever told you about the time me and my crew ran into a gator in New Orleans?"

Greer rolled her eyes. "Reuben, please," she said wearily. "According to your indelicately named associate, Booger, the reptile in question was an escaped pet iguana."

"Teeth," Rube said, pointing at the baobhan sith to emphasize his point. "That thing had *teeth*."

As I sat down, I said, "Since we're all supposed to be getting to know each other better, Rube, you can get the ball rolling. What's your story anyway?"

The raccoon grinned, displaying his own impressive set of chompers. "I was born a poor striped raccoon . . . "

Greer groaned. "Do not encourage him," she warned me.

"I'm serious," I said. "What's the true story?"

Rube sat up straighter and the teasing bravado disappeared from his voice. "I'm an independent contractor," he said seriously. "I work with the IRS as a containment specialist and do undercover jobs for the DGI. Raccoons can move around in the human world easily. We have a reputation as mischief makers and break-in artists. That means dodging the odd, stray coonhound and an occasional load of buckshot, but it's nothing we can't handle."

When he said "IRS," he didn't mean the tax wing of the federal government. Rube was referring to the International Registry for Shapeshifters, an agency that regulates shapeshifter/human interactions. They also clean up any evidence that might tip humans off to the existence of the Fae world.

From what I can tell, werecats are mainly in charge of the Registry aided by the raccoons. Together, they spend most of their time covering up werewolf transgressions, a sore subject with Festus who habitually refers to the creatures as "mongrel moon dogs."

After Festus had called in Rube's cleanup crew to take care of some evidence in the Malcolm Ferguson case, I learned that the raccoons maintain a computerized database of human sewer systems, a fact that Rube now confirmed for me.

"You'd be surprised how much of the human world is underground," Rube said, breaking into his happy, bantering tone again. "We can get pretty much anywhere undetected and get out the same way."

"I hope this isn't a rude question," I said, "but are you a shapeshifter?"

"Nope," he said. "What you see is what you get. We are Fae raccoons, and we are a law unto ourselves."

"That," Greer said, taking a drink of her whisky, "is an understatement."

Rube laughed. "Aw, come on, Red, you love me, and you know it."

Even if they were giving each other a hard time, I could tell this unlikely trio did share genuine affection and camaraderie. That told me they must be one hell of a team in action.

"So what do you do with the DGI?" I asked Rube.

Lucas stepped in with the answer. "His official job description is 'contract agent in charge of undetected entry, covert acquisition, and surveillance,'" he said gravely.

After thinking about that for a minute, I translated. "Breaking and entering, stealing, and snooping?"

"Exactamundo!" Rube said, slapping the table with his paw. "Job of a lifetime!"

"Doesn't that technically make you a crook?" I asked, trying not to laugh.

Rube clutched at his chest dramatically. "You wound me, Sister," he moaned. "You wound me to the core."

We all cracked up at that. Just then the barman delivered a tray full of food. I watched with fascination as Rube picked up a raw egg and neatly washed it in a bowl of water supplied for just that purpose. Using his teeth, he bit off the top of the shell, delicately spit it out on the plate, and then knocked the yolk and white back like he was taking a tequila shot.

"Wow," I said, "so it's true. You guys really do wash your food before eating."

"I may work in a sewer, Doll," Rube said, reaching for another egg, "but that doesn't mean I don't value good personal hygiene."

Lucas, on the other hand, apparently liked his eggs hard-boiled—and surrounded by sausage, breaded and fried—or so I found out when I asked him what the heck he was eating.

"Scotch Egg," he replied, munching happily.

"It's deep fried, but then they serve it cold?" I asked, wrinkling my nose. "That's disgusting."

"You wouldn't say that if you tried one," he said, wiping congealed grease off his mouth.

"I'll stick with the fries," I said, taking a thick, warm, golden potato wedge off the plate.

"Suit yourself," Lucas said. "Not everyone can be an epicurean like me."

Since Greer relied on a liquid diet, she hadn't ordered anything, but that didn't stop her from giving Lucas grief over his eating habits. "I agree with Jinx," she said. "I do not know how you survive on that disgusting tripe you call food."

"This from a woman so finicky she'll turn down anything but room temperature AB negative," Lucas shot back.

Sensing the conversation headed down a less than appetizing blood-related path, I said, "Your turn, Grayson. Rube clearly loves to talk about himself and Greer is totally out as a vampire. What's your deal?"

I hoped that was better than "what are you," which was the information I really wanted him to give me.

Lucas started to say something about how uninteresting he was, but Greer cut him off. "You're the one who suggested we get to know one another this evening," she said. "Answer the woman. Tell her about the Gwragedd Annwn."

The dragonlets used those same words back at the portal when we arrived in the Valley. I thought it might have been a Gaelic insult, but I was about to discover the real meaning.

Lucas swallowed his food, washing it down with ale. He seemed to be stalling for time, but I had plenty to give him—I waited. Finally, he said, "The Gwragedd Annwn are my people. I'm a Welsh water elf."

It was on the tip of my tongue to ask about pointy ears, but I managed not to say something that stupid, going instead with the fairly neutral and thoroughly curious, "Why would you be reluctant to tell me that?"

"Because I'm a halfling," he said. "My father was a water elf and my mother was a Druid. I haven't followed the traditions of either people. The Gwragedd Annwn are renowned healers, and the Druids are great scholars. Me? I'm just a guy who knows how to get things done—and I'm a really good swimmer."

His rakish smile returned with those last words, but I still detected uncertainty in his manner. There was obviously more to his history that Lucas didn't want to go into, and it didn't seem like the time for me to press for more detail.

"Okay," I said, "so I can't get rid of you by drowning. Good to know."

That touched off more laughter, which is what I intended. The conversation moved on to less charged topics. We ordered more drinks, and I allowed myself to be talked into trying a Scotch Egg. I'm pretty sure I clogged an artery—or several—but Lucas was right. Those things are delicious.

Even with everything that was going on around

Chesterfield and the Strigoi Sisters, I had fun that evening. My new friends were far less formal and formulaic than the other Fae I'd met.

Of course, the scene was a bar joke waiting for a punch line.

"A vampire, an elf, and a talking raccoon walk into a bar . . . "

But it was a good bar, as friendly and inviting as any neighborhood watering hole anywhere in the world. In the most incongruous of settings, I felt completely normal for the first time in days. In my gut, I knew the reprieve wouldn't last, so I settled back and enjoyed it while I could.

TEN

A cold blast of wind whistled down the High Street. Connor Endicott hunched into his wool jacket and turned the collar up. Normally on an evening like this, he would have preferred to stay indoors, but the allure of a waiting order of sketchbooks and pencils at Horatio Pagecliff's bookstore proved too strong.

The weight of the bundle under his arm reassured Connor that the walk had been worth it regardless of the weather. Was there anything more full of promise than a creamy blank page and a freshly sharpened pencil?

He wanted to dedicate an entire portfolio to sketches of the growing unicorn foal. The new filly would have to be raised largely indoors this winter due to the unusual timing of her birth. That would afford Connor the chance to bond with the newborn and study her development.

The Lord High Mayor brought the last surviving unicorns to Shevington roughly fifteen years ago. Since then, Ellis Groomsby, the town's stable master, had worked tirelessly with the sensitive creatures to put in place a viable breeding program. Connor now served as his principle apprentice.

Still thinking about how to ensure that the filly received adequate exercise, Connor spotted the sign for O'Hanson's Pub a few yards ahead. Couldn't he make time for a Scotch

Egg and a pint of ale? The idea of settling down at the table in the back by the fireplace appealed to him.

As he slowed his step and reached for the brass handle on the pub's front door, however, the nagging voice of his conscience stopped him. The biting wind would be much worse in a couple of hours, and he'd left Ailish at home nursing a cold.

An image of the Elven Grey Loris' enormous sad eyes rose in his mind. Normally, Ailish accompanied Connor wherever he went, sitting perched on his shoulder chattering happy commentary in his ear. But for the last two days, she'd sneezed and coughed—and complained loudly about taking the tonic Ellis prepared for her.

When Connor told his friend that he was going to Pagecliff's, she immediately reached for her red and white striped scarf.

"No, Ailish," Connor said. "The wind is blowing a gale, and you're sick. You have to stay here."

"Ailish doesn't like alone," she said defiantly. "Alone makes Ailish *sad*."

"You won't be alone long," Connor assured her, "and I'll get you some bananas and honey while I'm out."

That suggestion brightened her expression. "Sticky sweet honey?" the loris asked.

"Sticky sweet is the only kind there is, silly," he laughed.

"Silly Ailish will do alone for sticky sweet honey," she assured him bravely, before adding, "but hurry."

Connor's lips curled into a smile as he remembered the whimsical exchange. He rarely refused Ailish anything. He'd promised to return as quickly as possible. The Scottish Egg and ale would have to wait.

Truthfully, Connor had work to do anyway. He was finishing an embossed saddle on commission. The intricate patterns on the flaps were taking longer than he'd anticipated and he hated to miss a delivery deadline.

Quickening his steps, Connor made his way through the mostly deserted streets to the stables. As soon as he started up the stairs to his compact apartment over the tack room, he spotted Alish waiting for him at the open door.

The loris clutched a single pink tissue in her tiny hand. She greeted him with the mournful pronouncement, "Ailish's nose is running away."

Laughing, Connor took the tissue and wiped her face. "Ailish's nose is *running*," he said. "Not running *away*."

The loris sniffed and intoned solemnly, "If *away* is dry, *away* is good."

Connor held out his hand. "Come with me," he said. "I'll fix your bananas and honey. That will make you feel better."

Ailish climbed his arm and wrapped herself around his neck, clinging to Connor as he first deposited the parcel from the bookstore on his desk. In the kitchen, he opened the sack of groceries and put away his purchases, leaving out a large bunch of bananas and a jar of honey.

He peeled and sliced the fruit, poured the golden honey in a bowl, and settled Ailish on the sofa. After adding more wood to the fire, Connor went to his littered workbench beneath the dormer window. The smell of new leather and oil permeated the space, but in a pleasant way that he found both comforting and homey.

In truth, Connor had only lived two places in his life— his grandmother's cottage and the apartment at the stables. When Granny Endora died and left her house to Fiona Ryan, Connor had been secretly relieved. He liked his life exactly the way it was. He couldn't imagine living away from the animals or having to worry about matters of upkeep and getting along with the neighbors.

As a boy growing up at Endora's, Connor stole away to the stables at every opportunity. In the end, Ellis just put him to work. Then, when Connor turned 18, he moved in over the tack room. Fifteen years later, he was still there.

Just as he reached for a leather stamp, Connor heard heavy scratching at the window. Drawing back the curtain, he found himself looking straight into a set of glowing, jewel-like eyes.

"Oh for heaven's sake," Connor muttered, raising the sash. "Minreith, what are you doing out on a night like this?"

The dragonlet answered with a series of perfectly reasonable chirps.

"Yes, yes," Connor said, "I know. The stables are technically outside the city limits, and you're allowed to be here, but I already gave you a pan of scraps at dawn and it's cold out there."

Minreith turned his head, opened his mouth, and emitted a slender jet of flame.

"Okay, okay, *stop* that!" Connor said. "I know you have your own central heating system, you don't have to try to burn the place down proving your point. Come in, let me see if there's anything left you can eat."

Minreith delicately hopped through the opening, folding his wings flat against his body as Connor reached past him and closed the window. The dragonlet looked around curiously, spotted Ailish on the couch, and yodeled a greeting.

Ailish raised her paw in response and sneezed.

"She has a cold," Connor explained. "You better stay over here, so you don't catch it. When you sneeze, things have a tendency to go up in flames."

The dragonlet shrugged and settled himself on a clear corner of the workbench, watching as Connor went into the kitchen.

"I don't have any meat for you," he told the dragonlet. "How about some apples?"

Minreith's interested expression was all the answer Connor needed, but the dragonlet added a series of inquisitive clicks.

"Yes," Connor said, "there's cheese. You're a big moocher, you do know that, right?"

Shrugging again, Minreith caught the apple Connor tossed in his direction, holding it delicately in one talon as he nipped at the fruit with his sharp beak.

Rejoining his guest, Connor sat down two plates bearing both apple slices and hunks of cheddar cheese. "One for you," he said, "and one for me. Got it?"

Minreith gurgled reproachfully.

"Yes," Connor said, "I *do* think you'd steal my food. Unless it was broccoli."

From the sofa, Ailish said, "Broccoli green yuck." She emphasized her point by dipping a piece of her banana in the honey bowl and popping the whole dripping mess in her mouth.

"That will be enough out of you," Connor said. "It wouldn't hurt either one of you to eat more vegetables."

At that, Minreith swallowed his food and cackled a question at Connor.

"Brussels sprouts are an exception," Connor said firmly. "I won't eat those disgusting things either."

As Connor went back to work, Minreith launched into a description of the day's events in Shevington from the dragonlet point of view. Connor was only half listening to the gurgled and hissed narrative until something caught his attention.

"What do you mean the pretty lady from the human place?" he asked.

Minreith repeated himself and added the detail that the woman was with "the red vampire and the leather coat man."

"Are you talking about Jinx Hamilton?" Connor asked.

Minreith nodded.

"And she was with Lucas Grayson and Greer Mac-Vicar?" Connor said. "Really? Wonder what she's doing with the DGI?"

The dragonlet shook his head and let out a few more chirps.

"Oh my God, seriously? They're drinking at O'Hanson's?" Connor said. "I almost went in there on my way home. I'd like to get a look at this witch from the human world everyone is talking about. Maybe I'll ask Mrs. Ryan to introduce us one of these days. You know Jinx is her niece."

Nodding again, Minreith gulped down the rest of his apple and tapped the window with his beak.

"Are you sure you want to go back out there?" Connor asked. "You can sleep here tonight if you want."

Minreith shook his head, indicating he needed to get back to his flock.

"Okay," Connor said, "but you go straight back to your cave. None of this flying over the Valley at night spewing fire."

When the dragonlet protested, Connor said firmly, "It may be fun to convince people they see shooting stars, but then half the town thinks they've witnessed an omen and the Lord High Mayor has to settle them down. Barnaby has enough to deal with on a normal day without any help from you."

After Minreith left, Connor quickly became absorbed in his work again, finishing the embossing well after midnight. Putting his tools aside, he realized Ailish was curled up on the sofa snoring.

Since he had to be up at dawn to feed the animals and start mucking out the stalls, Connor knew he had to get some sleep, but he didn't want to wake Ailish who needed her rest. At the same time, however, if the loris awakened in the night and couldn't find him, she'd panic.

That just left him one option—joining her on the sofa. Being careful not to disturb his little friend, Connor carefully stretched out and pulled a blanket over them both. Ailish instantly curled up on his shoulder, wrapping one arm protectively around his neck.

Connor didn't know how long he'd been asleep when the sound of heavy knocking awakened him. Rubbing his eyes groggily, he answered the door to find Ellis Groomsby standing on the stairs.

"Ellis!" Connor said. "Did I oversleep? I am so sorry. I'll be right down."

"Slown down, Endicott," Ellis said. "You're not late. I'm better than an hour early, but I need to change your assignment for the day."

"Oh. Sure," Connor said. "What do you need me to do?"

"Get up to the new merfolk habitat and help with the introduction of the final aquatic lifeforms," he said. "The wind has died down, and the skies are still clear, but the work up there has to be finished before the first snow hits. You good with that?"

"Absolutely!" Connor grinned. "I've been dying to learn more about the sea creatures. Let me get my stuff together and I'll head out."

"Good man," Ellis said. "Stop by my office before you leave, and I'll give you the current work orders."

As he turned to go back downstairs, Connor said, "Uh, Ellis? Don't forget the unicorns need more bedding in this weather."

Ellis shot his young apprentice a bemused glance over his shoulder. "Connor Endicott," he said, "I'll have you know that I was working on unicorn conservation when you were in diapers."

"I know," Connor said sheepishly, "but Blissia did just foal."

"And she couldn't have picked a worse time to do it," Ellis groused. "Unicorns are supposed to foal in the spring."

"Which is why the little one should be kept . . . "

"For God's sake, Endicott," Ellis groused good-naturedly, "of course I'll make sure the filly is warm. Now get on with it, man!"

When Connor closed the door, Ailish, who was now fully alert and very interested, began to jump up and down with excitement. "Ailish go to see fish people!" she exclaimed breathlessly.

Catching her in mid-leap, Connor said, "No, Ailish doesn't. You're still sick, and there's a big storm coming. You have to stay here and help Uncle Ellis run the stables."

Both ears instantly sagged. "Grouchy Unca Ellis," Ailish pouted. "Phooey!"

Smothering a laugh, Connor said, "Ellis just pretends to be grouchy. You know you always have fun when you stay with him."

Brightening a little, the loris asked speculatively, "Unca Ellis have sticky sweet honey?"

"I will make sure Ellis has sticky sweet honey," Connor assured her.

"Okay," Ailish said, "but Connor hurry."

"I'll be back before you even know I'm gone," he said. "You don't have a thing to worry about."

ELEVEN

"I still don't see why I had to travel as a human," Festus groused, following Chase onto the elevator with a scowl, "or why I had to shave before you'd let me come."

"For the tenth time, Dad," Chase said, hitting the button for the second floor, "this is the only hotel I could get close to Chesterfield's shop, and it's not pet-friendly. You had to shave because you looked like a bum."

"Some women think stubble is sexy," Festus grumbled. "And I most certainly am not anyone's *pet*. I've got half a mind to get furry and shred the curtains for the hell of it. The cable package in this joint better be good, or they're getting a one-star review."

"For God's sake, Dad, we are not on vacation," Chase said. "The point is that we have a room with a window that opens and a nice handy tree outside so we can come and go undetected. You know, to do the job we were sent here to do?"

"Whatever," Festus said as the elevator doors opened. They stepped into a stereotypical hotel hallway. "How far did you say we have to walk from here to get to Chesterfield's?"

"About a block and a half," Chase replied, scanning the door numbers until he found their room. "This is it."

He inserted the card in the electronic lock and stood

aside to let Festus walk in first. Just beyond the threshold, a shimmering aura surrounded the old man right before he melted toward the floor. Within seconds, Festus, as his usual yellow cat self, stepped out of the pile of discarded clothing, stretched, and limped toward the nearest bed.

"Fold my stuff for me, will you, boy?" he said, springing onto the mattress.

Rolling his eyes, Chase said, "Sure, Dad. No problem."

"And when you're done, check the mini bar and see if they've got any decent Scotch in this place."

"No," Chase said firmly as he picked up his father's cast-off trousers. "Work first, whisky later."

Flattening his ears, Festus said, "When did you get to be such a tight . . . "

"Do not start with me, Dad," Chase warned.

Setting his mouth in a frown that turned his whiskers sharply downward, Festus said, "All I'm saying is that you most certainly do *not* take after *my* side of the family. Let's get on with it so I can have a drink."

Chase unzipped a side pocket on his suitcase and removed a quick release collar with a silver disc attached. "Fine," he said, "then you get to wear the RABIES tag."

Festus fixed him with an indignant glare. "I have never worn a collar in my life," he said, "and I do not intend to start now."

"You're the one who couldn't wait to shift," Chase said, "and I can't very well put the thing on myself after I make the change, so suck it up and stick your neck out."

While his father continued to complain loudly, Chase fastened the collar in place and pressed the tag between his fingers. The metal glowed slightly and then returned to normal.

"You're good to go," Chase said. "So far it seems to be functioning perfectly."

Festus frowned at his reflection in the large mirror

across from the bed. "Tell me again what this gizmo is supposed to do?" he said. "Damn thing makes me look like some kind of domesticated yarn chaser."

"You love yarn, and you know it," Chase grinned. "The Registry just started issuing these tags for field testing. Furl managed to score one for us for this job. RABIES stands for 'Residual Active Base Imprint Energy Scanner.'"

"I read the Registry memo," Festus said, "but as usual, Furl didn't make a damned bit of sense. Exactly what does this fool thing do?"

"It reads leftover energy signatures," Chase explained. "We'll use it to scan the interior of Chesterfield's store. It will show us the imprint of everything and everyone that has been there in the last 72 hours."

Festus studied the tag in the mirror with more interest. "Magic or tech?"

"A little bit of both," Chase said. "Ironweed touched off an explosion of hybrid ideas when he developed the GNATS drones and powered then with fairy dust. The RABIES designers used an enchantment to give the device the ability to scan for energy, but everything it records goes on a high-capacity memory chip."

Festus scrubbed thoughtfully at one ear with his paw. "Huh," he said. "Maybe those morons at the Registry have actually come up with something useful. So what happens to all the pictures we take with this thing?"

"They go to Barnaby and Moira for analysis."

"We don't get to look at them?"

"The tag emits a beam of light that will highlight everything it strikes," Chase said. "We'll be able to see the stuff in real time."

"Okay," Festus said grudgingly, "now I'm interested."

"I'll be sure to tell Furl you approve," Chase said sardonically.

Festus growled. "I never said I *approved*, I'm just a little more *interested* than I was five minutes ago. You're just assuming the damned thing will actually work. Are we doing Ionescu's office today, too?"

Chase sat down on the edge of the bed and began to take off his shoes. "No," he said. "Cezar gave us permission to look through Anton's papers. We can just walk right in the front door. No need to go sneaking around. We have an appointment with Anton's secretary tomorrow morning at ten. Then we're going to go see Miss Shania Moonbeam."

Festus snorted. "Her I can't wait to meet. I guess we're going to have to do all that on two legs?"

"We can't very well walk around Raleigh as mountain lions," Chase said, starting to unbutton his shirt. "And people tend to freak out when house cats start talking to them."

"Humans would be a lot better off if they *did* listen to their house cats," Festus said. "I discussed that very thing with Winston just the other day."

Chase froze. "Winston, as in Jinx's cat Winston?"

Unperturbed, Festus asked, "Do we know anyone else named Winston?"

Fixing his father with a look of horror, Chase said, "Does Jinx know you're talking to her cats?"

Festus laughed outright at that. "You think I've lost my ever-loving mind?" he said. "Of course she doesn't know. I go visiting when she's busy downstairs in the shop."

Intrigued in spite of himself, Chase said, "How are you getting over there?"

"Well, how do you think?" Festus said. "Through the AC ducts. The vent in her kitchen is loose."

Chase covered his eyes with his hands. "Dad, you cannot just break into her place like that," he groaned. "Seriously. Stop it."

"I am not breaking in," Festus replied complacently.

"I'm using an alternate means of entry. Besides, her crew is an interesting bunch. Talking to them gives me a chance to practice speaking Felinese without having to hang out in some back alley."

"Right," Chase said, "because you've always objected to alleys. How long has this been going on?"

Making a show of considering the question, Festus said, "Hmm. Let's see. Oh. Yeah. I remember. It started when you up and decided to break Jinx's heart without warning."

"That is *not* fair," Chase declared hotly. "You should know better than anyone why I had to break up with her."

"As usual, you're not listening," Festus replied. "I'm not arguing with the *why* of what you did. It's the *how* of the thing. I was worried about the girl. The best way to get the real scoop was to talk to someone who knows her in private. Women tell their cats everything. You know that."

When Chase didn't say anything, Festus said, "Well, do you want to know what I found out or not?"

"I'm not sure," Chase answered honestly. "Is it going to make me feel like more of a jerk than I already do?"

Festus shook his head. "Son, we're not talking about *you*. We're talking about Jinx."

Swallowing hard, Chase said, "You're right. What did you find out?"

"There were a lot of crying nights," Festus said.

"I knew that already," Chase replied flatly.

"Yeah," Festus said, "but what you don't know is that she doesn't hate you, so you can stop eating yourself up wondering about that."

Chase dropped his head. "How do you know she doesn't hate me?" he asked quietly.

When the old cat spoke again, his voice was more gentle. "Like I said, boy, Jinx talks to Winston and the others. She told them she knows you did what you thought was best, she just wishes you'd discussed it with her first. She wants the two of you to be able to work together and be friends. That's your opening."

Looking up, Chase frowned in confusion. "My opening?" he said. "My opening for what?"

"To settle down and be her friend like she wants you to be," Festus said, "That means not getting your back up every time Lucas Grayson smiles at the woman."

It was Chase's turn to scowl. "What am I supposed to do?" he asked sharply. "Sit there and watch him flirt with her?"

"That's exactly what you're supposed to do," Festus replied. "Lucas Grayson is not your enemy. For the love of Bastet, would you just tell me the truth about what happened between the two of you?"

"Leave it alone, Dad," Chase said, yanking off his shirt. "It's water under the bridge."

"Then why do you still want to take the guy's head off?"

Chase stood up and unbuckled his belt. "We need to get to Chesterfield's shop," he said tersely.

"Changing the subject won't make this situation better," Festus said. "If you won't tell me what happened, either get over it or resolve your differences with Lucas. I'm telling you, Jinx has had it with the attitude. We all have."

"I don't need to hear this lecture again," Chase said.

"If I were lecturing you, you'd know it," Festus said. "I'm trying to be your father and your friend. Don't make me have to speak harshly to you in front of everyone again the way you did last night. I don't enjoy doing that, son. Accept the reality of things and move on."

"Okay, fine. I hear you. Can we please just get going and not talk about this anymore?"

Regarding his son, who now stood before him in his underwear, Festus said, "Sure. But don't you think you ought to open the window while you still have opposable thumbs?"

Swearing under his breath, Chase padded to the window and opened it a few inches. Then the shimmering light covered his form and he shifted into a muscular, well-built Russian Blue.

As Festus jumped down off the bed, he said, "You putting on weight, boy? You're looking a little fluffy."

"I'm getting my winter coat," Chase said, jumping up on the window sill. "And with that beer gut, you're a fine one to be talking about someone's weight."

Joining his son on the window sill, Festus said, "Winter coat, huh? Keeping telling yourself that."

Gauging the distance to the tree limb outside the window, Chase effortlessly sailed across the space and hit the branch with a solid thud. Festus gathered himself and replicated the leap, nailing a perfect three-point landing.

"Still think your old man is fat?" he asked, grinning at Chase.

Chuckling, Chase led the way down the tree trunk. The two cats trotted side by side into the alley behind the hotel. Even with a pronounced limp, Festus matched his son's pace and stride.

As they made their way behind the buildings, Festus glanced around approvingly. "Good thing we're doing this on a Sunday," he said. "Fewer people out and about."

"Exactly," Chase said. "And we don't have to cross any streets. We're going in the back door at Chesterfield's."

Wrinkling his nose as they passed a restaurant dumpster, Festus said, "How did you manage that?"

"Furl sent Rube and his crew in last night to jimmy the lock on the backdoor and check for any enchantments or booby traps," Chase said. "The place is wide open."

"Which means we aren't going to find a blessed thing," Festus said.

"That's why you're wearing the RABIES tag," Chase said, sidestepping a wad of gum on the pavement. "We already know Chesterfield cleaned the place out, but hopefully the scanner will show us what *was* there."

Still annoyed at the silver tab slapping against his chest, Festus said, "Why didn't the Registry hang this RABIES thing off Rube's neck and let him take care of the recon?"

"You know they can't turn the coons loose with this kind of technology," Chase said. "Those guys are never more than one whisker away from committing a felony. Besides, they couldn't very well march into Anton's office or go talk to Miss Shania."

"Guess you have a point there," Festus admitted. "If raccoons could shapeshift, the damned striped goons would try to take over the world."

Glancing sideways at his father, Chase said, "You do drink with those striped goons, you know."

"Well, yeah," Festus said. "Nobody said they don't have good taste in booze."

Chase stopped in front of a lone door set in a red brick wall. "We're here," he said.

Standing up on his hind legs, he used his front paws to twist the knob, pushing at the same time. The door swung inward on well-oiled hinges.

Both cats slipped inside, and Chase pushed the door closed again. As their vision adjusted, they found themselves standing in a deserted back room.

"Good thing we can see in the dark," Festus said. "This guy wasn't big on natural lighting, was he?"

"Start the scanner," Chase said. "Let's see what Chesterfield was doing back here."

Festus scratched at the collar with his good hind leg. On the third swipe, the glow returned to the RABIES tag and a shaft of light emanated from the silver metal.

The beam illuminated an area roughly ten feet wide and fifteen feet deep in front of the spot where Festus was standing. A workbench covered with jeweler's tools appeared in the blue-gray glow.

"This must have been his workroom," Chase said. "There's the transom over the door just the way Glory described it."

As Festus played the scanner around the walls, the wavering outlines of a tall wooden cabinets with glass doors appeared.

"Can you make out any of the artifacts?" Chase asked.

"Yeah," Festus said. "That's a sextant, and that thing next to it is an astrolabe."

"A what?"

"An astronomical measuring instrument that came before the sextant," Festus said. "I think he's got these things arranged in chronological order of development."

"How do you know that?" Chase asked.

Festus laughed. "Give your old man some credit, boy. I do more with my time than just play Red Dot at the Dirty Claw."

As Chase watched, his father circled the room, scanning all four walls. When Festus returned to where he was standing, Chase asked, "Are we good to go into the front room?"

"Yep," Festus said. "Let's do it."

Chase leaned his weight against the door, shoving it open a few inches. He went through, had a quick look around, and then called for Festus to follow him.

Now that they were in the shop proper, more ordinary items showed up in the RABIES beam, although a few pieces displayed unusually intense energy signatures.

"Any of the stuff mean anything to you?" Festus asked, half an hour later.

"No," Chase said, "but we have plenty of experts to

analyze the scans. Let's go through the living quarters upstairs and then get out of here."

To their surprise, however, the second floor appeared to be completely empty.

"So he moved everything out longer ago than 72 hours," Chase said. "Interesting."

Behind him, Festus cleared his throat. "Not everything, boy."

"What do you . . . ?"

Chase's words died in his throat.

The RABIES beam highlighted a segment of the exposed brick in the apartment's living room. Glowing letters stood out on the rough surface.

"So sorry to have missed you," the message read, *"but I assure you, we will meet soon. Please lock the door when you leave. One can never be too conscientious about security, can one?"*

"Games," Festus muttered. "Always games with those damned Creavit."

"How could he have known we were coming?" Chase asked.

"How do the Creavit know anything?" Festus said. "Come on. We're done here."

With that, he turned on his paws and headed downstairs.

Chase moved to follow, but at the door he paused and looked back at the brick wall. He could no longer see the words, but the hair on the back of his neck stood up anyway. Chesterfield always seemed to stay one step ahead of them and that made Chase very, very nervous.

From downstairs, Festus yowled, "Get a move on, boy. I'm hungry."

Only partially shaking his sense of foreboding, Chase answered, "I'm coming. Keep your fur on."

The sun had already begun to set when the two cats

slipped back in the window of the hotel room. Chase shifted immediately, dressing in pajama pants and an old T-shirt before starting to upload the data from the RABIES collar.

The instant he was free of the scanning device, Festus started to groom furiously. "Where are you sending the files?" he asked between licks.

"To the Registry Dropbox account," Chase said. "The sooner they get them, the sooner we get some answers. You want to call for room service?"

"Sure," Festus said, jumping onto the desk and flipping the menu open with his paw. Then something occurred to him. "Are we expensing all this to the Registry?"

"Yes," Chase said. "Festus gave me a Registry credit card number. Why?"

"Oh, nothing," Festus said, knocking the phone, off the hook and pressing a button with his paw. "Hello . . . room service? Yes, this is Mr. McGregor in Room 210. What's the biggest steak on your menu? . . . Sixteen ounces? . . . Surely you can do better than that. What are my options for outside delivery . . .

"Dad!" Chase hissed. "What are you doing?"

"Hold on," Festus said into the phone, "I need to turn the TV down." Putting his paw over the mouthpiece he hissed back. "If I have to spend all day tomorrow as a human, I need sustenance, and the Registry can dang well afford meat. You in or not?"

Shaking his head, Chase said, "I'm in, but 16 ounces is enough for me."

"Lightweight," Festus muttered as he removed his paw. "Okay, if that's the best you can do, we'll take three 16 ounce porterhouse steaks with all the trimmings. Yes, yes, put it on the same card as the room. Now, let's talk single malt . . . "

TWELVE

When we stepped out of O'Hanson's, a gust of wind almost knocked us down. "Whoa!" I said. "Who turned on the air conditioning?"

"More like the deep freeze," Greer said. "I know you found flying with me a bit disconcerting, but would you mind if we used that method again to return to the portal? I don't fancy the idea of walking in this weather."

"Me either," I said. "Fly away."

Greer caught hold of me with one hand and offered the other to Lucas. "Ready to go, laddie?" she asked.

To my surprise, Lucas declined. "Naw," he said, "you two go on back without me. I need to do a couple of things here in Shevington. I'll be back in Briar Hollow in a few hours."

He didn't offer to explain what "a couple of things" meant, and since Greer didn't ask for more details, I didn't think I should either. We all said goodnight and then Greer and I rode the wind to the portal.

I didn't waste any time activating the opening. Normally I'd say the fairy mound stays cold year round, but our transition from the valley to the stacks was like stepping into a sauna that night.

"Brrr," I said, still shivering. "I didn't expect it to be so cold in the Valley this soon."

"You can't predict winter weather in the Valley," Greer said. "The sun will likely be shining tomorrow, but I'd wager the first snow isn't far away." She held out her hand again. "One more flight back to the lair?"

When I didn't move, she said, "Oh, dear. Air sickness?"

"No," I said, "it's not that. I was just wondering if you have any idea why Lucas stayed behind?"

"Ah," Greer said. "Our man of mystery. No, I don't know why he chose to remain in Shevington. The laddie is always one for his strange errands. I wouldn't worry about it. The better you come to know him the more you'll ignore his eccentricities."

Eccentricities? So far Lucas struck me as a routinely genial person. After what I'd just gone through with Chase, I wasn't sure I wanted to risk getting involved with another moody man. Greer seemed to read my thoughts.

"He's not a broody one like McGregor," she said, "and Grayson doesn't have a dark bone in his body. Like as not he just wanted to go have a word with Moira."

That wasn't what I was expecting. "Why would he talk to Moira behind our backs?" I blurted out.

Greer laughed. "You can't mistrust every man just because McGregor has been acting like a fool," she said. "Lucas is Moira's nephew."

Oh.

"Sorry," I said. "He never said that they're related."

"He doesn't bring it up often," Greer said. "Lucas likes to fancy he's made his own place in the world without trading on his aunt's position."

"Has he?" I asked curiously.

"He has indeed," Greer said, "but he's a discreet man under all that swagger, with a soft heart for family. Moira loves Barnaby, and Lucas loves Moira. He'd want to check on how they're both doing after the revelations about Chesterfield. Going to the Lord High Mayor directly wouldn't be proper in his estimation, so I imagine Lucas is talking with Moira now."

Discretion and a soft heart for family. Those were qualities I could deal with.

This time when Greer held out her hand, I took it.

Everyone had already gone to bed when we got back to the shop. I left Greer in her favorite chair by the fire. Knowing that the baobhan sith would be awake while we all slept allowed me to slip into my apartment without worrying about our safety.

When I glanced into the bedroom, four pairs of glowing eyes looked back at me, but none of the cats left the warm bed to join me on the couch. Neither of my parents stirred either.

Our temporary living arrangement couldn't go on forever, but until we had a better idea what Chesterfield and the Strigoi Sisters were up to, I preferred having my folks in Briar Hollow. Little did I know that Monday morning would visit us with a secondary problem—or maybe I should say the continuation of a problem I thought we'd already dealt with involving ghosts, baseball, and the town's dead mayor.

⟶⟶⟶

"Excuse me, are you the shop owners?"

Tori looked up from the counter in the espresso bar and into the heavily kohled eyes of a young woman dressed completely in black. Masses of bangle bracelets rattled at her wrists, and one nostril sported a delicate gold nose ring.

"I'm one of the owners," Tori said. "This is my mother, Mrs. Andrews. Can we help you?"

"My name is Mindy Mathis," the young woman said brightly, "and I just *love* your place. Are you Wiccan?"

Glancing at Gemma, Tori said, "Uh. No. We're kind of . . . what are we Mom?"

With a perfectly straight face, Gemma said, "Orthodox Druids."

Mindy frowned. "What does that mean exactly?"

"We only talk to oak trees, dear," Gemma said seriously. "Reform Druids revere any old shrub that comes along."

Coughing to cover up a giggle, Tori said, "How can we help you, Mindy? Did you want some coffee?"

"Huh? Oh. No," the girl said, as if she was struggling to remember why she'd even started the conversation. "I don't want to drink coffee, I want to *make* it. For you. For money."

Translating on the fly, Tori said, "You're looking for a job?"

"See!" Mindy said. "We're already *totally* on the same vibrational wavelength! Me working here is karmic. Tomorrow is Monday. I can start first thing."

The girl's enthusiastic outburst rendered Tori temporarily speechless. Stepping in to give her daughter time to recover, Gemma said, "I thought I knew everyone in town. Are you new here, Mindy?"

"Yes, ma'am," the girl said. "Me and my friends, Nick and Kyle, just moved to Briar Hollow. We're living in this cool old house that belonged to some dead guy named after a fish."

That kicked Tori's brain back in gear. "Fish Pike?" she asked.

"Yeah," Mindy said. "That's it." Then she leaned in and whispered, "You know he was murdered by a total psychopath, right?"

"I do know," Tori said drily, "since his body was found right outside our front door."

Mindy gasped. "Get. *Out!*" she said. "*Really*? Is it true the body was all arranged in a casket?"

"No," Tori said emphatically, "it is *not* true. He was just sitting on the bench."

"Well, what about . . . "

Before Mindy could share another wild rumor, Tori steered her in another direction. "Did you and your friends buy the Pike house?" she asked.

Clearly disappointed that Tori wasn't willing to share any grisly details about Fish's murder, Mindy said, "Oh, no. We couldn't afford to do that. We were just looking to rent some rooms or something, but then the realtor showed us the house. She said no one wants to live there because Mr. Pike was into weird stuff online. They say he met his killer in a chat room for people who think they can turn into mountain lions or something."

Not bothering to ask the identity of the ubiquitous 'they," Tori said, "That didn't bother you?"

"Oh no!" Mindy said. "We hope the place is haunted. That would totally kick our production into overdrive."

Gemma and Tori exchanged a sidelong glance.

"What are you producing?" Gemma asked.

"The HBH Files, Season 1," Mindy said proudly.

"And that stands for what?" Tori said.

"Haunted Briar Hollow," the girl replied. "We're planned to start with the courthouse ghost. They say he's this guy who used to be the town mayor. He killed himself with a fishing trophy."

"Don't let him hear you say that," Tori muttered.

"Excuse me?" Mindy frowned.

"Nothing," Tori said. "My business partner, Jinx Hamilton, isn't here right now. I can't consider hiring you without talking to her first. Why don't you come back in the morning and we'll see what she says."

———— ✦ ————

When Tori pulled me into the storeroom early the next morning and told me about Mindy I did not react well.

"The last thing we need to be dealing with is some

Goth-wannabe ghost hunter," I said. "Hiring her would be a bad idea."

"Maybe," Tori said, biting into one of Darby's bear claws, "but wouldn't it be easier to have Mindy here where we could keep an eye on her?"

Before I could answer, the brownie reappeared with a steaming pot of coffee. As he poured the fragrant liquid in my over-sized mug, I had one of my bright ideas. I'd rely on an unlikely ally to get me out of this one.

"Darby," I said, "did you hear what we were talking about?"

Regarding me with a scandalized expression, he said, "Mistress, I would never eavesdrop."

"Of course not," I said, "but did you *accidentally* hear what we were talking about?"

Cutting his gaze back and forth between us, Darby said, "Maybe the girl in black who was here yesterday?"

"You saw her?" Tori said.

"Yes, Mistress Tori," Darby said. "I saw and heard."

Darby isn't one to snoop, but if I had the power of invisibility like he does, I'd dang sure make use of it.

"Great," I said. "So what do you think? Should we hire her?"

The brownie looked shocked. "Mistress would like *my* opinion?" he asked.

"Yes," I said, "I would. Do you think we should hire her?"

Even though he seemed to have a lot of trouble working up the courage to speak, Darby said, "Yes, Mistress. I think you should."

Okay. That was a total backfire. I expected Darby to say no since I don't think he'd ever disagreed with me one time since I met him.

"You do?" I said, trying not to let my mouth hang open.

"Yes, Mistress," he said, appearing to gain confidence

in his answer. "I agree with Mistress Tori that it would be better to have the girl here."

From the triumphant grin Tori shot me, she knew I had been counting on Darby's support. "Looks like you're out-voted on this one, Jinksy," she said.

I could have pulled theoretical rank and said no, but that would have crushed Darby and sent him into a panic that he'd done something wrong—which Tori also knew.

"Fine," I sighed. "Hire her. But Mindy and her ghost hunting buddies are totally your problem. That means Howie, too."

The corners of Tori's grin wilted. No one liked dealing with the town's deceased chief executive Howard McAlpin who haphazardly haunts the courthouse. He's such a politician, he gives politicians a bad name.

Never one to be daunted, however, Tori rallied quickly. "No problem," she said. "I've got this."

File that under "famous last words" and stay tuned.

After Jinx and Tori finished their breakfast and left the store room, Glory and Rodney emerged from the shadows on the shelf behind the couch.

"Darby!" Glory called. "Can you come here a sec?"

The brownie jumped at the sound of her tinny voice. "Mistress Glory!" he said. "You frightened me!"

"Shhhh!" she hissed. "Keep your voice down. Come closer."

Since he was too short to reach the shelf on his own, Darby carried a step ladder across the room and wrestled it open. When he climbed to the top, he was on eye level with the mini witch and her rodent companion.

"Hello, Rodney," he said. "Mistress Glory. Do you have a problem I can help with?"

"We don't have a problem," Glory said, her face going

chartreuse with excitement. "We have an opportunity."

Beside her, Rodney nodded vigorously.

"I'm sorry, Mistress," Darby said. "I don't understand."

"Don't you ever get tired of all the others having the adventures and fighting the bad guys?" Glory asked.

"No," Darby said honestly. "I am afraid of the bad guys."

Glory put her hands on her hips. "I've seen you be plenty brave when you need to be," she declared.

"When my friends were in danger," Darby said earnestly, "but not because I wanted to be brave."

"Nobody *wants* to be brave," Glory said. "People are always brave because they have to be. I'm terrified of Mr. Chesterfield, but I think he *likes* that I'm terrified and that makes me mad."

"Surely you do not want to face Mr. Chesterfield!" Darby gasped.

The glow on Glory's face faded a bit at that suggestion, but she still plowed ahead. "No," she said, "of course not, but I think it's time the three of us showed the others that we can pull our weight around here."

Darby frowned. "You want me to pull my weight. Pull it where?"

Rodney put a paw over his eyes and shook his head, which only made Darby frown more.

"Did I misunderstand, Mistress Glory?" he asked.

"'Pulling your weight' is just an expression," Glory explained. "I want us to do something that shows everyone we really are part of the team."

"How are we going to do that?"

"Operation Stowaway!" Glory said. She leaned toward the edge of the shelf. "Here's what I have in mind."

THIRTEEN

When Chase and Festus arrived at Anton Ionescu's office they found a funeral wreath on the door and a tearful secretary named Miss Frobisher dressed in black waiting for them.

"Mr. Ionescu was a great man," she said mournfully. "I'm devastated by his death."

"Our condolences on your loss," Chase said. "We appreciate that you agreed to help us at such a difficult time."

"Mr. Ionescu's brother explained that this is a matter of utmost importance to the family. I'm happy to do everything I can," she said. "Please follow me."

The woman led them down a hallway paneled in dark, expensive wood. Removing a key from her pocket, she opened a door to reveal an opulent office filled with baronial leather furniture and expensive works of art.

"If you need or want anything," she said, "just press Ext. 42 on the phone."

After Miss Frobisher excused herself, Festus reached up and jerked the knot of his tie down, undoing the top button on his shirt. "Scratch what I said about never wearing a collar, boy," he muttered. "These damned nooses are worse."

Loosening his own tie, Chase said, "For once, I agree with you."

Venturing deeper into the office, Festus let out a low whistle. "Would you get a load of this joint! Wonder what Ionescu was charging Chesterfield by the hour?"

"I think it's safe to say Anton wasn't doing any pro bono work," Chase said. "How do you want to tackle this?"

Spotting the overstuffed leather desk chair, Festus' eyes lit up. "Why don't you take the file cabinets?" he said. "I'll go through the desk drawers. We wouldn't want to miss anything."

"Of course not," Chase said drily, opening the top file drawer. "I am in awe of your thoroughness."

Festus made a point of ignoring his son, plopping down in the chair and giving the rollers an experimental push instead. "What are we looking for anyway?" he asked.

"Your guess is as good as mine," Chase said, thumbing through the files before deciding to lift a double handful out en masse. "I guess we'll know it when we see it."

The men fell silent as they began to go through Ionescu's paperwork and possessions. After about an hour, Festus said, "Boy, you have any interest in a locked drawer?"

Chase, who was sitting on the floor with a stack of documents in his lap, looked up. "I do," he said. "Which one?"

"I almost missed it," Festus said, sliding the chair back and pointing toward the left side of the desk. "It's this little skinny thing here in between the top drawer and the file compartment. Can't be good for much more than a few sheets of paper."

"Interesting," Chase said. "Why am I guessing Miss Frobisher doesn't have the key to that one?"

"Oh," Festus said, rubbing his hands together in gleeful anticipation, "that doesn't matter. Let your old man handle this one. It's been awhile, but sometimes fingers *do* come in handy."

As Chase watched, Festus bent two large paper clips. "These desk locks aren't good for much," he said, inserting one of the wires in the top of the mechanism. Grimacing, he twisted the other wire and was rewarded with a solid click. "Ha!" he said triumphantly. "Told you! I've still got it!"

"Yeah," Chase said, getting up and joining his father, "but I'm worried about what 'it' might be."

"Mind your manners or I'll get furry and box your ears," Festus said, opening the thin drawer and removing a single manilla folder. "What do we have here?"

He placed the folder on the desk blotter and opened it. The top sheet was a glossy 8" x 10" photograph of an intricate necklace.

Chase picked up the picture and studied it while Festus scanned the letter lying underneath it.

"Anton was negotiating to buy the necklace," Festus said. "From a Mr. John Smyth. Spelled with a 'y' no less."

"That screams alias," Chase said.

"Completely," Festus said. "The letter says you're looking at 'an antique oval amulet approximately 5 centimeters in length and 3.8 centimetres in width on a rose gold chain.' How big is that in English?"

"About 2 inches by an inch and a half," Chase said.

"Says here that Ionescu was negotiating with Smyth with a Y on Chesterfield's behalf to buy the necklace."

"Does the letter describe the stone?"

"It does," Festus said, reading again. "'Dark rowan amber encasing a trio of rowan berries.' And there's an inscription on the back."

"Which is?"

"'*The rejuvenation of that which has faded*,'" Festus replied. "Does that mean anything to you?"

"No," Chase said slowly, "but it seems too much of a coincidence that the Amulet of the Phoenix is also made of amber. Has the sale already taken place?"

Festus scanned the remainder of the document and then flipped through the other sheets in the folder. "I don't think so," he said. "Smythe was supposed to call Ionescu on Saturday morning to discuss the terms of the sale."

"And Anton died Friday night," Chase said. "What else is in the folder?"

Festus held up a second photograph. The image showed a slender young woman with long blonde hair.

"Who is she?" Chase asked.

"Katrina Warner," Festus said. "She owns a bookstore on the Royal Mile in Edinburgh up near the castle."

Laying the two photos side-by-side on the desk, Chase said, "I wonder if she's somehow connected to the amulet?"

"Well," Festus said, "I'm just going out on a limb here, boy, no pun intended, but the name of her shop is Rowan Bough Books."

Taking out his phone, Chase said, "I'm going to photograph all these documents for Lucas and Greer. Then we're going to look behind every picture frame and book in this room. If Ionescu was hiding anything else, we're going to find it."

Just before noon, Anton's secretary knocked on the office door. Festus hastily shoved the book in his hand back on the shelf and sat down in the desk chair as the woman entered the room. Chase, who had been peering behind an oil painting of a landscape made a show of studying the brush strokes on the canvas.

"Pardon me," Miss Frobisher said, "but if you gentlemen are still working, may I order in some lunch for you?"

Brightening at the mention of food, Festus said, "Absolutely. I'd kill for a bacon cheeseburger and a beer."

"Dad," Chase said, "we don't want to be any trouble to Miss Frobisher."

For the first time since they'd arrived at the office, the sad-eyed woman actually smiled. "Mr. Ionescu loved bacon cheeseburgers," she said. "There's a little place around the corner that he swore was the best in the state. I'll call for a delivery now. Shall I add fries?"

"Two double orders," Festus said, seizing the moment before Chase could stop him.

While they waited for the food to arrive, Miss Frobisher produced a white tablecloth, which she draped over the coffee table in the office's seating area. Next she laid out silver flatware and crystal pilsner glasses. "You'll find a selection of beer in the refrigerator there in the cabinet," she said, indicating what looked like a bookcase from the outside. "I'll bring the burgers in as soon as they're delivered."

She left again, and Festus eagerly explored the bar fridge. "Gaelic Ale!" he crowed happily. "The Romanian bloodsucker had taste after all."

"Lower your voice!" Chase hissed. "And could you be a little less gleeful about raiding a dead man's beer cooler?"

Festus fixed him with a perturbed glare. "I'm not raiding anything," he said. "The lady gave me permission. You want one?"

"Is there anything non-alcoholic in there?"

Festus extracted a bottle of mineral water. "This suit you, Mr. Straight and Narrow?"

"Yes," Chase said, catching the bottle that Festus tossed to him. "And as for the straight and narrow part, don't you think one of us should be sharp when we talk to Miss Shania Moonbeam?"

Twisting the top off his ale and taking a long pull, Festus said, "Better you than me. Sober is the last state I want to be in to meet some crackpot dame named Shania Moonbeam."

Chase sat down in one of the arm chairs. "Doesn't it bother you that we're camping out in the office of a man who hired a psychopath to try to kill us?" he asked.

"Nope," Festus replied, claiming the second chair. "The psychopath is dead. Anton is dead, and we're drinking his beer. That feels like a win to me."

Just then, the office door opened and Miss Frobisher came in carrying a silver tray with two plates dwarfed by massive paper-wrapped burgers flanking an enormous cut-glass bowl filled with fries. "Will there be anything else, gentlemen?" she asked, putting the platter down in the center of the white table cloth.

"No, thank you," Chase said. "This is great. Won't you join us? There's enough food here for an army."

"That's kind of you," Miss Frobisher said, "but I'm a vegan."

As the door closed, Festus mumbled, "I knew there was something off about that dame."

"Not everyone is a carnivore," Chase pointed out as he began to unwrap his burger.

"The trustworthy ones are," Festus replied, biting into his burger and smiling happily. "I just may live," he announced.

As they ate, an odd thought suddenly occurred to Chase. "You know, Dad," he said, "this is more time than I've spent with you in human form in years."

"Don't get used to it," Festus shot back. "I'm not a huge fan of the bipeds."

Chase started to say, "You haven't been since Mom died," but thought better of it. Instead he said, "Does the hip hurt more when you're in your human form?"

Festus washed down a mouthful of food and opened a second bottle of ale. "Yeah, I can't get my weight off the damned thing unless I'm on three legs."

"You must hate him," Chase said quietly.

"Chesterfield?" Festus said, biting into a fry. "Yeah, I do, but not because he lamed me. He's a reckless fool, working magic in front of humans, playing fast and loose with dangerous artifacts. He sees nothing but his own self-ish plans. The risk of exposing our hidden world means nothing to him. Your mother died rather than betray our true nature. You think I'm going to just stand by and watch some Creavit scum out all of us while the humans break out the pitchforks and torches? Not a chance."

"And yet Barnaby let Chesterfield off with probation back in '36," Chase said. "What the heck was that all about?"

"Good question," Festus said. "After Moira and I got Chesterfield contained, we put him in a holding cell in the In Between. Power was just radiating off that guy. Thirty-six hours later? Moira tested him with the touchstone and he couldn't get it past bright blue. She decided he'd been juiced up on something when he fought us and that he really wasn't such a big deal wizard after all. I didn't buy it then and I don't buy it now."

"So what did Barnaby do?" Chase asked.

"He kept Chesterfield in that holding cell for a month," Festus said, "and tested him six ways from Sunday. Never one time did the guy register any real, viable power. Chesterfield came off as just a garden variety, low-level wizard. Started whining about how he'd gotten in over his head, said he'd never do it again, claimed he just wanted to live quietly among the humans. Damned if Barnaby didn't buy it. The whole story was a load of bull."

"What makes you say that?" Chase asked. "I mean if Chesterfield passed all those tests, maybe Moira was right that he was using something to augment his powers the day you fought him."

"Not a chance," Festus said, "and you know why?"
"Why?"
"Because I had to shift every single day for three months before my hip stabilized and now there's scar tissue in there."

Chase blinked. "You never told me that," he said. "Shapeshifters don't scar."

"No, we don't," Festus said, "but I did."

———

When Chase pushed open the door of Miss Shania Moonbeam's Divinatory Emporium, a gong sounded.

"Oh, brother," Festus grumbled. "Here we go."

"Behave," Chase said, plastering on a smile as a short, round woman draped in layers of diaphanous, neon fabric emerged from the back room.

Instead of the fake gypsy seer accent they expected, Miss Shania said brightly, "Well, hey y'all! You looking to have your fortune told? Or maybe I can read the the bumps on your heads?" She turned to Festus, "Your grandpa looks like he has a real bumpy head."

"*Grandpa*?" Festus growled.

"This is my father," Chase said smoothly. "Festus McGregor. My name is Chase. We were sent by a former client of yours, Glory Green."

"*Glory!*" Miss Shania gasped. "Oh my goodness gracious! I have been worried *sick* about that girl. She just up and disappeared. Didn't even give notice over at the state archives. Did she follow her dreams and start singing like Elvis? If she did, I'm gonna be *green* with envy."

"'Green' being the operative word," Festus said.

Miss Shania frowned, "I'm sorry. What did you say?"

"Nothing," Chase said firmly. "He said nothing. Glory did start a new life. She's in . . . retail . . . working with a friend of ours. She told us that you know a local antiques dealer with a reputation for acquiring hard-to-find items."

The woman's face wilted. "Mr. Chesterfield," she said. "You know he just up and died, right?"

"Did he now?" Festus said. "And when did this tragedy occur?"

"Just a few days ago," she said, "and his people cleaned his shop right out. Didn't even have the decency to put a funeral wreath on the front door. I think they must be Yankees. They don't do like we do down here when it comes to the dead. "

"His people?" Chase interrupted. "He had family?"

As if she'd been caught with her hand in the cookie jar, Miss Shania pursed her lips and said, "Well, now don't *quote* me on that part. I'm just assuming it was his people that did it because he must have left all that stuff to somebody and now the whole store is just as empty as a cat house on Sunday morning."

Trying not to smile, Chase asked, "How did he die?"

"I'm afraid the voice didn't tell me that," Miss Shania said. "Sometimes they leave stuff out if the channel is bad. I'm sure you understand."

"Oh," Festus purred, "we *do*. It's so hard to get good reception from the other side."

"It *is*!" Miss Shania said. "Worse than trying to get through on your cell phone when you're back in the sporting goods section down at the Walmart."

Shooting his father a murderous look, Chase said, "Would you mind telling us what the voice told you?"

"Oh," she said. "That's easy. It said, 'Tell anyone who asks that Irenaeus Chesterfield is dead.' Came through just clear as a bell." Then her lip began to quiver. "But it scares me," she said. "I think that voice was the Angel of Death himself."

"Why do you say that?" Chase asked.

"Because since Mr. Chesterfield died, the voice in my head is gone. I think the Grim Reaper took his life and my gift, too."

FOURTEEN

Mindy showed up not long after Tori and I finished breakfast. I was looking approvingly at the receipts for the weekend; SpookCon1 was definitely a success. Magic crisis or not, we did have bills to pay. When the bell on the front door jingled, I looked up to see a young girl dressed in black with an incongruously bouncy demeanor coming toward me.

"Hi!" she said, holding her hand out. "Are you Jinx? Tori told me I had to see you about being hired in the espresso bar. Is this a good time?"

As much as I might have wanted to object to the girl on sight, that simply wasn't possible. The phrase "infectious personality" describes Mindy perfectly.

"Sure," I said, shaking her hand. "Tori tells me that you have experience working as a barista? Can you tell me about that?"

Five minutes later, I'd already decided that in the coffee department Mindy's qualifications put ours to shame. Who knew a certain large, overpriced chain had so many advanced training courses?

"So you worked as a barista while you were finishing college?" I asked.

"Yes, ma'am," she said.

That made me wince. "It's just Jinx," I said.

Mindy grinned. "Sure thing," she said. "Yeah, I graduated last spring with a degree in film studies. Me and my friends, Nick and Kyle, are hoping to have a hit with the HBH Files. That stands for 'Haunted Briar Hollow' by the way. If we can go viral, who knows what might happen."

Hoping to "go viral" might not sound like the most solid business plan, but it's a standard "best practice" for a millennial like Mindy.

"Are Nick and Kyle looking for jobs, too?" I asked.

"Nick is working for the old couple in the corner grocery," she said.

"George and Irma," I supplied. "And Kyle?"

"He's going to try to get hired at the pizzeria."

Given my suspicions about Pete, that didn't sound like the greatest idea in the world, but at least all three of them would be on the square where we could keep an eye on their activities.

"Okay," I said, "you're definitely qualified and we could use the help, so you're hired. Go on over and tell Tori I said to get you started."

"Thank you so much!" Mindy enthused. "This is going to be *awe*-some. I won't let you down. I promise." Then, leaning in a little, she whispered, "By the way. Your aura's looking sort of muddy. Are you getting enough sleep?"

Taken aback, I said, "Actually, no. I got in late last night."

"Don't worry, Boss," she said cheerfully, "I'll brew you something herbal that'll fix you right up."

Unless "herbal" meant coffee, Mindy had a lot to learn about my beverage tastes.

Over lunch with the Moms in the storeroom, Tori practically glowed about our new hire. "My God, Jinksy," she said, "Mindy took the espresso machine apart and cleaned the nozzles—without even looking at the manual. I thought it was working fine, but then she pulled a shot that was just this side of heaven."

"Gloat, why don't you?" I said. "Let's not forget that Super Barista is in town to look into hauntings, including his Late Honor the Mayor, which could mean trouble for us. Has she mentioned the YouTube ghost video yet?"

The baseball video. Yeah. Let me tell you what happened with that.

Two Bigfoot hunters in town for SpookCon1 stumbled on a spectral baseball game at the high school field. Baseball is Beau's new obsession, and since most of the people he knows are dead, he organized his cemetery friends in a league.

The ghosts didn't realize they'd gotten an extra jolt of energy after they were exposed to the entire electricity-eating Ionescu clan. The experience made the spirits just corporeal enough to show up on video, including a shot of Duke charging the camera with teeth bared, which had people calling him a "hellhound."

"Mindy hasn't brought the video up," Tori said. "Besides, most of the comments on YouTube are running in favor of it being a hoax. I think it's actually good for us in terms of the tourist trade."

Yeah, except for one little dead detail.

"What about the fact that one of the guys who shot the video has gone missing?" I said. "It's only a matter of time before the whole story turns into one great big urban myth/unsolved mystery *thing*."

We all grew quiet at the mention of the "missing" boy. The Strigoi Sisters killed him and left his body in an alley. At my insistence, Greer transported the remains to a different location where they could be found and returned to his family. So far there had been nothing on the news about the discovery, but we all knew it was coming.

"Deal with one thing at a time, Norma Jean," Mom counseled quietly. "Greer said the boy's death would look like an accident."

An "accident" with four neat puncture wounds in his jugular. Still, Mom was right. We couldn't deal with something that hadn't happened yet.

Tori wisely decided to change the subject. "So," she said, "dish already. How was your big night out in Shevington?"

"Cold," I said. "Mom, you weren't kidding about winters in the Valley."

She laughed. "No," she said, "I wasn't, but wait until you see how beautiful it is at Christmas time."

Even though we hadn't found a way to reunite the whole family, Mom was already determined we would be spending Christmas with my brother and no one wanted to oppose her on the idea. Gemma saved me from having to make a response with a neat deflection.

"Where did you all have drinks?" she asked.

"O'Hanson's Pub," I replied.

"Oh!" Mom said, sounding like an eager little kid. "Do they still make Scotch Eggs?"

"For heaven's sake!" I laughed. "Is everyone in love with cold, deep-fried, sausage-wrapped eggs?"

In one voice, Mom and Gemma both said, "Yes!"

Never one to leave food on the table, Tori said, "Do we need a girl's night out at O'Hanson's so I can try one?"

"That would be so much fun!" Mom said. "Let's do it when things settle down. Did you have fun, honey?"

"I did," I said. "Rube joined us."

Gemma snorted. "Now you're drinking with raccoons. What are we going to do with you, young lady?"

"He did most of the drinking," I said. "I swear that guy has a hollow leg."

"Most raccoons I've ever known have *four* hollow legs," Gemma observed wryly. "They aren't known as wild animals for nothing."

Tori wasn't interested in discussing mammalian drinking habits. She steered the conversation right back to Lucas. "So what about Mr. Tall Dark and Fedora?" she asked. "He was flirting with you big time Saturday night in the lair."

Blushing, I said, "He was not."

"Chase sure thought he was," she countered. "Festus almost had to put his claws out to make him behave."

"That's Chase's problem," I said, and then added, "but I did find out something about Lucas I didn't know. He told me he's half Gwragedd Annwn."

Tori shook her head. "Never heard of that one. What does it mean?"

"It means he's a water elf," Mom said. "What's the other half?"

"Druid," I said. "So what's the big deal about water elves?"

Mom and Gemma exchanged a look. "Are you going to tell her?" Mom asked.

"Tell me what?"

"The Lady of the Lake was Gwragedd Annwn," Gemma said.

Which meant absolutely nothing to either me or Tori, who said, "CliffsNotes, please?"

"The Lady of the Lake gave Excalibur to King Arthur," Gemma said. "The Gwragedd Annwn are old and noble Fae. Lucas comes from a distinguished magical lineage."

She didn't use the word "royal," but the implication was there.

"He didn't seem to want to talk about it," I said. "Greer told me that Lucas likes to be taken on his own merit rather than because of his family. Moira is his aunt."

"Really?" Mom said. "I knew Moira was half elf, but I didn't realize she was a water elf. That explains her interest in merfolk culture."

Just then my cell phone beeped. It was a text message

from Chase. "They've finished in Anton's office and sent some pictures to Greer and Lucas," I said, reading from the screen. "They're going to talk to Miss Shania, then check out of the hotel and head back. Chase says Anton's secretary is really broken up about his death."

"Have you told Cezar about the girls yet?" Gemma asked.

Oh God. To be truthful, that hadn't even crossed my mind. "No," I admitted. "I haven't."

"Honey!" Mom said. "You have to get on the phone and talk to him this second. The girls could be a terrible threat to all of his people. What if they try to turn more of the Ionescus into *Strigoi mort blasfematoare*?"

Crap.

I agreed to call Cezar immediately. We cleaned up the remains of our lunch, and the others left me alone in the storeroom to place the call.

On Friday night, just before he'd supervised the removal of Anton's body, Cezar Ionescu gave me his private number. He answered on the first ring. "Good afternoon, Miss Hamilton," he said. "How may I help you?"

"You can start by calling me Jinx," I said. "There's been a development."

As briefly as possible, I explained about the sighting of Seraphina and Ioana as well as Chesterfield's role in their rescue.

"This is not good," Cezar said.

Uh, yeah. I got that part.

"Anton's burial is scheduled for Thursday," Cezar said. "Because he was a public figure, he cannot simply disappear. The body has been staked, but we will still have an open casket service. When the human sense of propriety has been satisfied, the beheading will occur and Anton's soul will be at rest. Should the girls choose to disrupt these plans at any juncture, the consequences could be serious."

We agreed that Chase, Lucas, Greer, and I would attend the service to help with security just in case the Strigoi Sisters decided to pay their last respects. Cezar made it clear to me that he saw peace with the Fae world as a valuable asset for the Ionescus. That made our list of potential enemies shorter by one. Not bad for a Monday.

———∞∞∞———

When Kelly came out of the storeroom with Tori and Gemma, her husband was waiting for her. "Hi, honey," Jeff said. "Can I talk to you for a sec?"

"Sure," she said. "What's up?"

When he hesitated, Gemma said, "Come on, Tori. Let's go check on Mindy and see how she made it through the lunch run."

As they walked away, Kelly frowned at her spouse, "Jeff, is something wrong?"

"No," he grinned. "I think something might be very right. Come with me."

To Kelly's surprise, he led her outside and down the sidewalk past the cobbler's shop, stopping in front of the vacant store on the corner. "What do you think?" he said.

Perplexed, she said, "About what? An empty building?"

"An empty building that's *for sale*," he corrected her.

Kelly's jaw dropped. "You're not seriously thinking about buying it, are you?"

"I am," he said. "Well, that is, if you agree. I met the owner at the Halloween carnival. He actually has two buildings for sale on the square. This one and the old hardware store over there on the corner. The price is good and I'm tired of being on the road all the time. This would put us closer to Jinx so you all can do your . . . thing . . . and I've always had it in the back of my mind that running a sporting goods store would be fun."

"But where would we live?" Kelly protested.

"There's an apartment over the store," he said. "I have the key. You want to see it?"

Not having the heart to throw a damper on his enthusiasm, she said, "Sure. Why not?"

Jeff dug in his pocket and came up with a key on a white tag. He unlocked the front door and they both stepped into the abandoned retail space. Unlike Jinx's store, this building had large windows on the front and side, flooding the ground floor with light. A staircase in back led upstairs to a newly remodeled apartment.

"Oh!" Kelly said, running her hand along the granite counter in the kitchen. "This is nice."

"Come look at the view," Jeff said, drawing her toward the living room where the windows afforded an unobstructed view of the mountains. "Pretty sweet, huh?"

"It is," Kelly agreed. "But, honey, you have six dogs."

"So?"

"Six dogs in an apartment over a store?" she said. "Isn't that kind of crazy?"

"This place is at least twice as big as where Jinx lives, and she has four cats," he said. "Besides, the city park is just two blocks down that way and they have a brand new dog run."

Kelly put her arm around his waist. "When did you track all this information down?" she asked.

"This morning," he said. "I wanted to have all my ducks lined up before I showed you. If we sell my truck, that will cover most of the down payment, and what we get for the house should bring the mortgage payments down to nothing. What do you say, honey? How about we have us an adventure and shake up our lives a little?"

"Wouldn't you say my returning to the magical world has done a pretty good job of shaking things up already?" she asked.

Drawing her closer, he kissed her on the forehead. "In a real good way," he said. "You're happier than I've seen you since . . . "

"Since we had to give Connor up," she said quietly.

"Yeah," Jeff admitted. "Since then. But we're getting our boy back, honey. If we live here, that puts us closer to Jinx and to him. What do you think?"

"I think it's the most wonderful idea you've ever had," she said, laying her head on his shoulder. "Let's do it."

Mindy finished wiping down the counter and reached up to precisely re-align the cups with the edge of the shelf. She'd offered to work into the evening, but Tori assured her that she'd done more than enough for her first day.

If Nick hadn't sent a group text saying he was onto something big, Mindy might have protested more, but now she couldn't wait to get back to the house to hear what he'd found.

As she gathered up her things, Mindy dropped her purse and book in the new Witch's Brew tote bag Tori gave her as a "welcome to the shop" gift. Then she stopped and stared at the bag. She could have sworn that the flying witch graphic only appeared on the front side.

Shrugging, she picked the bag up, completely oblivious to the black-and-white rat who slipped into the tote as she turned to leave. Nor did she see the back door stand open just a fraction longer than normal when she stepped into the alley to walk home.

Without realizing it, Mindy had passengers *and* a stalker. Operation Stowaway was a go.

FIFTEEN

Barnaby Shevington listened as Greer MacVicar described the documents discovered in Anton Ionescu's office. When she finished, he said, "Tell Jinx and the others that Moira and I will be joining you this evening in Briar Hollow to discuss this matter in detail."

The baobhan sith's green eyes flickered with unanswered questions. "Of course, Barnaby," she said smoothly. "In the meantime, Lucas and I will try to find out more about this John Smythe person, presuming, of course, that we can determine his real identity."

Barnaby waved his hand and broke the signal originating from the lair. He could have used the same enchantment to arrange the call he now needed to make, but for that conversation, appearances would matter greatly. That meant using Moira's mirror.

"Innis," he called out, "I'm going for a walk and then I have business in the human realm. Don't wait supper for me."

The matronly brownie materialized out of thin air. "You're not eating enough," she declared stoutly, "and you'll catch your death of cold out there."

"Yes, yes, Innis, so you tell me repeatedly," Barnaby said. "If anything of importance comes up, I'll be in Briar Hollow."

Shrugging into his greatcoat, he took leave of his disapproving housekeeper and headed around the corner and down the hill to Moira's workshop, exchanging greetings with passing townsfolk along the way.

Dewey, Moira's dwarven assistant, answered the door, staring up at Barnaby from knee level. "We're busy," the dwarf said gruffly.

"Dewey!" Moira said sharply. "Do not speak to the Lord High Mayor that way!"

Completely unfazed by the reprimand, Dewey said, "Well, we *are* busy."

Smiling tolerantly, Barnaby said, "It's fine, Moira. If you are in the middle of something, I can go to madam Kaveh's for coffee and come back later."

"Nonsense," Moira said. "That will be all for now, Dewey. I'll call you when I need you."

The stout, barrel-shaped dwarf stalked away muttering something about "schedules" and "focus" before going into the garden and closing the door behind him with a resounding thud.

Barnaby and Moira both burst out laughing.

"He doesn't approve of me, you know," Barnaby said, stepping inside.

Moira went to him and took his coat. "I know," she said, offering him a kiss. "But *I* do approve of you. Very much."

Barnaby took her hand and allowed himself to be led to a chair by the fire. "What were you working on when I interrupted you?" he asked.

"More breathing potion for the workers helping with the construction of the merfolk city," she said. "They've chosen a name for the settlement by the way. The city will be called Qynn. It means 'happy, strong, and graceful.'"

Leaning forward to warm his hands, Barnaby said, "A most fitting appellation, who chose it?"

"Lute himself," Moira said. "When the various committees could not agree upon a name, he exerted his executive powers. No one thought to argue with him."

Barnaby chuckled. "Why would they? Most of the merfolk cannot remember a time when he was not their leader. Do you think the pace of the work pleases him?"

Drawing her own chair closer, Moira said, "Lute's great age and wisdom have granted him almost infinite patience. I cannot imagine him being displeased with anything."

"I almost envy him that," Barnaby said. "More than 500 years in the waters of the deep ocean, witnessing the violence of storms, the demise of ships sinking to the ocean floor, the battles men have waged in their fragile surface vessels, and still he remains solid as a rock."

Moira laughed. "He would tell you he's done nothing more than stay in his shell and continue to swim. Lute has a most droll sense of humor."

Barnaby shook his head. "Would you ever have thought a leatherback turtle, even a Fae one, would have a humorous streak?"

"No," Moira admitted, "but Lute is the only great sea turtle I have ever known." Then, studying Barnaby's face carefully, she said, "My darling, did you really walk down here against a stiff north wind to discuss aquaculture with me?"

"You know me too well," he said. "I came to tell you that the McGregors found proof that Irenaeus has been seeking to acquire the Amulet of Caorunn."

Moira set back heavily. "But how can that be possible?" she said. "Surely the Witch of the Rowan has ensured the security of the amulet."

"Apparently she has not," Barnaby said, "and that is why I have appeared on your doorstep and why I must ask you to come to Briar Hollow with me this evening. And, of course, I would not miss an opportunity to sit with you by the fire on a cold day."

She smiled. "If all we had to do was sit by this fire, how lucky we would be. I assume that tonight we must tell them about both amulets, the Phoenix and Caorunn."

"I fear so," he said, "but first we must make a call, one that requires a grander scale than a mere magical channel."

"My mirror is at your service," she said, "but to whom will this call be made?"

"Reynold Isherwood."

A long second passed punctuated only by the crackling of the fire before Moira said, "So, the situation has become that serious."

Barnaby nodded gravely. "I fear it has," he said. "You heard Greer MacVicar's theory about how Irenaeus developed his temporal shifting device. He combined elements derived from multiple artifacts of power. What could that madman do if he fused the energies of two or more of the amulets?"

"I honestly cannot answer that question," Moira admitted. "So far as I know, the amulets have never been assembled in a single location."

"Irenaeus had the Amulet of the Phoenix and lost it when he allowed Brenna Sinclair to draw on its powers," Barnaby said. "He must know Colonel Longworth relies on the amulet to remain corporeal. I know Irenaeus. He undoubtedly believes he can retrieve the amulet any time he wishes, an act that would now visit great pain upon Jinx. That alone would appeal to his sadistic nature. Now Festus and Chase have found evidence that Irenaeus authorized Anton to negotiate for the purchase of the Amulet of Caorunn."

Moira stared into the fire. "The merging of the oak and the rowan," she said slowly. "Interesting."

"What are you thinking?" Barnaby asked.

"Many things," she said. "I must consider the alchemical ramifications of such a combination. After we speak with Reynold, I will require some time with my books."

"Time I will happily sit staring into these flames," he said tiredly. "I've been doing a great deal of that these past few nights."

"I know," Moira said softly, "but you cannot blame yourself. The Amulet of the Phoenix was missing for centuries."

Barnaby sighed. "There is no need for such careful speech, Moira. The amulet disappeared when it was ripped from my murdered wife's neck by her killer. I have never wanted to believe Irenaeus killed Adeline, but I fear that tonight I will be called upon to explain how I have handled things, and in so doing, to tell Jinx and the others everything."

"In truth," Moira said, "would it not lighten the burden on your soul? You are guilty of nothing but thinking better of those who did not deserve your faith in them."

"Perhaps," he said, "but we can speak of all that later. Now I think it's time to contact Reynold."

Moira raised her hand and beckoned to an ornate standing mirror sitting at ground level below the alcove that held her desk. The mirror obediently glided toward her, positioning itself in front of their chairs and to the right of the fire.

"I hope this works," she said. "It's been a very long time since we initiated contact with the Elders."

As Moira softly chanted the calling spell, a small mass of smoke formed in the center of the mirror's silver surface. The vapors wavered, lengthening then contracting before the amorphous cloud coalesced to reveal the interior of the Ruling Elders' council chamber. The Executive Elder, Reynold Isherwood, tried and failed to hide his shock.

"Lord High Mayor, Alchemist, greetings," he said stiffly. "This is quite a surprise."

"Greetings Chief Elder," Barnaby said. "And if we may drop the formalities, allow me to say you are looking well, Reynold."

Isherwood raised an eyebrow. "As are you, Barnaby," he said. "For men of our age and experience, we seem to be holding up well. But you, dear Moira, you are as ageless as always."

Moira smiled. "Still gallant, I see," she said. "How is Thomasin?"

This time Isherwood's smile was genuine. "Still far too good for the man she married."

"Please give her my best wishes," Moira said. "I hope to see her again one day."

"That is her hope as well," Isherwood said. "We both feel that this schism between the New and Old Worlds must be healed."

Capitalizing on that opening, Barnaby said, "Then we begin with a point of agreement, which, unfortunately, leads me to pose a difficult question. Why did you not inform us that the Amulet of Caorunn had been stolen?"

Isherwood's features hardened. "Perhaps for the same reason you failed to tell us that the Amulet of the Phoenix had been found."

Barnaby shook his head. "Reynold," he said, "let us not immediately retreat into an angry impasse. Forgive me. The story of the Amulet of the Phoenix entwines so closely with my own history that I confess I have rather come to think of it as my own. For that, I apologize."

Isherwood inclined his head. "Given your late wife's station in service to the Mother Oak," he said, "I quite understand that sentiment—even in the face of what I assume is your understanding that the amulets belong only to the trees from whose blood they were formed. For my own pugnaciousness, I beg your pardon."

Barnaby smiled disarmingly, choosing to ignore Isherwood's attempt to lecture him.

"It is refreshing to see that even as we advance in years, we can still summon the fires of our youth to *be* pugnacious, Reynold," he said. "Let us try again. When the Amulet of the Phoenix resurfaced, I spoke in private with the Mother Oak about how to appropriately handle the matter. It was on her counsel that I acted. In truth, given the centuries of strained relations between the continents, I did not think to contact you."

Although he seemed loathe to admit it, Isherwood could not hide his curiosity. "May I be privy to the Mother Oak's position regarding the reappearance of her amulet?" he asked.

"She told me that the amulet would naturally fall into the hands of its next rightful steward," Barnaby replied, "and I believe that it has."

"And who might that person be?"

"A confidante of the Witch of the Oak," Barnaby replied.

"Which would be Fiona Ryan," Isherwood said.

Barnaby looked at him appraisingly. "You seem to know quite a lot about Shevington's sphere of influence given that we have not officially communicated with the Ruling Elders since the 16th century," he said.

"One hears things," Isherwood smiled.

"One has not apparently heard that there is a new Witch of the Oak," Barnaby said, barely keeping an edge out of his voice. "Jinx Hamilton, Fiona's niece, has come into her powers. She is the one for whom the Mother Oak has waited."

This time Isherwood made no attempt to hide either his astonishment or his knowledge of Shevington. "You have repaired the break in the line of Knasgowa?" he asked.

"I repaired nothing," Barnaby said. "The Daughters

found their own way back. Now, I have been forthcoming with you. I ask the same courtesy in return regarding the Amulet of Caorunn. What has become of it?"

Isherwood's countenance took on a hooded quality. "How, may I ask, did you learn of the amulet's status?"

A frown creased Barnaby's face. "Really, Reynold, this sparring about our covert means of information gathering will get us nowhere. We have both expressed our belief in the need for a spirit of accord. I suggest we begin to actually work from that position."

Isherwood looked as if he wanted to snap back, but reining in his temper, he said tightly, "Your point is well taken. Forgive my tone, but an answer to my question would be helpful."

"Very well," Barnaby said. "We have reason to believe that Chesterfield has been negotiating the purchase of the amulet through a rather common thief based in Edinburgh."

Isherwood sat up. "Does Irenaeus have the amulet?" he asked urgently.

"I truly do not know, Reynold," Barnaby said, "but to speak honestly with the Witch of the Oak and with those who work beside her, I must have some sense of the seriousness of the threat we are facing. It seems that Irenaeus plans to move against the Grid. Are any of the other amulets missing?"

Any shade of pretense disappeared when Isherwood answered. "They are not, Barnaby, and the Amulet of Caorunn must not be allowed to fall into Irenaeus Chesterfield's hands."

In spite of his best efforts, Barnaby could not stop himself. "I warned you, Reynold. I told you the Creavit heresy would threaten the integrity of the entire magical world."

The man stiffened visibly at the criticism. "Not all Creavit are evil," he said. "There are many distinguished made families in Europe who have shown great dedication in working with us to *craft* the integrity of the magical world."

"Can you be completely certain of that, Reynold?" Barnaby asked softly. "The Creavit are creatures of infinite patience."

A sardonic smile twisted Isherwood's features. "Well, you would certainly be in a position to know that, wouldn't you, *Barnaby*?"

With a dismissive gesture, Isherwood broke the enchantment and the mirror went blank. Moira quietly reached for Barnaby's hand. "Do not let his words affect you," she said. "Have no doubt about who you are."

Entwining his fingers with hers, he said, "I know who I am, but now I must summon the courage to speak of who I was and pray that Jinx and the others do not judge me harshly for it."

Sixteen

Glory breathed a sigh of relief when Mindy put the tote bag down in the living room of the newly cleaned and hastily "decorated" Pike house. During the jostling walk from the shop, the corner of Mindy's book had jabbed Glory in the ribs with every other step.

But it wasn't just the cessation of the rocking and poking that made Glory feel better. She instantly felt Rodney's paw give her three taps from the other side of the canvas— their pre-agreed signal that all was well. Glory had genuinely feared for her rodent friend's safety inside the bag.

Little did Glory know that Rodney had made the trip from the shop to the house inside Mindy's purse. Pleased with himself that he'd found a cushioning wad of tissues and a leftover corner of a granola bar for a snack, the rat thought everything about Operation Stowaway was going great—until he stepped in an open tube of lipstick at the bottom of the handbag.

Not wanting to leave magenta tracks all over the interior, Rodney was forced to stand in the makeup until his right hind leg was purple up to the first joint. Snagging one of the tissues and balancing precariously on the other leg, he scrubbed furiously at his stained fur. Then, wanting to hide any evidence of the mishap, he shredded the tissue and piled the remains on top of the offending lipstick.

Just then, Mindy put the tote down with a thud and Rodney happily climbed out of the purse and up the spine of the book to signal Glory that he was okay. Stained, but okay. Then he cautiously peeked over the top of the bag, only to duck down quickly when Mindy came out of the kitchen followed by two young men.

"I'm telling you it's *better* than the baseball video that's already on YouTube," one of the boys said. "I've actually identified the ghost."

"Geez, Nick," Mindy said excitedly. "Would you quit talking about it and just show us what you got?"

"I was so busy working with the video I forgot to plug my laptop in," he said. "The battery's dead."

"No problem," Kyle said, taking out his computer. "Where's the file?"

"It's already on the YouTube channel. I was just waiting for you guys to see it before I hit publish."

Kyle clicked a few keys, and then all three young people crowded around the screen. From his vantage point, Rodney could see the picture in the gap just under Mindy's elbow. The night vision picture showed an image of a baseball field.

"When did you shoot this?" Mindy asked.

"A little bit before dawn this morning," Nick said. "I couldn't sleep, and I wanted to scout out the baseball field. I never dreamed I'd get any evidence at that time of day, and then I had to get to the grocery store early to help George with a delivery, so I didn't have a chance to process the footage until I got off work."

As they all watched, the lone figure of a man slowly materialized at home plate. He wore an old-fashioned baseball cap, which he slowly removed before raising his hand and rubbing his face. As he turned to look into the camera, the screen froze and split. The ghostly image on the right sat next to a black-and-white photograph of what appeared to be the same man.

"Oh. My. *Gawd!*" Mindy breathed. "Who is he and how did you find that picture?"

"I just got lucky," Nick admitted. "Since he's in uniform, I thought maybe he got killed while he was playing. There's a list on Wikipedia of baseball players who more or less died in action. I just started clicking through looking at photos."

"So who is . . . er. . . was he?" Kyle asked.

"His name is John Lewis Dodge," Nick replied. "He was playing for the Mobile Sea Gulls in the Southern Association League when he was hit in the face by a baseball. Dodge was just 27 years old. Talk about a lousy break."

Kyle leaned closer to the screen to study the two images. "So Dodge just played in the minors?" he asked.

"Nope," Nick said, "he played two seasons in the majors, then went back to the minors in 1913."

Mindy pushed Kyle aside to get a closer look for herself. "I don't get it," she said, squinting at the screen. "If this guy played for an Alabama team, what's his ghost doing in Briar Hollow?"

"Beats me," Nick said, "unless the other baseball spirits are attracting additional ghosts."

"Aw, come on," Kyle said. "If we haunt it they will come? There's zero precedent for that."

"Which," Nick beamed, "is the beauty of it. This is the perfect way to launch our paranormal series—with something no one has ever seen."

"Or will believe," Kyle pointed out.

To Nick's consternation, Mindy agreed. "Yeah," she said. "And, well, doesn't this look kind of lame up beside the other video? That guy got two whole ghost teams playing an actual game. This is just a lone ghost with a sore face."

Her comment elicited a howl of protest from Nick, and

the three of them launched into a vigorous debate about the merits of the video. The distraction gave Rodney the opportunity he needed to jump down from the bag. He paused just long enough to give Glory a questioning thumbs up. Even though she was plastered flat on the side of the tote, Glory answered with the same gesture.

Then Rodney dove under the skirt of the easy chair whose bulk was holding the tote upright and continued to listen as the trio of ghost hunters argued. After several minutes, Nick grudgingly agreed not to publish the video in favor of staking out the ballfield as much as possible over the next few nights to try to capture more footage.

"So does this mean we're not going to look for Mayor McAlpin's ghost?" Kyle asked, closing the lid of his laptop.

"I think we put him on the backburner for now," Nick said. "George and Irma told me a little bit about the courthouse haunting, and I gotta say, if the ghost is McAlpin, he's not very good at his job. Most of the time people only see the bottom half of him. When he first showed up, he was just a disembodied pair of shoes."

Mindy looked confused. "How could anyone look at a pair of ghost shoes and know who was wearing them?" she asked.

"Get this," Nick grinned. "McAlpin had issues about being short. He had his shoes built up. That's how they know the ghost is him."

"Oh my God," Mindy giggled. "A Hushpuppy haunt!"

"If McAlpin is this lame in the afterlife, he must have been some piece of work when he had a pulse," Kyle said. Then, struck with sudden inspiration, he said, "Come on guys, that's enough work for one night. Let's throw a pizza in the oven and watch some *Big Bang Theory*."

Two supreme pizzas and six episodes later, only soft snores and the occasional burp could be heard from the couch and recliner. Rodney stuck his head out and then surreptitiously tiptoed farther into the room. When he verified that all three of the humans were sound asleep, he signaled Glory, who peeled herself off the tote, breathing deeply to re-inflate herself.

When she was three dimensional again, she gestured toward the front door, and Rodney nodded vigorously.

Looking around uncertainly, Glory whispered, "Darby?"

Instantly the brownie appeared beside her. Glory pointed again toward the door, and Darby nodded. Climbing astride her broom, she made room for Rodney to ride behind her, then slowly elevated them to eye level with Darby as they advanced toward the front door.

When Darby reached for the knob, Glory made ready to slip through the opening, instantly throwing her broom into high gear when a six-inch gap appeared. At the last second, however, she realized the screen door was still closed. Pulling back sharply, she threw herself into a backward loop. Rodney held on for dear life, but lost his grip and went flying through the air and straight into Darby's outstretched hand.

Righting herself, Glory shrugged and mouthed the word, "Sorry!" indicating that Rodney could get back on the broom.

Wide-eyed and indignant, Rodney shook his head and scampered up to Darby's shoulder where he planted himself with a firm grip on the collar of the brownie's shirt.

Glory shot him an irritated glare and formed the word "chicken" with her lips.

In response, Rodney stuck his tongue out and stayed where he was.

Darby quietly pushed the front door open another few inches and unlocked the screen. Once they were outside, he moved to close the door but froze when he heard

Mindy's voice. "Which one of you losers left the front door open?" she demanded sleepily. "You trying to get us murdered in our sleep?"

Without waiting for her accomplices, Glory zoomed across the yard and out of sight. Darby blipped into invisibility and took Rodney with him. A block from the house, Glory slowed down, hovering just out of the glow of a street lamp.

"Darby! Rodney! You guys okay?" she hissed.

A disembodied voice to her left said, "We are fine, Mistress Glory. May we please go home now?"

Ducking to dodge a moth, Glory said, "Absolutely. Wait until we tell the others what we found out. They're never going to doubt us again!"

"You went *where*?" I spluttered. "What were the three of you *thinking*? What if someone saw you, or worse yet what if something *ate* you?"

Drawing himself up to his full three-feet, Darby said, "Mistress, if I may be so bold, I survived for centuries in the cemetery guarding Knasgowa's grave."

"In an alternate dimension, hidden from the world, where nothing could hurt you," I shot back. "Not the same thing at all, Darby. Not. Even. Close."

That got me nothing but a pouting and slightly defiant brownie.

"And you!" I said, turning to Rodney. "You are supposed to be the responsible one here. How could you let them talk you into this?"

Without hesitation, the rat pointed at Glory, tossing her straight under the wheels of the bus.

"Glory," I said, "this caper was your idea?"

Crossing her arms defensively, Glory said, "It wasn't a caper. It was a covert operation to gain information about

Mindy and the other ghost hunters. We heard you talking about the need to keep an eye on them and decided to help. You never let us do anything."

That rendered me temporarily speechless. "What on earth are you talking about?"

"Just because we're little, you think we can't be part of the team and fight evil and all that *stuff*," Glory said, warming to the topic. "We decided to prove you wrong. So there."

The fact that Mom, Gemma, and Tori were all doing their best not to bust out laughing was not helping move this conversation along in the slightest.

"How, exactly, have you proved me wrong?" I asked.

Shifting her hands to her hips, Glory proceeded to tell us everything they had seen and heard in the Pike house. When she was done, I sat down heavily on the couch. Rodney, who was sitting on the arm, reached over and patted me consolingly. That's when I noticed his hind leg was purple.

"Do I even want to know what happened with that?" I asked, pointing at his leg.

He shook his head.

"Yeah," I said. "That's what I thought. So, on top of everything else, we have another ghost video to deal with. Perfect. Just perfect."

Tori cleared her throat. "Uh, Jinksy, Beau and I are really the ones who got this ghostly baseball thing started in the first place. Why don't you let us check this Dodge guy out and see if we can make this all go away?"

"Good idea," I said. "Away as in *far* away. Far, far, away."

"No problemo," she assured me. "We're on the case."

Before I could tell her that didn't really make me feel better, Barnaby and Moira showed up, and we were suddenly wading in a veritable sea of "problemos."

SEVENTEEN

When Barnaby and Moira arrived in the lair, I excused myself to go upstairs and get Dad and Beau. They had been manning the shop since we sent Mindy home at 5 o'clock. We had no customers, and the square appeared to be deserted. I turned the "Closed" sign around, switched off the lights, and sent Chase a text saying he and Festus should join us.

By the time I went back downstairs, Festus, who was usually full of jovial wisecracks, appeared around the corner from the passageway. He walked silently through the seating area and assumed his favorite spot on the hearth with his back to the room.

Chase came in and greeted everyone. As he passed me, I asked in a low voice, "What's up with the old man?"

"Beats me," he said. "He was fine this morning, but his mood has gotten worse and worse all day. Probably just a hairball. It'll come up sooner or later."

Since I wasn't keen to talk about the regurgitation habits of werecats, I changed the subject. "Where are Greer and Lucas?" I asked in a regular tone of voice.

"Here," Greer answered, stepping out of the stacks followed by Lucas. Both carried armloads of leather-bound volumes. When they dropped the books on the work table, the force of the landing raised a cloud of dust around the weighty tomes.

Curious, Beau lifted the top book and read from the spine, "*A History of the Second Crusade as told to Fr. Gilbert by a Knight of the Templar Cross.*" He opened the cover almost reverently. "My heavens," he said, "this is an illuminated manuscript."

Barnaby moved to stand beside him. "You cannot imagine the hours monastics like this man labored in the medieval scriptorium to produce such manuscripts. During both Reformations, human and Fae, zealots threatened the destruction of works such as this for perceived heresies. We salvaged what we could, safeguarding the manuscripts here and in other repositories around the world."

"A work of intellectual heroism," Beau said, cradling the book in his hands. "This is simply magnificent."

"You have an interest in such things, Colonel Longworth?" Barnaby asked.

"I do, sir," he said. "One fueled by both my current circumstances and as a matter of personal curiosity."

"Then you must come to Shevington and spend time with me in my private library," Barnaby said. "We can discover what common interests we might share."

"It would be my honor, sir," Beau said, carefully replacing the volume, "but I fear we bibliophiles are forcing our companions to wait for an explanation of your presence here this evening."

Barnaby looked around as if he'd forgotten the rest of us were in the room. "My apologies," he said, bowing slightly, "an addiction to research is my greatest failing. Let us begin."

When we were all seated around the fire, I said, "So I guess the two of you are here because of what Festus and Chase found in Raleigh."

"Yes," Barnaby said, "the scans from the RABIES collar confirmed everything Greer and Lucas had already surmised about the specific focus of the inventory Irenaeus Chesterfield amassed over the past few years. The artifacts we saw all relate to time and navigation."

We all exchanged puzzled looks. The Lord High Mayor and the resident alchemist came all the way to Briar Hollow to give us confirmation of what we already knew?

Before I could say anything, Festus broke his silence. "That's it?" he asked sarcastically. "What about that fancy rowan necklace thing Chesterfield was trying to buy? You have some slick explanation for that?"

The nasty, accusatory tone of the words wasn't lost on us, but I think everyone was too shocked to say anything.

Barnaby shifted in his chair. "I'm afraid," he said, "that is a rather more complicated story."

"Aren't all of your stories complicated?" the old cat said sharply. "Run it past us. I think we're bright enough to keep up."

Chase winced. "Dad," he said, "show a little respect."

"Oh, I'm plenty respectful, boy," Festus said, "but I've also been doing me some thinking, and I don't like what I've come up with. Two amulets made of amber both associated with particular trees, one of which is sitting in the dead center of Shevington? I'm thinking that's not a coincidence and I'm thinking his Lordship the Mayor here knows all about it."

I'll give Barnaby credit. He didn't flinch.

"Your thoughts are correct," he said gravely.

"Oh," Festus said, "I'm not done. In fact, I'm just getting warmed up. When the Amulet of the Phoenix surfaced, you acted like it was nothing more than a magical trinket Chesterfield just happened to get his paws on, but wasn't exactly the truth, was it?"

No one said a word or even dared move as the yellow cat and Barnaby Shevington stared at one another.

"No," Barnaby said softly, "that was a lie. The Amulet

of the Phoenix is no mere trinket. Although its story has receded into our mythology over the past several hundred years, it is one of the great artifacts of Fae culture. The fact that it was in Chesterfield's possession is not insignificant."

Without blinking, Festus said, "Who had the amulet before him?"

"My late wife, Adeline," Barnaby replied. "Until the Amulet was taken from Brenna Sinclair, I had not seen it since my wife's murderer ripped it from her neck on the 6th day of April, 1580. Darby recognized it instantly when it was seized from Brenna because he was in service to my daughter, Knasgowa. I dreamed of returning the amulet to her as she also guarded the Mother Oak. We were never able to locate it during her lifetime."

My mother looked at Barnaby with something akin to awe. "Knasgowa was your daughter?" she said. "But that means you're our . . . "

"Grandfather," Barnaby said, "though many times removed now."

"That's all warm and fuzzy, Gramps," Festus said, "but let's get back to business here, shall we?"

The tension in the room ratcheted up like a race car going from zero to sixty. Festus clearly had no intention of stopping what amounted to his interrogation of Barnaby. All the rest of us could do was sit there and watch.

"As you wish," Barnaby said. "Pray continue."

"Did it occur to you that Chesterfield might be the wizard who killed your wife?" Festus asked.

"It did occur to me," Barnaby replied, "but I could not face the idea that . . . that . . . my own brother killed Adeline."

Anger filled the amber eyes that remained locked on Barnaby. "Now we're getting down to it," Festus purred. The sound was low and menacing. "Just so we're sure everybody is on the same page here. While the rest of us have been fighting and bleeding to protect the Fae world from discovery, you chose to protect your sorry brother instead. Do I need to remind you that my wife died rather than betray our kind, Barnaby? If that's even your name."

My grandfather faced his accuser with an ashen face. "You need not remind me," he said. "And, no, my name is not Barnaby Shevington although I have lived as that man since 1560 when I first met Adeline. She believed, as did everyone who knew me, that I was born in 1540. In truth, I entered this world in 1125, the eldest son of Fae parents. My name then was Barnabas Chesterfield. Irenaeus is my younger brother by five years. Until this moment, only Moira has known the entire truth of my identity."

Festus fixed her with his gaze. "So what's your excuse, Alchemist?"

Since I'd been watching Barnaby's face, I hadn't seen how angry Moira was becoming. She answered Festus in Gaelic and he spit back a razor-edged retort. That's when Barnaby held his hand up. Even in their anger, Festus and Moira obeyed the unspoken command.

"Enough," Barnaby said. "I make no excuses for my behavior, but if I may, I will tell you the whole story. Then you may judge me as you will."

He was looking at Festus as he spoke. Anger radiated from the old cat, but even enraged, Festus is a fair man. He nodded at Barnaby to continue.

As the eldest son of a 12th century Fae family, Barnaby enjoyed all the privileges of the heir apparent. He would inherit his father's land and wealth, while the younger son was destined to study with the familial alchemist. All was well, and even happy, in the Chesterfield clan until young Irenaeus failed to develop his magical powers.

As the boy grew, he became more and more an outcast. In 1144, without his father's permission, Irenaeus apprenticed himself to a Templar Knight and went to the Second Crusade. After the Siege of Lisbon, he became obsessed with the science of the "infidels" and went to Egypt to study.

"I knew nothing of my brother's fate until 1180 when he contracted with a demonic entity for his powers," Barnaby said. "Irenaeus was the first Creavit. His defection to the powers of darkness killed our parents and blackened the family name. My grief and disillusionment drove me into seclusion. I lived and worked with the Fae monastic scholars who created the kind of manuscripts the Colonel and I were just admiring. For more than 350 years I removed myself from the affairs of the Otherworld. But then, one day in 1560, while paying my respects to the Mother Tree, I met the *Quercus de Pythonissam*—the Witch of the Oak—an incomparably lovely woman named Adeline Moore. It was for her that I reinvented myself."

"And you promptly lied to her," Festus said flatly.

"Only in part," Barnaby said. "Adeline knew I was a Fae noble who had lived as an exile. I met in private with the Ruling Elders and reclaimed my lands and titles. Adeline gave me the strength to pick up the discarded fragments of my life. She gave me hope. I took my mother's surname, Shevington, and altered my given name, but . . ." his voice faltered. "I wanted her to think well of me. I was afraid to tell her the truth about Irenaeus. My cowardice cost Adeline her life."

I had to clear my throat before I could speak. "What was your brother doing while you were rebuilding your life?"

"Leading the Creavit heresy," Barnaby said bitterly. "When Irenaeus sold his soul, he set in motion the chain of events that culminated in the Fae Reformation. I realized I bore a responsibility to fight him and his kind. All of that notwithstanding, however, no evidence pointed to his involvement in Adeline's murder. I simply could not bring myself to believe him capable of such a crime."

"And 1936?" Festus asked. "How do you explain that?"

"Irenaeus asked me for clemency, saying he wished only to live a scholarly, contemplative life," Barnaby said. "It was a longing to live in peace apart from the affairs of the world I understood well. We tested his powers and they appeared to be minimal. I granted him probation because he is my blood. That was a terrible mistake, one against which you warned me, Festus. You were right, and I am most heartily sorry for my error."

Festus worked his mouth back and forth, considering my grandfather's words. "I can't fault a man for standing by his own blood," he said finally, "but I swear to you, Barnaby Shevington, if one person in this room comes to harm because you're hiding anything else from us, you will answer to me."

I know the difference between a threat and a promise. That was a promise.

"There are no more secrets," Barnaby said. "We must act swiftly and together to locate and recover the Amulet of Caorunn."

"The what?" I asked.

"The necklace in the photograph from Anton's office," he said. "That is the Amulet of Caorunn, shaped from the blood of the Mother Rowan and holding in its heart three berries from her branches. If my brother were to possess it and to join it with one of the other amulets, the consequences would be dire."

Oh, man. I cannot tell you how much I hated to ask the next question.

"Exactly how many amulets are we talking about here?"

"Thirteen in total," Barnaby said. "Together they form the Coven of the Blood. If Irenaeus were to possess any number of them, Moira believes he could sever the realms."

I didn't like the sound of that. "Which means what?" I asked.

"It means that Chesterfield could cut the world of the humans away from the Otherworld," Moira said. "Creavit magic would assume control of this world, and we would be powerless to stop it."

EIGHTEEN

When Irenaeus Chesterfield entered the time loop in the pizzeria, he found Seraphina and Ioana circling the empty restaurant like starving dogs. Both Strigoi rushed to him, falling to their knees and whimpering.

"Please," Ioana begged, looking up at him with eyes sunken and crazed from hunger. "Please, we must eat. You said if we went to the carnival with you and did as you said, we could feed. We did everything you told us to do. *Please*."

Chesterfield stared at her impassively, seemingly impervious to the piteous pleading. The terrified creature at his feet might as well have been a scientific specimen in a petri dish.

"Fascinating," the wizard murmured. "Trapped within a single second of time, yet subject to ravening hunger."

Through cracked lips, Seraphina whispered, "We're starving. We'll do whatever you want us to do, but we must eat. It's been days."

Chesterfield's brows went up. "And your perception of time remains intact!" he said. "I would not have thought that possible. You offer endless insights for my considera- tion. And you are quite correct. Days have passed. Almost six of them, in fact. I believe your last meal was that unfor- tunate young man in the alleyway. You really should have grabbed a snack before staging that carnival drama with the child."

Ioana shuddered. "Have pity," she moaned. "We will die."

Chesterfield leaned down and placed his index finger under her chin, forcing the Strigoi to look at him.

"Ah," he said in a silky whisper, "but therein lies the sheer beauty of this experiment. You will not die. That is unless I decide to be merciful and take your heads off. Absent that benevolent intervention, you will simply exist here in an eternal prison of starvation and madness."

Seraphina laid a hand on her cousin's shoulder to quell the terrified sobbing. "I don't think that's what you're going to do," she said, confronting Chesterfield directly. "Why would you go to the trouble of rescuing us from the lightning just to watch us suffer?"

Curling his lips in a feral smile, Chesterfield said, "Because it amuses me."

"I'm sure it does," Seraphina replied, her voice shaking, "but there's more to you than that."

The wizard pushed back the sides of the old-fashioned frock coat he wore and shoved his hands in his pockets. "Is there now?" he said. "Please enlighten me with your superior knowledge of my motivations. Why did I rescue you?"

"Because you see a purpose for us in your greater plans," she said. "My father spoke of you. He said you were the most ruthlessly practical man he had ever known."

Chesterfield considered her words. "Anton was not without his perceptive abilities," he admitted. "I am, indeed, a practical man, but only in the face of demonstrable benefit. Here are your only options, Strigoi. The rules of your feeding program are as follows. If I free you from your cage for one half hour, you may feed on the proprietor of this establishment. You may not, however, kill him, and you most certainly may not mesmerize him and make him your human servant. If you dare defy me, you will suffer the consequences."

Eagerly seizing on his words, Ioana begged, "Oh, please, please, sir. We will not defy you."

Dismissing her coldly, he turned back to Seraphina, "It is not this babbling fool with whom I am concerned," he said. "She has neither spirit or initiative. You, dear Seraphina, are a different matter. You have both a mind and a degree of resolve. You are the one I do not trust."

Though a tremor passed through her body, Seraphina did not avert her eyes. "I am also practical . . . master," she said. "We will not defy you. *I* will not defy you."

With that, she lowered her gaze to the floor and waited.

After a long moment, Chesterfield brought his hands together, clapping in slow rhythm.

"At last," he said, "the proper deference. Well played, young woman, well played. Your performance has won you a trial run. My exit from this space will trigger a release spell of 30 minutes' duration. I have no desire to watch as you indulge your baser instincts, so I caution you now to pace yourselves. You must make Peter last, as he is the only human you will be given for the immediate future. Hide the evidence of your meal on his person, and leave him capable of attending to his business. We do not need to raise suspicion among the locals."

Seraphina bowed her head again. "As you command, master."

Chesterfield removed his watch from the pocket of his vest, opened the case, and then paused with his thumb over the winding crown. "Do not make me regret this clemency," he warned. "I have no patience for insurrection." Then, clicking the crown, he disappeared.

Ioana instantly leaped to her feet and started toward

the living quarters behind the dining area, but Seraphina stopped her. "Let me go!" the girl shrieked. "I must eat."

"Stop," Seraphina ordered. "We both must eat, but we must also use this time we have been given. We will turn the human and make him our own."

The words were enough to halt Ioana's mad dash. "Seraphina, we can't do that!" she whispered hoarsely. "If we defy Chesterfield, we will never eat again."

"If we do not defy him," Seraphina hissed, "we will become his slaves. Do as I say, Ioana, unless you want to face *my* temper."

From the back room, a man's voice called, "Hello? Is someone there?"

"I'll do anything," Ioana whispered, "just please, *please* let me feed."

"We will both feed," Seraphina said softly. "But we will do it my way." Then, raising her voice, she called out gaily, "Oh, hi! We are just so sorry! We thought you were open for business. We're looking for something to eat."

"Sure," Pete called out, "hang on. I'll be right there."

<hr>

The confrontation between Festus and Barnaby stunned us all. I have no doubt Barnaby would have given us the same information had he been left to his own devices, but the force of the werecat's questioning laid bare the real impact of my grandfather's decisions.

Irenaeus Chesterfield wasn't just "a" bad guy, he was *"the"* bad guy. The first Creavit. A murderer. The driving force behind a vendetta against my family—well, his *own* family. That was the part that left me speechless. Chesterfield was my great uncle? No way I saw that coming.

Greer and Lucas got most of the details right in their research, except Chesterfield was never human. He was Fae and suffered from what amounted to a birth defect;

one that made him a jealous, envious outcast. Plus, he wasn't "associated" with a wealthy family, he was their very own, personal black sheep.

Here we thought his rescue of the Strigoi Sisters constituted the major problem at hand. Now all that was shoved to a back burner in the light of his designs on the Amulet of Caorunn, possibly the Amulet of the Phoenix, and probably the eleven others we'd just learned about. I mean seriously, is any good likely to come out of something called the "Coven of the Blood?"

Moira explained the name was simply a reference to the sap given by each Mother Tree to form the amber used in the corresponding amulet, but that only touched off a furious spate of mental math in me. If there were thirteen amulets, there had to be thirteen Mother Trees.

When I said as much, the alchemist nodded. "There are," she said. "Collectively, they're called The Coven of the Woods."

Which meant there were thirteen witches and probably thirteen staffs like Dilestos, the sentient walking stick Amity Prescott gave me right before I visited Shevington for the first time. Dielstos was made from a branch of the Mother Oak.

And somehow all of those objects—all of us—supported and worked with—or for—the Grid . . . which held reality together . . .

That was about the time my brain shifted into overload. Channeling the same kind of commanding response that led Barnaby to halt the barrage of questions Festus had been firing at him, I held up my hand and said, firmly, "Stop! Enough!"

All the voices in the lair fell silent. Everyone looked at me.

"This is too much for one night," I said. "We need to stop. If the Strigoi are going to put in an appearance, it will be at Anton's funeral on Thursday. We have almost two days to get a crash course in the Grid. Right now, I think we could all use some time to just absorb everything we've learned tonight."

My words seemed to relieve my grandfather. From everything I knew about Barnaby, he was a private man who liked nothing more than to spend quiet hours in study. This conversation must have been hellish for him.

"Are you all staying here tonight?" I asked.

"I cannot," Barnaby said. "The merfolk migration is in its final stages, and the auguries are predicting a major winter storm in the coming days."

Moira laid a hand on his arm. "Go," she said, "I will stay here and do what I can to help. Dewey will bring my mirror to your office. That will allow us to contact you with clarity regardless of the conditions in Shevington."

Barnaby frowned. "But do you not require two mirrors?"

She smiled tolerantly. "We are sitting in the middle of a Fae archive, Barnaby. I assure you there is a suitable mirror here that I can activate."

Which is how we came to have a full-length, gilded mirror in the lair—I hope with an unlimited data plan.

Before Barnaby left, he crossed to the hearth and held his hand out to Festus. They spoke in Gaelic, so I can't tell you the exact content of the conversation, but in the end, the old cat put his paw out, and they shook.

Then Barnaby had a few quiet words with Moira before he turned to Mom and me. "Would the two of you do me the honor of walking part way to the portal with me?" he asked.

"Of course," Mom said, rising from the sofa. Dad didn't turn loose of her hand as she stood up, watching her with a worried expression. Leaning back down, she said, "Let me go, Jeff. It's fine."

Reluctantly he released her hand, but I felt Dad's eyes on us as we walked away with Barnaby.

For the first hundred yards or so, no one spoke. Then Barnaby ventured tentatively, "If there is anything either of you wishes to say to me, please do so."

Without breaking stride, Mom reached for his hand. "When I was a little girl," she said, "and you used to come down to the big meadow below the city to fly kites with all the kids, you always brought me candy."

Out of the corner of my eye, I saw my grandfather swallow hard. "Completely against your mother's wishes," he said.

"One afternoon," Mom went on, "you told me that I reminded you of a little girl you had known once. Who was that?"

"My daughter," Barnaby said roughly, "Knasgowa. I flew kites with her in that same field when she was a child. Her people, the Cherokee, had never seen such a thing. She called her kite Wind Dancer."

Mom stopped and turned toward him. She was crying. "Why didn't you help me?" she asked in a broken voice. "Why didn't you stop Anton from cursing me? Why didn't you protect my baby?"

I would have preferred to leave them alone, but there was no place to go.

"Kelly," Barnaby said, tears spilling from his eyes, "I did protect Connor the only way I could, by arranging for him to be brought to Shevington. You had already forsaken your magic because of the accident with the girls. The Guardian of the Oak must be willing. We could not compel you to fill that position. The Mother Tree would not allow it."

"Has it all been a game?" Mom asked, choking on the words. "Have we all been dancing on Chesterfield's strings?"

Barnaby looked down at their clasped hands. "Chester-field . . . Irenaeus . . . my brother," he said haltingly. "I wanted to believe that he could turn away from the darkness. Please understand that I remember him as a boy before any of this happened."

He looked up, and Mom nodded at him to continue.

"You saw the presence of your magic as a burden you could not bear," Barnaby said. "For my brother the opposite was true. Being denied the heritage of his powers destroyed him. For whatever he has done in his long life, it all began from tremendous personal pain, rejection, and disappointment. Forgive me for wanting to see him as he once was. Forgive me for wanting to afford him a better life."

Mom reached for Barnaby. As they embraced, she whispered, "How have you stood it all?"

His voice came out muffled against her shoulder. "I have stood it all," he said, "because I believe that everything that has happened was meant to occur, that we all walk a path toward a shared purpose. I believe in hope, dear Kelly, and in love. It is from that I draw my sustenance."

NINETEEN

I'd like to tell you that after all that drama, we got on point, worked out a grand scheme to stop Chesterfield in his tracks, dealt with the Strigoi Sisters, and immediately started planning the holidays. End of story.

Yeah. Not so much.

After Barnaby's stunning revelation, we all went to our respective corners to recover. I heard my parents talking quietly in the other room, and Mom's quiet crying, but then I fell into an exhausted sleep.

The next morning, I dressed quietly so as not to wake them and headed downstairs to find Gemma and Mindy already setting up the espresso bar.

Since we couldn't very well talk in front of our new hire, I said, "Morning. How'd you all sleep?"

Mindy immediately launched into a description of some experiment in "lucid dreaming" she was trying, while Gemma answered with, "About like you'd expect."

No argument from me on that one.

A sharp rap on the front door diverted my attention. "Dang," I said, "someone must need their coffee."

I crossed the distance to the door and opened it to be greeted by a rather officious man clutching a large manila envelop. "Gemma Andrews?" he asked briskly.

"She's in the back there," I said, stepping aside. Something about his manner gave me a really bad feeling about where this was all headed.

Gemma came out from behind the counter to meet him.

"Are you Gemma Andrews?" he asked bluntly.

"I am," she said. "What can I do for you."

He handed her the thick brown envelope. "You've been served," he said. "Have a nice day."

With that, he turned on his heel and marched out.

"Uh oh," Mindy said, as Gemma undid the clasp on the envelope. "This can't be good. Did you get a look at his aura? Spiking red all over the place. Total warning sign."

Just then, Tori came out of her micro apartment. She stopped when she saw the look on her mother's face. "Mom?" she said. "What is it?"

Gemma had to try twice before she managed an answer. "Your father just had me served with divorce papers," she said flatly. "Excuse me. I have to go to Cotterville."

From the stairway, Mom said, "Gem, wait," but she was too late. Even as Mom rapidly descended the last few steps with Dad right behind her, Gemma was out the back door.

"Jeff," Mom said, "stop her."

Dad barreled past Mom and after Gemma, with the four of us crowding in the doorway to watch. He got one hand on the door, before Gemma threw the car in reverse, backed into the alley, and sped off in a cloud of dust.

Dad turned back toward us. "Do you want me to go after her?" he asked.

"Tori?" Mom said. "What do you think?"

Her face ashen with shock, Tori said, "No. This is between them. Mom will call us if she needs us."

Scrap Andrews didn't look up when he heard a step at the open door of his office. "You get that shipment stowed?" he asked, assuming he was speaking to the lumber yard manager. Instead, a thick sheaf of legal papers sailed into his field of vision, knocking the pencil out of his hand, and landing with a resounding thump on top of his desk.

"You want to tell me what the hell that's about?" Gemma demanded. "And while we're at it, who have you been buying *Obsession* perfume for?"

Looking up into his wife's angry face, Scrap's expression hardened. "How do you know I've been buying *Obsession*?"

"Let's just say I have my ways," Gemma said. "Answer the question."

Calmly retrieving his pencil, Scrap said, "Your 'ways' are exactly what got us here, and for your information, that perfume was a gift for a nice, *normal* lady I've been seeing."

Gemma opened her mouth to speak, clamped it shut again, then finally said, "Do you even care that you're breaking your daughter's heart?"

"I'm divorcing you," Scrap said, "not Tori."

"Tell her that," Gemma snapped.

"I'd be happy to," Scrap retorted, "but she won't take my calls."

"Because you wouldn't take hers for a week."

Scrap stood up and offered the papers back to Gemma. "You'll need these when you hire a lawyer," he said coldly.

Gemma took the documents, but then said, in a calmer voice, "How long have you been thinking about this?"

"Since I met Mary Ann," he said.

Gemma frowned, then grew red in the face when realization dawned. "Mary Ann Marshall?" Gemma said. "You're old enough to be her father, not to mention the fact she's gone chasing after every man in three counties. Did you have to take up with a complete slut?"

Scrap stiffened. "I don't appreciate you speaking that way about my future wife," he said archly.

"For the record," Gemma said tersely, "your *current* wife doesn't *appreciate* being cheated on and lied to."

At that, Scrap at least had the grace to look ashamed of himself. In a more subdued voice, he said, "I am sorry about that part, Gemma, but I haven't been happy in a long time."

The placating attempt fell on deaf ears.

"Well, Scrap," Gemma said hotly, "God forbid that you not be happy. That's certainly worth destroying a 35-year marriage without even trying to work it out with your wife *and* alienating your only child in the process."

An uneasy look came into his eyes. "Please don't tell Tori about Mary Ann," he said. "I'd like to do that myself, so she understands what really happened."

"I'll just bet you would like to do some snow job on our daughter," Gemma said, "but you know what? She's smarter than you realize and I'm done protecting you, especially after the way you've reacted to the truth about the powers that Tori and I share. I don't think you give a tinker's damn in hell about magic. That was just an excuse to file for divorce so you could be with your little bimbo."

The hard look returned to Scrap's eyes. "Be careful, Gemma," he said, "or I might not protect you either."

"That two-timing weasel," Mom said hotly. "He's going to need protecting when I get done with him. How old is Mary Ann Marshall anyway?"

Tori, looking like she wanted to throw up, supplied the information. "Twenty-eight," she said. "She was two years behind me and Jinx in school."

When Gemma came back two hours after her abrupt exit, the four of us went upstairs to talk in private. From

Gemma's description, her encounter with her husband had been ugly from the start but then turned vaguely menacing.

I didn't want to be insensitive, but if Scrap made good on his veiled threat, he could cause us all a lot of trouble—a commodity we already enjoyed in abundance.

"Do you really think Scrap would make good on his threat about outing you and Tori?" I asked.

"Who knows what he'll do," Gemma said angrily. "The man has lost his damned mind."

As much as I hated to put it on the table, this couldn't be allowed to get to the damage control stage. We needed to think about prevention.

"Uh, then don't we have to . . . do something . . . to keep that from happening?"

Beside me, Tori gasped, "You want to kill my father?"

Normally Tori doesn't go straight to extremes, but her nerves were more than a little frayed.

"For God's sake, Tori," I said, "of course not. I mean don't we have to put some kind of spell on him to make him forget about the magic?"

"Oh," she said, "sorry. I kinda *do* want to kill him so I thought that's where you were going."

Even though she was completely serious, the rest of us cracked up. Our shared laughter bled some of the tension out of the air. We were sitting in my living room, each with a cat in our laps.

I'd like to tell you my furry crew showed up in sympathetic support of Tori and Gemma, but honestly, they just saw four idle pairs of hands available for petting duty.

"Jinx is right," Gemma said, idly rubbing Yule's ears. "We can't run the risk of Scrap saying anything."

"Or Mary Ann," Mom said.

"Why would Mary Ann . . . " Gemma stopped and settled her mouth in a firm line. "I didn't consider that," she said tersely, "but you're right. Excuse me; I'm going to get another cup of coffee."

All of our minds had instantly gone to the same place, and mine, at least, could have used a dose of brain bleach at the thought of pillow talk between Scrap and his girl-friend. I can't imagine what that image was doing to Gemma.

"Uh, why don't Tori and I go downstairs and let you guys talk," I suggested to Mom.

"I think that's a good idea, honey," Mom said. "We'll be down in a little bit."

Gemma stood mindlessly swirling the coffee in her cup with a spoon when a voice behind her said, "You planning on churning that coffee?"

Shaking her head, Gemma laid the spoon down on the counter. Then she felt her friend's hand on her shoulder. "The girls are gone," Kelly said. "You can go ahead and have that cry you're holding in."

Gemma laughed, but the sound came out mixed with a sob. Still staring at the coffee, she said, "How could he, Kell? Was I that bad of a wife?"

"Don't be ridiculous," Kelly said. "Scrap was that bad of a husband. Come on, honey. Sit down so we can talk."

Obediently, Gemma picked up her cup and crossed to the small breakfast table, accepting the tissue Kelly held out to her as they both claimed a chair.

"Jinx is right about putting a spell on Scrap," she said, "and we have to do it immediately."

"I know."

"Can we put a wart on Mary Ann's nose while we're at it?"

"No," Kelly said, "but I wish we could."

Twin tears rolled down Gemma's face. "What am I going to do now?"

"This may not be the right time to tell you this," Kelly said, "and we haven't even told Jinx yet, but Jeff and I are going to buy the empty store next door to Chase's place."

Gemma's features wilted even farther. "How can I stay in Cotterville without you?" she asked, her lower lip trembling.

"You don't," Kelly said. "You take Scrap for every cent he's worth, including the house, which you sell so you can buy the old hardware store on the corner. The same guy has both buildings listed. You can finally open that apothecary shop you've been talking about since we were kids. I know it's a lot of change at once . . . "

Gemma interrupted. "Stop," she said, dabbing at her eyes. "You don't have to sell me. It's perfect."

Kelly blinked. "Just like that?"

"I'm not the one who upended our lives," Gemma said firmly. "Scrap did that, and long before I told him about the world of magic."

"True," Kelly said slowly. "But don't you need to think about this some more?"

"No," Gemma said. "If I do, I'll doubt myself, just like always, and this time, that's not happening. Moving over here to be with my . . ." her voice broke. "With my real family is just what I need. But it could be months before the divorce is final and I have the money, what if the building sells before then?"

"Oh," Kelly smiled, "I don't think it will be months. We may not be able to put a wart on Mary Ann's nose, but I think we can manage to ensure that Scrap goes along with everything you want in the divorce."

"Kelly!" Gemma gasped. "That would be an unethical use of our magic!"

"More unethical than a man cheating on his wife?"

Kelly asked, arching her eyebrow. "I don't think so. Besides, it won't be unethical if we word the spell the right way. After all, we're just interested in keeping the peace."

"My God," Gemma said, "Jinx is right. You're a changed woman."

"You're dang right I'm a changed woman," Kelly said firmly, "just like you're going to be. We're done apologizing and being penalized for our magic, especially by men."

For the first time that day, Gemma laughed. "Should I warn Jeff about that?"

"Jeff is handling everything just fine," Kelly said. "He wants to run a sporting goods store and I completely support him in that—and he completely supports me being back in the Fae world. Scrap is a different story."

Dabbing at her eyes again, Gemma sat up straighter. "Well," she said, "I guess that settles it. We have to wear those new t-shirts Tori ordered for the shop."

"What new t-shirts?"

"The ones that say, 'Badass Feminist Witches Unite.'"

In the alley below, Tori paused at the trash cans as laughter floated down from the open windows of Jinx's apartment. Through her own tears, she smiled. "Best friend magic," she whispered. "Works every time."

TWENTY

We didn't find out for another week or so what Mom and Gemma cooked up that day in my apartment. All we knew is that when they came downstairs, Gemma was herself. Tori went to her mom and gave her a hug. "You feeling a little better?" she asked.

"I am," Gemma said, "and I'm starving. How about we get pizza from the Stone Hearth?

With Mindy there, we couldn't let Darby cook for us, and all my suspicions about the guy aside, Pete made a mean pie.

I placed the call, and Dad retrieved the food, coming back in the shop balancing four large, flat cardboard boxes.

"That guy Pete looks awful," he said as he deposited the boxes on one of the tables in the espresso bar. "He can barely put one foot in front of the other."

"Oh?" I said, eyeing the food suspiciously. "Do you think we should eat these?"

Dad laughed. "Don't be a germaphobe, honey. He said he got ahold of something bad at the Halloween carnival and just hasn't been able to shake it yet. I know how he feels. I've hit some bad truck stops in my day."

"Do you think maybe we should check on him later?" Mom asked with concern. "He does live alone after all."

"I'll mention it to Chase," I said. "They've gone biking

together a few times, so I guess that makes them friends."

Getting some food in us definitely helped everyone's mood, as did the distraction of appearing normal for Mindy's benefit.

After a little covert pumping, Tori was able to determine the ghost hunting trio was indeed "onto something major" but wouldn't be publishing any evidence just yet. That meant they were sticking by their decision to hold the video of John Dodge.

The fact that the young ghost hunters had been able to capture the deceased ballplayer on film at all still bothered me—a lot. The original spectral baseball video we could explain thanks to the jolt of juice the spirits received from the Ionescus. This one was different.

Greer suggested we were seeing an overall rise in paranormal energy levels in and around Briar Hollow commensurate with the increased Fae presence in the area. On the one hand, that was good for the courthouse square association's goal of turning the town into a paranormal destination, but it also meant we were going to have to get serious about controlling and coordinating manifestations. One more thing to add to the "to do" list.

After we finished lunch, Gemma decided to take out her excess energies via a manic round of cleaning that had the unintentional effect of putting Darby into a major pouting fit. Not only had the brownie been denied the pleasure of preparing lunch for us, he was now being treated to the sight of someone scrubbing areas where he never let so much as a speck of dirt appear.

Every time I went into the storeroom for something, he materialized and demanded to know if his work was considered substandard.

Between keeping up the ruse for Mindy and trying to manage Darby's wounded ego, I gave up at 3 o'clock and sent our lone, non-magical employee home. That left us free to put Dad in charge of the shop and head down to the lair—with a snack request to Darby delivered with assurances of starvation.

The olive branch worked. The brownie immediately brightened and said he would prepare something wonderful.

Given the state of things in the lair, sustenance might be needed. Basically, the whole team was in a state of total disorganization.

After everything we learned the night before, I guess I shouldn't have been surprised. There were so many topics we needed to explore, no one—not even Moira—had a firm handle on where to start. She had, however, located and activated the standing mirror and checked in with my grandfather.

Beau informed me privately that Barnaby did not look as if he had slept, but was otherwise "quite himself." If I was worried about him, I can't imagine how Moira must be feeling.

When I called for ideas about how we could start making some progress, suggestions started flying thick and fast. That's when Glory put her fingers in her mouth and let out with an ear-piercing whistle that sent Duke diving under Beau's feet.

"Would you *stop* doing that!" Festus roared. "Cats have better hearing than humans *and* dogs put together. If you're hurting the dead mutt's ears, you're *killing* mine."

"Sorry," Glory said, "but you were all talking at one time, and I need you to *hush* and listen to me for a change."

With his ears still lying flat, Festus said, "We're listening, and you danged sure better have something to say."

"I do," Glory said. "Research is what I did for a living. We have to start with what we know and connect the dots from there. All we know for sure is that Mr. Chesterfield wants the Amulet of Caorunn. It's made of amber, and so is the amulet the Colonel wears. That's a connection. If this were my project, I'd find out what oak and rowan might be able to do together before I worried about anything else."

Her approach was so simple and obvious, we all just kind of stood there sheepishly, until Moira said, "Precisely. That is where I began my preliminary research when we learned about the Amulet of Caorunn in the first place. I think we have all allowed ourselves to become . . . distracted . . . in the face of so many revelations. So, shall we get to it? Gemma? Tori?"

Let me break down for you what we did know at that point.

Rowan or "Witchwood" is associated with the element of fire. When the Strigoi Sisters first showed up on the scene, Greer outfitted us with rowan amulets as a means of protection. Oak, on the other hand, is associated with sovereignty and water.

Beau, who had been spending the morning reading about trees in the human realm, shared something interesting about oaks. They are the species most likely to be struck by lightning, surviving the blasts with remarkable resiliency.

All trees, even those here in our stream of time, are remotely connected to the Mother Trees and exhibit a degree of sentience. I had some personal experience with that, having once connected with the consciousness of an aged hickory. The tree communicated with me through impressions rather than words. That did not detract, however, from the depths of its aged wisdom, leaving me with the indelible memory of the deep roots of its presence.

We don't do trees any service when we plant them by themselves to shade some lonely corner of the front yard. According to Beau, trees make friends with each other in a natural forest. In such a setting, they will even continue to feed the stumps of their felled companions for decades. They also rely on intricate defense mechanisms against predators like insects and birds, signaling one another when a threat is at hand.

Since we all agreed that understanding more about the life of trees in the human realm was important, Glory settled down to work with Beau on that subject.

Greer immersed herself in the history of the Second Crusade. Barnaby told us that after the only real Crusader victory of that campaign, which occurred in Lisbon in 1144, Irenaeus disappeared into Egypt to study the "science of the infidels."

The magical artifact that crippled our friend Myrtle and robbed her of her powers, the Orb of Thoth, was fashioned in Egypt from metal taken from a meteorite that damaged the step pyramid at Saqqara around 2630 B.C.

I'd had a psychometric chat with the interior guardian of the orb who told me Chesterfield "appropriated" the artifact and used it as a weapon without fully understanding its purpose. Then came the kicker.

"Mark my words," the guardian said, "Irenaeus Chesterfield must not recover the orb. Should he ever come to understand its true potential, all will be lost."

So riddle me this, Batman.

What would happen if Chesterfield got ahold of some or all of the amulets from the Coven of the Blood *and* the Orb of Thoth (currently hidden in the depths of the ocean)? No one could answer the question, but just asking it scared the heck out of me.

Glory's suggestion got everyone back on track. A kind of studious air of concentration fell over the group. Mom went upstairs to mind the store with Dad since we'd be open into the evening.

Festus, predictably, offered to work with Greer, and Chase set about expanding our existing drone surveillance while coordinating security for Anton's funeral with Cezar Ionescu. When I stopped to look at the multiple drone feeds on the big screen TV, Chase said quietly, "How are you doing after last night?"

"Okay," I said. "It's a lot to take in. But honestly, I'm glad Barnaby told us. At least now Chesterfield doesn't seem like such a random villain. We have a lot to learn, though, to get ahead of him."

Gesturing around the room, he said, "At least it's a matter of divide and conquer now."

"So I'm not the only one?" I said.

"Only one what?" he asked.

"To not know about the Grid?"

"Hardly," Chase said. "Everyone in the Otherworld knows the Grid exists, but to really understand how it operates? The roles of everyone and everything involved? That's pretty esoteric stuff. Plus, Shevington has been cut off from the Old World Fae since the 16th century. The Mother Oak is as much a defector with the rest of us."

I hadn't thought about that. "But she never disconnected from the Grid, did she?" I asked.

Chase shook his head. "I don't think that's even possible, but how the separation affected her interactions with the other Mother Trees? I have no idea. I'm not even sure Barnaby and Moira do. You have to understand, Jinx, Shevington is re-entering the broader Fae world. For Barnaby to contact the Ruling Elders? That's huge."

If you're having a hard time keeping up with the intricacies of Fae politics, join the club.

"But I thought the Elders contacted him about being an ambassador or something," I said. "Isn't that why I'm supposed to take over as mayor some day?"

"Yes," Chase said, "but that was all arranged through diplomatic correspondence delivered back and forth by couriers. The 'talks' have taken years. Glaciers move faster.

To actually dial up Reynold Isherwood for a face to face? That's the huge part."

"Okay," I said, "I get that, but it's also kind of cool. I mean, Chesterfield pretty much caused the Fae Reformation in the first place, but now defeating him may bring everyone back together."

Festus, who had apparently been listening to our conversation, jumped from Greer's work table to the back of the couch nearest to where Chase and I were standing. "Don't be so sure about that," he said.

"What do you mean, Dad?" Chase asked.

"A lot of the Creavit back in the Old World assimilated," Festus said. "Claimed that whether they had bargained for their powers or not, they wanted the magical community to function as a whole. They have money and influence—even intermarried, but their magic still isn't natural."

"Come on, Dad," Chase said, "aren't you being a little prejudiced?"

Setting his mouth in a firm line, Festus said, "No, boy, I'm not. All Creavit magic comes from a deal with the Darkness. Period."

Just then, Darby came by with an enormous platter of food that caught the old cat's eye. "Hold up there, Short Stuff," he said as he walked down the back of the couch. "Let me get a look at what you've got there."

As we watched, Festus directed Darby to fill a plate for him. I asked Chase in a low voice, "Do you think he's right?"

"Dad has a lot of connections," Chase admitted. "You may have noticed he's not one to play by the rules. Plus, Chesterfield is the only known Creavit who settled in America. That has to be because of Barnaby, which I don't like one bit."

I'd already thought about that, and I didn't like it either.

Lucas, who was standing at the edge of the stacks, caught my eye and beckoned. "Excuse me," I said to Chase, who, for once, managed not to bristle when he saw where I was headed.

Lucas and I were the only two people in the lair at the moment who weren't occupied with either research or tactics. To my considerable surprise, he asked me to go to the Valley with him.

"Are you out of your mind?" I said. "I can't just run off to the Valley and leave all of this."

I really didn't like the suggestion that I wasn't doing anything useful, which must have shown on my face.

"Sucks, doesn't it?" Lucas asked with a wicked grin.

"What?" I said, annoyed and a little amused at the same time.

"When the team is doing everything they need to be doing, and the boss isn't necessary at the moment," he replied.

"I am *not* the boss," I protested.

"Sure you are," he said, "and until this outfit gets their answers lined up, you're just twiddling your thumbs. I really do need to go to the Valley, and there's no reason in the world why you can't go with me."

He was right, but I wasn't ready to admit it yet.

"What do you need to do in Shevington?" I asked.

"I have to talk to Furl at the Registry and then pay a courtesy call on a relative," he answered.

"A relative?" I asked. "What relative?"

Since Lucas had yet to admit he and Moira were family, I was surprised he'd so casually mention other of his kin.

"My Uncle Owain," Lucas said. "He serves as head architect for the merfolk city. Since Owain is the eldest surviving male in our line, Moira kinda cuffed me around the ears for not calling on him to pay my respects. He's her half brother, you know."

Okay, so maybe he wasn't being secretive after all.

"Moira is your aunt?" I asked innocently.

"Greer told me she told you," Lucas replied. "I should have mentioned it myself. I just don't like to make a big deal about it."

His manner was so open and honest; I started to warm to the idea of a trip to the Valley in his company. "So paying this courtesy call is important?" I asked.

"Yeah," he admitted, "it's a whole big Elven etiquette *thing*. I'm running the risk of insulting Owain if I don't show up soon."

Then something occurred to me. "Wait a minute," I said. "Does that mean I get to see the city? Like from underwater?"

"Qynn," he said. "That's what they've named the place, and, yes, it does."

"And how do we get there?" I asked.

Sensing that he had me, Lucas said, "That's a surprise. You have to come with me to find out."

That did it. I was hooked.

"Oh, fine," I said, trying to act put upon and failing. "Let me see what the others think."

Clearing my throat, I said, "Hey guys, I'm thinking about going to the Valley with Lucas."

I swear to you, no one even looked up—okay, Chase flinched—but my ego still got taken down a few notches.

Walking over to Beau, I tapped him on the shoulder. "Did you hear me?" I asked. "I'm going to the Valley with Lucas."

"Hmm?" the Colonel said, glancing away from the page. "Oh, yes. Safe journey." Then, turning back to Glory, he said, "Now, regarding this matter of rhizomes . . ."

Lucas chuckled. "Told you," he said.

"Harumph," I muttered. "Let me at least get Tori's attention."

Crossing to the alchemist's corner, I took Tori by the arm and steered her clear of the table. "Excuse me," I said. "I need a minute."

Gemma and Moira gave identical dismissive waves. Dragging Tori out of earshot, I told her where I was going, and then said, "Look, I don't care how intense things are right now, you and Beau get that other thing taken care of while I'm gone. Understand? I want a report when I get back."

"Like I said, Jinksy," Tori grinned. "No . . ."

"Don't say it," I warned. "Every time you tell me there's no problem, there's a problem."

You know what they say. Just because you're paranoid doesn't mean they're not out to get you, and in this case, my paranoia was completely on target.

TWENTY-ONE

Beau slipped off the Amulet of the Phoenix and handed it to Tori. Bending down, he put his hands on either side of Duke's head. "Do you understand what we need you to do, boy?" he asked, fondling the dog's ears.

Duke's tail happily lashed back and forth, passing through the leaves on the ground rather than scattering them. "Good boy," Beau said. "Off with you now."

As they watched, the ghost dog bounded across the ball field straight for the spot where Nick had set up his camera equipment for the evening. When Duke came even with him, the dog intensified his energy. Nick bolted upright with a start, knocking soda cans and potato chips off his makeshift table.

Duke ran to the edge of the field, fading with each step, then repeated the maneuver, this time standing still and staring at Nick as if willing him to follow. Just as Tori had guessed he'd do, the young man snatched the video recorder off the tripod and took out after Duke who began to slowly and skillfully lead him away from the field.

When the pair disappeared around the corner, Tori and Beau walked quickly to home plate. "Hello?" the Colonel called out, his voice sounding oddly hollow. "Who walks among us in this place?"

They waited but heard nothing.

"Maybe he's not here tonight," Tori suggested. "We can't risk standing out here in the open much longer."

"Let me try once more," Beau said, clearing his throat. "Please, if you are with us this evening, I have need of a word with you regarding the game of baseball."

That did the trick.

Beside Beau the night air wavered and a man wearing an old-fashioned baseball cap materialized. "Who are you?" he asked, staring at Beau. "Can she see us?"

"She can," Tori said. "Are you John Lewis Dodge?"

The new arrival blinked. "How do you know that?"

Deciding the real explanation was too difficult, Tori said, "Everyone knows how you died in that game in 1916 when Tom Rogers smacked you in the face with a base-ball."

On reflex, Dodge scrubbed at his face. "Is that what happened?" he said. "All I remember is waking up with my face hurting. Took awhile, but I finally figured out I was benched for good."

"If I may," Beau said, "I am Colonel Beauregard T. Longworth, late of the Army of Northern Virginia. I met my demise some 50 years before your own, so I have some experience in these matters. Are you here because you need assistance moving on in your journey?"

Dodge frowned. "Moving on? No. I'm here looking for Hiram."

"Hiram Folger?" Tori asked.

Dodge grinned. "That's him! I knew old Hiram when he was playing for the Durham Bulls. Fact is, we're some kind of distant cousins on my mama's side. Anyhow, I heard Hiram was playing in a league on this side, and there's several of us who want in. Since I knew Hiram, the others sent me to get in touch with him."

"Oh my," Beau said weakly. "How exactly did you learn of Hiram's activities?"

"My grave is down in Cave Hill Cemetery in Louisville," Dodge said, adding, "that's Kentucky. You ought to come visit sometime, Colonel. We got about 5,000 dead boys down there that fought for the gray like you. How come you're not in uniform no more?"

"A complicated story, Mr. Dodge," Beau said. "Pray continue."

"Well," Dodge said, "Harry Clay Pulliam is buried down there with us."

Beau's grave expression instantly transformed to one of rapt interest. "*The* Henry Clay Pulliam?" he said excitedly.

Dodge nodded. "The one and only. He's a great man, Mr. Pulliam."

Tori cleared her throat. "Uh, boys, I hate to break up this little impromptu fan club meeting, but who exactly is Henry Clay Pulliam?"

Looking mildly scandalized by her ignorance, Beau said, "Mr. Pulliam was the sixth president of the National League. He served from 1903 until his unfortunate demise in 1909. His work in settling disagreements between his own organization and the American League was quite instrumental in leading to the creation of the World Series."

Dodge whistled appreciatively. "Dang, Colonel, for an old dead guy, you know your baseball."

Seemingly oblivious to Dodge's clueless insult, Beau beamed with delight. "Thank you, young man. I am a most avid . . . "

Tori cut him off. "Hold on," she said. "Let's get back to Pulliam. What does he have to do with all this?"

Dodge answered placidly. "Oh, after Mr. Pulliam blew his brains out, he'd been kind of dissatisfied in the afterlife."

Beau nodded in commiseration. "As is always the case

with the suicides," he said sadly. "They seem rather universally restless. Except for those who succumbed to sleeping tablets, of course."

Interested in spite of herself, Tori said, "Really? What's up with them?"

Beau shook his head. "Nightmares," he said, "of the lurid sort that leads to shrieks and wails."

"Must be awful for the neighbors," Tori deadpanned.

"Quite," Beau agreed, with Dodge nodding in baleful agreement.

"Okey dokey then," Tori said, "back to Pulliam."

"Oh, right," Dodge said. "Henry's excited for the first time in decades. Never occurred to him to get a league going on this side. He's drawing up a list of dead recruits, talking about setting up the dead majors. Why ole Pete Browning himself is buried right down there with us. Can't get a much better start than that."

"The Louisville Slugger?" Beau exclaimed. "Oh, I should very much like to meet him!"

"Beau . . . " Tori said, but the warning came too late.

"We can make that happen," Dodge said. "So I can tell Harry you'll get him and Hiram together?"

"Uh, guys . . . "

Completely ignoring Tori, Beau said proudly, "As it happens, I am the organizer of the Briar Hollow Spectral Sports League."

"You are?" Dodge said. "Well, that's just perfect! I'll come back tomorrow night and bring Henry with me. We good to meet here?"

In the distance, Duke howled, the signal that Nick was headed back to the field.

"Uh, no, actually," Beau said hastily. "It would be much more felicitous for us if we could hold these talks at the local cemetery."

"Now, wait a minute . . ." Tori protested.

"We can find it," Dodge said confidently, already starting to fade from sight. "See you at midnight."

As he dematerialized, Tori said, "Beau Longworth, I cannot believe you . . ." The sound of Duke's approaching howls stopped her.

"We are not done with this discussion," she hissed, handing her companion the Amulet of the Phoenix, "but right now, we have to get out of here."

"There is no time," Beau said, slipping the chain over his neck. "Follow my lead."

The instant he was solid enough to do so, he offered Tori his arm. She took it, and together they strolled across the grass like they were simply out enjoying a walk on a crisp autumn evening.

As they reached the sidewalk, Nick rounded the corner, camera still in hand. Skidding to a stop in front of them, he said, "Oh, uh, hi, folks. Out for a walk?"

"Indeed," Beau said, "winter will be upon us soon, and we do enjoy these bracing evenings."

"Uh, yeah, right," Nick stammered. "Did you see anything run by here?"

As Duke trotted up and sat down beside his leg, Beau said, with a completely straight face, "We did not. Was there something in particular for which you were searching?"

"Uh, it's hard to explain," Nick stammered. "Thanks anyway. Good night." With that, he started back down the sidewalk, swinging his head from side to side as he went.

Patting Tori on the hand, Beau said, "A most successful evening, wouldn't you say, Miss Tori?"

"No, I would not say," Tori replied crossly. "And guess what? *I* am not going to be the one to give Jinksy this news. No way, no how."

Paling at her words, Beau said, "Now that is rather a hard line to take, Miss Tori."

"Don't. You. Even," Tori said. "I swear to God you're acting like you want to play in the Dead Majors."

When Beau didn't reply, she stopped walking to gape at him openly. "You do!" she accused him. "You want to play ball with them!"

"Well," he hedged, "it is rather the chance of a lifetime."

"You know what, Beau?" Tori said. "You better thank your lucky stars you're already dead, because when Jinksy hears about this, she's gonna be mad enough to kill you all over again."

Lucas and I stood on the shore of the man-made lake in the upper valley. Dark clouds filled the mountain passes to the north, and the sharp breeze made the idea of going into the water unthinkable.

So far, my time in the Valley with Lucas had actually been fun. This was the second time he'd given me a mental break from the pressure of the Chesterfield situation, and I admit, I was grateful.

First, Lucas had taken me to the Registry office, which is located at the bottom of the same street that houses the Dirty Claw. Since the entire building was filled with large and small werecats, I immediately understood why the mildly disreputable bar is filled with boozy, furry patrons at all hours of the day and night.

A Siamese secretary showed us into Furl's office, which was a study in spontaneous organization and shredded cardboard.

"Sorry," Furl said, batting a pile of the material off of one of the chairs in front of his desk. "I destroy cardboard when I need to think."

Taking in the thick coating on the floor and in the corners, I said, "You must have a lot to think about."

Furl is a Scottish Fold in his small form. When he laughs, his eyes crinkle closed, and his whiskers twitch. "You sound like my brothers," he said. "But Merle does the same thing with newspapers and Earl has a thing for those twisty ties that come off bread sacks. What can I do for you folks today?"

Lucas reached into the breast pocket of his duster and took out a document, which he laid flat in front of Furl. As the werecat scanned the contents, I couldn't help but notice the way the fur started to stand up on his neck.

"Why does the DGI need files on Creavit shape-shifters?" he asked. "That's a chapter of our history we put to bed a long time ago."

Oh, great. Another wrinkle on the whole, "made" magic thing. The Fae world really needed someone to step up and write *Creavit Magic for Dummies*.

"Hold on," I said. "I don't mean to be out of order here, but what do you mean Creavit shapeshifters?"

Furl's tail flicked back and forth. It was the first time I'd ever seen him display anything that might be taken as annoyance. "Some humans who contracted for their powers chose to become shapeshifters," he said, "mainly were-wolves. The last one was killed in the 17th century. That is, unless the DGI has information they're not sharing with the registry."

Lucas held his hands up placatingly. "Calm down, Furl," he said. "We don't have any evidence that any of these beasties are still roaming around, but I am interested in Creavit werewolf activity in the south of England around 1580."

1580? That was the year Adeline Shevington was killed. I started to say something, but an almost imperceptible shake of the head from Lucas stopped me.

Clearly relieved, Furl said, "Whew! That long ago? Don't scare me like that, buddy. It'll take awhile to dig up the data, but I think I can find what you need. I'll shoot you an email when I get it together. You two have time to run up to the Dirty Claw with me? The special of the day is nip nachos."

"No can do," Lucas said. "We have to make a trip to Qynn."

Furl shuddered. "Water," he said, "not my favorite thing. Stay dry, you two."

Now that we were standing on the shore of the sea, I recalled those words to Lucas. "Furl warned us not to get wet," I said, "but I don't see how we're going to manage that. I thought you'd have a submarine or something waiting for us."

"Ha!" Lucas scoffed, holding out his hand. "Subs are for amateurs. Be prepared to be dazzled, fair lady."

"What are you up to?" I asked suspiciously.

"Like I said, it's a surprise. Take my hand, and you'll find out. You do trust me, right?"

What was I supposed to say to that? I took his hand, instantly feeling warm power envelop my body. The weight of the cold air disappeared from my skin, and I could no longer feel the wind.

"You can swim, right?" Lucas asked, leading me into the water.

"Yes," I gulped, tightening my grip on his hand as the bottom fell away under my feet.

"Don't be scared," he said, "as long as you're holding my hand, you'll be able to breathe just fine. You won't even get wet. You ready?"

This time all I managed was a nod, but when he went under, I went with him, instinctively closing my eyes. After a few seconds, Lucas said, "Jinx, you're not going to see much like that."

Cautiously opening first one lid and then the other, I saw Lucas floating in front of me in a soft halo of aquamarine light. The waterproof aura flowed down his arm and over our clasped hands to surround me as well.

"Wow!" I said, my voice echoing slightly in my ears. "This is amazing."

"No," Lucas said, pointing with his free hand. "*That* is amazing."

There, lying on the bottom of the lake, sat a massive domed city. The superstructure itself was complete, but inside I could make out multiple construction projects in progress. On the outer edge of the city, teams of what I thought were horses pulled materials toward domed entrances. Then I looked closer. The "horses" had flippers and long serpentine tails.

"What are they?" I asked.

"Huh?" Lucas said. "Oh. The Kelpies? They're water horses. And you see those seals there? Those are Selkies. Once they're out of the water, they take human form. You're not in Kansas anymore, kiddo."

Half expecting to see some deep sea version of the Lollipop Guild show up, I said, "So, are we off to see a wizard?"

"Nope," Lucas said, kicking forward and propelling us into a gentle dive, "a turtle."

TWENTY-TWO

When Lucas said "turtle," my mind went to a hard-shelled creature roughly the size of a breakfast plate. Instead, I was introduced to a massive leatherback whose bulk rivaled a VW Beetle—one with grayish-black paint and rows of pale spots.

"He rarely gets out of the water," Lucas whispered as we approached the pond where Lute serenely floated listening to progress reports from his engineers. "The old boy probably tops 1,500 lbs. and he really doesn't have feet, just flippers. There are ponds and canals constructed throughout the city for his convenience."

Keeping my voice low as well, I said, "Honestly, I thought the whole city would be underwater."

"Portions of it are," he explained, "and from what I understand, multiple chambers can be flooded and drained according to need. Many of the merfolk breathe in both water and air."

I started to answer when a sonorous voice boomed out, "Lucas! Come talk to an old reptile, and bring that pretty woman with you."

Lute had spotted our approach. His beaked face broke into what I took to be a smile because the tiny, elliptical eyes squinting at us twinkled with good humor.

We stepped into a dry area that jutted into the pond.

The space was lined with seats facing toward the water and reminded me of a half-submerged conference table. When we sat down, we were on eye level with the massive sea creature

"Lute," Lucas said, "allow me to introduce Jinx Hamilton. Jinx, this is Lute, the leader of the merfolk settlement."

The turtle raised one thick flipper, which I accepted with a slight shake. "Hi," I said. "It's a pleasure to meet you."

"The pleasure is all mine," Lute replied. "Barnaby has spoken of you. He tells me you're quite something, young lady. What are you doing hanging around a scoundrel like Lucas?"

The turtle's easy banter seemed to be inviting me to play along, so I did. "I've been wondering that very thing myself," I said, throwing a teasing glance toward Lucas. "Is he as bad as I think he is?"

Lute shook his head, raising little ripples on the surface of the pond. "Worse," he said regretfully, "much worse. There are mermaids in this city who start crying the instant he walks in a room."

I think Lucas would have jumped between us if it hadn't meant leaping into the water. "Well, okay then!" he said. "We don't want to keep you, Lute. I know you have a lot to do."

The turtle laughed so hard water sloshed over the edge of the pond. "You know what they say, Lucas, guilty shark, bites first." Then, gliding closer to me, the old turtle said, "Truth be told, the boy runs backward from the ladies. I'm delighted to see him in your company. Always running around, this one, jumping from one portal to the next, taking every exotic assignment. Settle him down a bit, will you? Everybody needs to just float in calm water sometimes."

I mentally filed that last bit away as possibly some of

the best life advice I'd ever received. Before I could respond, a man's voice spoke from behind us. "A useless endeavor. My nephew has made it his life's purpose to swim against the tide."

Lucas turned toward the newcomer, sweeping off his hat and actually going down on one knee and bowing his head. "Uncle Owain," he said, "fare thee well?"

"I do, nephew" the man replied. "And how fare thee?"

Looking past Lucas, I saw a tall, reed-slender man dressed in leather clothing that would have looked more at home in Sherwood Forest than an underwater city. In fact, Owain had a total Robin Hood thing going, right down to the pointy beard shot through with silver.

"I am well," Lucas said, rising. "Allow me to present the *Quercus de Pythonissam*, Jinx Hamilton."

Something told me to stand as well. When I did, Owain bowed at the waist, and said, "Madam, forgive me, I did not know, or I would have spoken to you first. Owain Kendrick, at your service."

"Uh, no problem," I said. "Pleased to meet you."

Lucas grinned. "Now that we've scared her half to death, Uncle, can we loosen up?"

"We can indeed, you rascal," Owain said, drawing Lucas into a manly man hug and pounding him on the back. "I told Moira to get you down here to say hello before I had to come to the surface and find you myself."

"My apologies," Lucas said. "The DGI has been keeping me busy. But seriously, you've outdone yourself this time, Uncle! This place is amazing, even better than the tree city."

Tree city? I made a mental note to ask Lucas about that one later.

"I couldn't agree more," Lute rumbled. "He captured my vision for Qynn perfectly."

Owain tried to deflect the praise, but he flushed with

pleasure all the same. "I merely had the honor of drawing up the plans," he said, "and of working with exceptional artisans from Shevington."

"Show these fine folks around, Owain," Lute suggested. "I need to swim down to the seabed gardens and check in on the planting." Swiveling his head toward me, the turtle said, "Traditionally we leatherbacks survive on jellyfish, but as I have no quarrel with the creatures, eating them seems rather unnecessarily aggressive, wouldn't you say?"

"If I were a jellyfish I'd sure think so," I agreed earnestly. "What do you eat?"

"Seaweed," Lute said genially. "Ever tried the stuff? Highly nutritious. What we'll be growing here will be completely free of human contamination."

"What kind of contamination?"

Lute's eyes grew sad. "More things than I can tell you, young lady," he said. "Everything from medical waste to nuclear radiation."

"That's awful!" I said. "I had no idea."

"Most on land do not," Lute said, turning slowly and paddling away. Just before he disappeared under the surface, he called over his shoulder, "Come back soon, Jinx Hamilton, and often."

As the water stilled again, an overwhelming sense of awe filled me as I realized I had just been in the presence of both greatness and true benevolence.

"That," I said, looking at Lucas, "may have been the most amazing experience of my life."

He and Owain both laughed. "Lute has that effect on people," Owain said. "For a creature who has lived five centuries, he remains remarkably light at heart, though deeply saddened by the impact of humankind on the great oceans."

"Is that why he decided to seek sanctuary in the Valley?" I asked.

"Yes," Owain said. "The sea people are losing the fight to protect the integrity of their home waters. Lute believed the time had come to continue the fight from a more secure base, one that would help to preserve the best of merfolk culture. Shall we have that tour Lute suggested?"

Lucas and I walked with him through the streets and along the canals of Qynn, a city whose graceful curves and flowing structures mimicked the lines of the sea environment lying beyond the the protective bubble. Everywhere, incorporated in the architectural decorations, I spotted objects from the human realm—ship's figureheads and wheels, harpoons, anchors, buoys, and even ancient gold coins no doubt plucked from sunken treasure chests.

When I asked Owain about the items, he said, "The merfolk are great collectors. For centuries, they derived all their knowledge of mankind from the things that sank into their world from the surface. There is not a wreck lying on the seabed they have not explored. Lute was one of the first to see the great vessel called *Titanic* after she sank on a cold winter's night in 1912 with 1,503 souls lost. He cannot tell the story even now without weeping for them."

Owain continued to point out rescued artifacts as we strolled down the long central boulevard flanked by flowing canals filled with sea creatures busily going about their business. I was passing the time of day with a lovely purple octopus when a commotion at the far end of the promenade made me look up.

A young man ran toward us, his voice rising in volume as he came nearer. "Owain!" he cried. "Owain! You must come. There has been a terrible accident."

Catching the boy by the arms, Owain commanded, "Steady, man. Steady. Tell me what has happened."

Gasping for breath, the worker said, "We were bringing the last dolphin pod through the Atlantic portal. There was a new man on the team, a fellow from the Shevington stables. He misjudged the current and got caught in the suction."

"Is he alive?" Owain asked urgently.

"I truly do not know," the boy said. "One of the dolphins dove after him. We could not reach them before the portal closed. It will not open again for six hours."

Cold foreboding ran down my spine. "What was his name?" I demanded, catching hold of the messenger myself and almost shaking him. "The name of the worker from the stables? What was it?"

Blinking, the boy said, "Endicott, ma'am. I think his name was Connor Endicott."

I felt the weight of Owain's gaze on me. "Do you know this Endicott?" he asked. "Is he of importance to you?"

"He is," I replied woodenly. "He's my brother."

Everything after that still blurs in my mind. I remember Lucas taking hold of me and steering me as we hurried to an airlock that would give us access to the water outside. Owain pressed a small bottle of iridescent liquid in my hand saying, "Drink this. It will allow you to breathe underwater on your own."

I did as I was told, experiencing a cascading warmth similar to the earlier sensation when Lucas took my hand. Together we entered the inland sea. Then, I was beyond the confines of the dome, swimming between Owain and Lucas toward the work site. Two large pillars marked the portal's location. Groups of workers clustered around the area along with a pod of approximately 25 dolphins. One of the creatures broke away and came toward us.

"Owain," the dolphin said, in a high-pitched, clicking voice. "Please accept my personal apologies for this incident. I could not reach the humanoid in time."

"We know you tried, Delphinus," Owain answered. "I understand one of your number went through with him?"

The dolphin nodded. "Capensis was nearest to the man

and dove with him through the torrent of the portal."

"Torrent?" I said. "Is it really that bad?"

Delphinus answered me with deep compassion. "Humanoids are somewhat less capable than we of negotiating the current," he said gently.

As I looked at his sinuous form, easily nine feet of powerfully packed muscle under tough gray skin, tears came to my eyes. "Is my brother dead?" I asked in a choked voice.

"Your brother?" Delphinus asked, tilting his head to the side. "Forgive me. I did not know. Capensis is our strongest swimmer. If anyone could successfully safeguard the boy through the portal, it would be he."

Lucas, who had been hanging suspended and still in the water near Owain throughout the conversation, spoke up. "There has to be something we can do," he said.

"Sadly, not for six hours," Owain answered. "The portal can only be opened according to a set schedule so as not to alert the humans on the other side and to maintain the correct volume and salinity here in the Sea of Qynn."

"There are other portals," Lucas said with determination. "Can you give me the coordinates of the opening on the other side?"

"Of course," Owain said, "but what are you planning to do?"

"Get back to Shevington and find another way to reach Jinx's brother," he said. "That is if you're up for the plan, Jinx?"

Up for the plan? I only had one question. What were we waiting for?

TWENTY-THREE

Wednesday morning Chase stood at the front window of his small apartment staring across the square at the pizzeria. Not hearing from Pete after leaving multiple messages bothered him. The fact that Jinx was still in Shevington with Lucas Grayson bothered him even more. True, they left late the day before, and there was the time difference . . .

From behind him, the sound of something solid hitting the floor accompanied by a splashing noise broke Chase's reverie. Turning, he found Festus sitting placidly on the breakfast table. On the floor in front of him, an overturned glass and a spreading pool of orange juice explained the noise.

With a colorful exclamation, Chase dove for a roll of paper towels to halt the spill before it reached the carpet. "For God's sake, Dad," he said. "Why did you do that?"

Lifting one paw and examining the state of his claws, Festus said, "Waking you up, boy. I finished the bacon and eggs on your plate. Did you not think to make a proper breakfast for your poor old father?"

"Right," Chase muttered, throwing the soggy paper towels in the trash and taking a plate out of the oven, "spare me already. I kept yours warm. You could have just asked."

Festus chuckled. "Naw," he said. "This was way more fun. So were you staring out the window thinking about Jinx being up in Shevington with Lucas?"

"For your information," Chase said, "I was thinking about Pete. I left him three messages last night. He didn't call me back, and he's not outside sweeping the sidewalk like usual. I haven't known him to miss a morning since he bought the place."

"Then get your butt over there and check on him," Festus said. "You planning on pouring my coffee, or do I have to turn the pot over, too?"

Grumbling, Chase fixed a bowl of coffee and cream. When he put the dish down in front of his father, he said, "You know, there's nothing keeping you from shifting and fixing your own breakfast."

Festus looked up, licking a stray bit of scrambled egg off his whiskers. "You want me wandering around the apartment buck nekkid?" he asked. "Because I'll be happy to do that."

Chase held his hands up in surrender. "Fine. You win. I'll do the cooking."

"That's what I thought," Festus said, lapping at his coffee. Between slurps, he asked, "Didn't Pete give you a key to his place?"

"He did," Chase said thoughtfully.

"Keys are meant to be used," Festus observed. "So use it."

Draining the last of the coffee in his cup, Chase said, "I think I will. Can you please not make any more messes while I'm gone?"

"No promises," Festus replied, licking the butter off his toast. "You know I get bored easily."

Groaning inwardly, Chase went downstairs and let himself out the front door, then locked it again. At the far end of the block, George lifted one hand off the broom he was using and waved. Chase returned the gesture, glancing at his watch—7:00.

He stepped off the curb and crossed to the opposite corner, striding rapidly past the closed stores as he approached the Stone Hearth. With every step, his sense of foreboding seemed to grow.

Finding the pizzeria locked up tight, Chase cupped his hand and looked through the window. At first, he didn't think anything was out of the ordinary until he saw one sneaker-clad foot protruding from the base of the counter. His heart pounding, Chase rummaged in his pocket and found the key, still attached to the paper tag from the hardware store where Pete had it cut.

The unused key fit stiffly. Chase had to fiddle with the mechanism, being careful not to break the stubborn metal off in the lock. Finally, a solid click rewarded his efforts. Stepping quickly into the shadowed interior, he called out, "Pete? Pete, you okay, man?"

No answer. Feeling sick, Chase slowly approached the protruding foot, stepping cautiously to the side and looking around the corner. Pete lay on his back, open, cloudy eyes staring at the ceiling. The gray pallor of the man's face told Chase all he needed to know, but he still knelt down and laid his fingers against the icy skin to feel for a pulse. Nothing.

Sitting back on his heels, Chase said in a choked voice, "Aw, Pete. Damn it. Why didn't you call someone?"

As he stared at the corpse, fighting back tears, something brushed against Chase's cheek. Startled, he wheeled around, putting down a knee to steady himself. But instead of confronting the intruder he expected, Chase saw nothing but empty air. Or did he? Squinting, he stared into the space, letting his eyes go slightly out of focus. Had something there moved?

After several seconds, Chase shook his head. "Come on,

McGregor," he muttered, "man up. Quit jumping at shadows. It's not like you've never seen a dead body before."

Taking out his phone, he started to call the Sheriff's Office and then stopped. This might be the only chance he would have to search for evidence to clear Pete's good name with Jinx and the others. The poor guy wouldn't be any more or less dead in half an hour.

Leaving the body, Chase let himself in the living quarters at the back of the building. What he found there puzzled him. A stack of freshly folded laundry sat on top of the dryer. The dishes in the drying board were all scrubbed clean. A partially completed model of a tall ship stood in the center of a work table in the bedroom amid a litter of tiny, precise tools. The bed was even made.

All perfectly normal, but wasn't Pete supposed to have been sick for the last few days? Chase would have expected to find evidence of that—open bottles of Pepto, pillows, and blankets on the couch, the remains of bland meals. The refrigerator contained a half-eaten pizza supreme with jalapenos. Definitely not stomach bug comfort food.

And then there was the unease Chase couldn't shake. He could swear someone or some *thing* was watching him. He couldn't put his finger on it, but even apart from the body lying in the front room, something about the place just wasn't *right*.

Still, he saw nothing to tie Pete to Malcolm Ferguson, Irenaeus Chesterfield, or the Strigoi Sisters. It was time to involve the authorities.

Chase went back to the dining room to make the call, sitting quietly with Pete while he waited for Sheriff Johnson to arrive. When the big man let himself in the front door, he got straight to business. "Again with the dead bodies, McGregor? Where is he?"

"Behind the counter, John," Chase said. "I didn't touch anything."

The Sheriff walked back and looked at the corpse. "Not a mark on him I can see," Johnson said. "You say he'd been sick?"

"We ordered pizzas yesterday," Chase said. "Jinx's Dad picked up the food. He told us Pete looked awful. When Jeff asked if he was okay, Pete said he ate something at the carnival that made him sick and just couldn't get over it."

Shoving his hat back on his head, Johnson said, "You ever had food poisoning?"

"No," Chase said, "never had the pleasure."

"I have," Johnson said. "Damned stuff will make you want to die, I just never thought about anybody actually dying from it. We'll have the coroner take a look at the body, but nothing I see makes me think this was a crime."

"Me either," Chase said, "but it's a damned shame. Pete was younger than me."

Johnson shook his head. "Sure is," he said, sounding as if he wanted to cry. "I am going to miss that man's thick crust pepperoni."

Within an hour, the news of Pete's death was all over town. Hypochondriacs immediately flooded the local doctor's office, terrified that they, too, had eaten mysteriously fatal festival food.

At noon, Irma charged into the Witch's Brew, beckoning furiously for Tori to join her. "I have to talk to Jinx right this minute," the woman said breathlessly. "We could have an epidemic *and* a liability issue on our hands."

Tori glanced at Mindy. "You got this?" she asked.

"Sure thing," Mindy said, adding, "and good luck." The girl was clearly relieved she wasn't going to be the one dealing with the agitated old lady.

Tori joined Irma just beyond the seating area in the espresso bar, hopefully out of hearing range of the paying customers who were now far more interested in potential scandal than their lattes.

"What do you mean a liability issue?" Tori said, purposefully speaking quietly to get Irma to do the same. Thankfully, it worked.

"Pete got food poisoning at the Halloween carnival," Irma whispered. "What if his people up and decide the committee murdered him by accident?"

Struggling to keep a straight face, Tori said, "I think 'murder by accident' is called manslaughter, and we have absolutely no idea what Pete ate, when he ate it, or if that's what really killed him. The sheriff told Chase the coroner has to have a look at the body."

"That won't happen until sometime tomorrow," Irma said. "There's a line all the way out the door over at doc's. Living patients pay him more than dead ones. People are scared to death we've got a botulism outbreak in town."

Tori drew in a long breath and willed herself to be patient. "Irma, honey, I worked in a cafe for more than ten years. Tom made us take health classes from the state every year. If anybody in town had botulism, the symptoms would show up in 18-36 hours. This is Wednesday. The carnival was Saturday night. Is anybody else actually sick?"

Irma paused, counting on her fingers, and seemed to relax as the numbers added up. "Well, no," she admitted, "but diseases are sneaky. I really need to talk to Jinx right this minute."

"I'm sorry," Tori said, "but she's not here."

All the color drained from Irma's cheeks. "Oh, Lord," she said, "she's upstairs dying of the botulism, isn't she?"

"No, she is not," Tori assured her. "Jinx had to run over to Cotterville on family business. She'll be back later, and I'll have her call you, I promise."

Irma hadn't even reached the front door when a voice

beside Tori said softly, "Mistress Tori, the red-haired vampire wishes to speak with you."

Making a show of straightening a display of coffee cups, Tori said, "You can call her Greer, you know."

"Not until she gives me permission, Mistress," the brownie whispered. "I am afraid of vampires."

Tori had to admit that his feelings weren't completely unfounded, but they'd have to discuss that later. "Thank you, Darby," she said. "Tell her I'll be right down."

Tori finished fidgeting with the inventory for appearance's sake, and then went into the storeroom where her mother and Kelly were unpacking a new shipment of essential oils.

"Hey," she said. "Either one of you up for creating a diversion? Greer wants to talk to me down in the lair and I don't know how long I'll be. I don't want Mindy asking questions."

Kelly looked up from the packing sheet in her hand. "We have to come up with a plausible reason to come and go in the basement *and* keep Mindy from going down there."

"I know, I know," Tori groaned. "I wasn't thinking about lair logistics when I suggested we hire her, and you have to admit, she pulls an amazing espresso shot."

"She does," Gemma agreed, "when she's not babbling about people's auras. Apparently I am getting back to my usual magenta self."

Without cracking a smile, Tori said, "Now see, I would have pegged you for aubergine."

"Or maroon," Kelly said, studying her friend closely. "With maybe a little burnt orange around the ears."

"That will be enough out of both of you," Gemma grumbled, reaching for her purse and keys. "I need to go to Wally World for cleaning goods, so I'll take the Junior Ghosthunter with me. What does Greer want to talk to you about?"

"Beats me," Tori said. "I know Chase was going to go down to the lair to tell everyone about Pete. I've been dealing with Irma who is hysterical about an epidemic of Sneaky Botulism."

The Moms exchanged a look. "Excuse me?" Kelly said. "What is Sneaky Botulism?"

"Probably a made-up mom disease like that thing you used to threaten us with when we were kids," Tori said. "Remember?"

Gemma made a dismissive sound. "Ha! Miss Smarty Pants," she said, "that just shows how much you don't know. The Itch is real. Our mothers threatened us with it and their mothers before them."

"Right," Tori deadpanned, "generational lying, 'cause that makes it all okay.' Just like I'm supposed to believe eating raw cookie dough will give me worms."

Kelly giggled. "That one was a lie," she admitted, "but only because we wanted the cookie dough for ourselves."

Tori shook her head. "Shameful. The both of you. Just shameful. You'd take cookie dough right out of the mouths of your own children?"

"Dang straight we would," Gemma said. "Nobody ever said I was bucking for Mother of the Year. When it comes to chocolate chip, it's every woman for herself."

Turning to leave the room, Tori paused at the threshold. "Uh, Mom, they sell cookie dough at Wally World, don't they?"

"Already way ahead of you on that one," Gemma said. "I'll get two rolls. Now go. It's not nice to keep a vampire waiting."

Tori grinned. "Don't be so sure about losing out on that Mother of the Year thing," she said.

As Gemma bustled past, she gave her daughter a quick peck on the cheek. "Don't have the trophy engraved yet," she said. "I haven't decided if Kell and I are going to share or not."

Tori waited until Gemma and Mindy were out the back door and Kelly was in charge of the espresso bar to head down to the lair. Gloomy expressions greeted her all around.

"Uh, oh," she said, "I'm guessing this is not a wake for the dear, departed Pete. What's going on?"

Greer spoke for the group. "We've just received a message from Jinx in Shevington," she said. "Her brother was working at the merfolk city, and there was an accident."

Tori paled. "Oh God, he's not . . . "

Moira cut in. "Do not assume the worse," she said. "All we know is that he was sucked through the ocean portal into the human realm. The Valley is caught in the midst of a severe winter storm. Jinx and Lucas cannot reach the portal to return here, so they are going after Connor on their own. Jinx asked that you be the one to break the news to her parents."

Tori stared at her numbly. "How am I supposed to do that?" she asked.

"Gently, my dear," Beau said, "gently. If you wish, I will come with you."

"Yes," she said, "I think that would be a good idea, but we have to wait until mom gets back from running errands. I'm not about to give Kelly news like this without Mom there."

When only silence met her words, Tori studied the faces around her. "Okay," she said, "spill. What else is going on?"

Greer cleared her throat. "We may have a bit of a containment issue on our hands."

"Meaning?" Tori asked.

"After hearing Chase's description of finding the dead pizza man," Greer said, "I believe he may have been killed by the Strigoi Sisters. We must covertly visit the local mortuary tonight so I may examine the body."

"Covertly visit?" Tori said. "I think that's called 'breaking and entering.' And this is necessary why?"

"If the Strigoi killed him, he will rise again and walk among the living, of course," Greer answered.

Tori plopped down heavily on the nearest sofa. "Right. Of course, he will," she said. "Perfect. Just freaking perfect."

Twenty-Four

Lucas and I emerged from the Sea of Qynn in a world turned white. Ten inches of snow fell while we were underwater. As the warm envelope of magic evaporated from my skin, the bitter wind sliced through me making my teeth chatter.

"How are we supposed to get back to Shevington in this?" I asked Lucas, raising my voice to make myself heard above the storm.

Moving to block the worst of the gusts with his body, Lucas leaned down, speaking against my ear. "We use Plan B," he said.

As I watched, he reached into an interior pocket of his duster and drew out a small bottle literally labeled "Plan B." Squinting, I saw that the vessel contained a minuscule amount of umber-colored powder.

"What is it?" I asked, moving closer to the shelter of his body.

"Dried baobhan sith blood," he said. "It will let us take the flight, but I only have enough left for one trip. I have to warn you, I'm not very good at steering. You better hang on."

Lucas put his free arm around me, and it seemed only natural that mine should encircle his waist. His body was hard with muscle and unbelievably warm.

"Why aren't you freezing to death?" I asked, leaning into him.

"Elven blood has its advantages," he chuckled. "Are you ready?"

"As ready as I'm ever going to be," I replied.

I saw Lucas uncork the bottle with his thumb. Jerking upward, he covered us with the red powder, which curiously did not blow away with the wind. Instead, the particles expanded, covering us in a slowly spinning cloud. Lucas began to chant. The words of the incantation made the dried blood move faster, almost as if we were caught in a centrifuge.

"Hold on," Lucas shouted. "Here we go!"

When he told me he wasn't good at steering, Lucas didn't come close to preparing me for the maelstrom we entered. Unlike my flights with Greer, I saw nothing because I closed my eyes and prayed we'd just land in one piece. We did, with a bone jarring thud. Thankfully Lucas took most of the impact. Still, we wound up in a tangled heap at the base of the Mother Tree.

I felt more than heard the voice of the Oak in my mind. "Nice landing," she said.

"Everyone's a critic," I grumbled, sitting up and tentatively testing my limbs.

Beside me, Lucas who was doing his own systems check, said, "Excuse me?"

"Nothing," I said, looking across the street at the well-lit windows of my grandfather's house. "You may not have stuck the landing, but you hit the bull's eye on the target."

"I aim to please," Lucas grinned, "pun intended."

He stood up carefully and offered me his hand. I accepted, letting him haul me to my feet. "I take it you don't use that stuff often?" I asked.

"I do not," Lucas said. "The last time I resorted to Plan B, there was a werewolf, a raccoon, and a shotgun involved."

As we set off across the street, I said, "Yeah. I hate it when that happens."

"Me, too," Lucas said. "You do not want an armed raccoon ticked off at you."

I almost asked and then decided we didn't have time.

Innis answered the door, took one look at my thin coat and nearly blue skin, and went into matronly overdrive. "What on earth are you doing out in weather like this wearing *that*, child?" she demanded, drawing me inside and all but pushing me into the fireplace. Over her shoulder, she barked at Lucas, "Wipe your feet."

"I'm fine, Innis," he said, obediently scrubbing his boots on the mat. "Thanks for asking."

The brownie retrieved a heavy wool shawl from the back of a nearby chair and draped it around my shoulders. "Where is my grandfather?" I asked, huddling into the thick fabric. "We need his help."

"I am here," Barnaby said, emerging from his study. "Owain just told me what happened. How did you get here so quickly?"

"Dried baobhan sith blood," Lucas replied.

The answer seemed to surprise Barnaby, but all he said was, "Do you have more?"

Lucas shook his head. "That was the last of it."

"Then we have a problem," Barnaby said. "The drifts are already too bad to pass into the lower valley. The portal to Briar Hollow is cut off."

Come on! I already knew from conversations with Chase that there was more than one way in and out of the Valley. "I don't want to go to Briar Hollow," I said. "I want to find Connor. Can't we use another portal?"

"We have the coordinates for the Atlantic portal's opening in the human realm," Lucas said. "If you have a map, we can consider our options."

Barnaby disappeared into his study and came back with map—from AAA no less—of the state of North Carolina.

"Triple A?" I asked. "Seriously? When was the last time you needed roadside assistance?"

"Their maps are excellent," Barnaby said defensively. "Earl acquires them for me. He likes to vacation in human form. I believe his term for the excursions is 'road trip.' As I understand the pastime, it involves aimlessly driving a motor vehicle while listening to loud music and consuming low-quality food."

Well, who knew? Earl was a werecat after my own heart.

Lucas plotted the portal's position and pointed to a spot in the waters off a large green area on the map. "That's it," he said. "According to Owain's coordinates, Connor would have surfaced there."

I pointed to the shaded blob. "What is that?" I asked.

"It says 'Alligator River National Wildlife Refuge,'" Lucas replied.

Barnaby had retrieved a second map from his study. This one, drawn by hand on aged brown paper, was covered with red "X" marks. He compared the two maps and then said, "Oh dear. I do hope that is not a literal reference to alligators."

The magical world blindsides me a lot, but I knew exactly what was coming next. "Okay," I said, "I'll bite. Why?"

"Because the nearest portal to the point where Connor went into the water lies at the eastern edge of the wildlife refuge," Barnaby answered. "Here."

Why wasn't I surprised? We were already up to our backsides in proverbial gators. Real ones didn't seem like much of a stretch.

"It doesn't matter," I said. "If that's the only way to get to Connor, then that's where we're going."

Barnaby reached for my hand. "My dear," he said, "this will only put you in the vicinity of where Connor would have come through the portal. You do realize that he could be anywhere or . . . "

I interrupted him, my voice choking on the words. "Dead," I said. "I know perfectly well he could be dead, but you cannot ask me to go back to my mother after everything she's been through without some kind of answer, Granddad. You know I can't do that."

Barnaby still looked deeply troubled, but he didn't argue with me. "Let me contact Ironweed," he said. "Perhaps we can at least improve your chances by sending you through the portal with GNATS drones to aid with the search."

"That's a good idea," I agreed. "While you're doing that, I want to see where Connor lives."

"Of course," Barnaby said, "but why?"

"When we find Connor, he's going to be scared and confused," I said. "I want to know how to connect with him. I can't just blurt out that I'm his sister and expect him to believe me and trust me."

Neither Barnaby nor Innis would let me go back out in the building snowstorm without a better coat. The brownie bundled herself up until she looked like a barrel with feet and went out on the square, returning in minutes with a package wrapped in brown paper. Undoing the string, I held up a gorgeous long coat in regal blue. To my surprise, it fit perfectly.

"Oh, Innis," I said, "this is beautiful. What do I owe you?"

The brownie blinked. "Owe me?" she asked. "I charged it to Mr. Barnaby, like everything else."

Barnaby waved his hand. "Consider it an early birthday gift."

That stopped me in my tracks. "You know when my birthday is?" I asked.

"Of course, I do," he said, sounding mildly offended. "Connor was born December 3, 1982, and you were born December 6, 1985."

When I started to cry, both men exchanged utterly horrified looks. I collapsed into a chair sobbing. It was Innis who patted me comfortingly on the hand all the while dispensing tissues.

"Good heavens," Barnaby said, "I . . . uh . . . what did I . . . why . . . "

He spluttered to a stop and looked helplessly at Lucas who shrugged in equal ignorance.

Taking pity on them both, I managed to explain. "I d-did . . . didn't . . . know his birthday. I want him back, Granddad."

At that, I dissolved all over again. I didn't see my grandfather squat down in front of me. I only knew he was there when I felt his hand on my knee. Wiping my eyes, I looked through my tears at him and repeated myself, "I want him back."

"Then go get him, Jinx," Barnaby said earnestly. "I have complete faith in your abilities to accomplish anything. Go get your brother."

Not "quit crying like an idiot" or "are you sure you're up for this." No. He said he had complete faith in me. Barnaby trusted me to go through a portal into the middle of what sounded like a gator infested swamp and come back with Connor. My tears began to slow. I put my hand over his and nodded.

"Good," my grandfather said. "Now, go with Lucas to the stables. Ellis will be expecting you and will let you into Connor's apartment. I will coordinate with Ironweed. We will meet back here in an hour."

I don't know what I expected to see in my brother's apartment, but what I found made me yearn to know him all the more. Beautifully drawn, unframed sketches of life in Shevington covered the walls.

Connor has a good eye. He doesn't just see form, he recognizes and renders the inner spirit. I detected skill in the hands of the weaver, mirth in the eyes of the old lamplighter, and focus in the posture of meditators beneath the branches of the Mother Tree.

On the worktable under the window lay pieces of intricately tooled leather, the parts of a saddle that would, when complete, be a work of art in itself.

"He does custom work for clients," Ellis Groomsby explained, watching me as I traced the patterns lovingly with my index finger. "There's none in the land that can turn out leather work like Connor. He never mentioned that you're his sister."

"He doesn't know," I whispered. "I wanted to come here so I would know how to make him believe me when we meet."

Pattering feet sounded on the stairs. I barely had time to register a blur of gray before a monkey-like creature wrapped her arms around my neck.

"Bring Connor back to Ailish! Ailish loves Connor."

"His pet," Ellis explained. "She is an Elven Gray Loris. They are inseparable, but Connor insisted she stay home while he worked at the inland sea. The poor thing's been nursing a cold. He didn't want her out in this weather."

Pulling back slightly, I looked into the enormous dark eyes. "Hi, Ailish," I said. "I'm Jinx."

"Pretty lady Connor's sister?" the loris asked.

"I am. And you're his friend?"

"Ailish is Connor's best friend," the tiny creature corrected me. "Pretty lady bring Connor back?"

Gently stroking her head, I said, "I'm sure going to do

my best, little one. Try not to worry, okay? Do you want me to tell Connor anything when I find him?"

"Tell Connor Ailish never ask for sticky sweet honey again," she said, tears falling from her eyes. "Tell Connor Ailish will eat green broccoli yuck."

Both Lucas and Ellis looked away to keep from laughing.

"Green broccoli is definitely yuck," I agreed. "Now let me give you to Ellis, so I can go find Connor."

"No!" the creature wailed. "Ellis works. Ailish lonely. Ailish afraid. Ailish not want Ellis!"

Suddenly an idea occurred to me. I looked at the stable master. "May I take her to my Aunt Fiona for now?" I asked.

Ellis smiled with relief. "That's a wonderful idea," he said. "The poor wee thing is used to more company than I can give her right now. I'm sorry, but there's just too much to do caring for the animals in this weather."

"Do you have a coat, Ailish?" I asked.

The loris hopped out of my arms and returned with a red-and-white striped scarf. "No coat," she said. "Stripey thing."

"Jump up here on the table so I can fix the stripey thing for you," I said.

Ailish complied, and I carefully arranged the scarf. "Are you ready?" I asked.

In response, the loris climbed my arm and tucked herself inside the neck of my coat. "Ready!" she said. "Ailish have adventure now!"

———⁂———

"Well, of course the little darling can stay with me," Aunt Fiona said. "Do you like molasses cookies, Ailish?"

The loris cocked her head to the side. "What molly lashes?" she asked curiously.

"Molasses," I said. "It's like sticky sweet honey, but darker."

That set the creature's head bobbing up and down. "Sticky sweet good," she declared. "All colors."

Fiona laughed. "Oh, you are fun! Go to the kitchen with Stan and we'll all make a batch of cookies."

Ailish craned her neck back and looked at the eight-foot tall Sasquatch standing in my aunt's living. "What are Stan?" the loris asked, sounding awed.

"I'm a Sasquatch," he said gently. "Some people call me a Bigfoot."

Ailish leaned out of my embrace and looked down. "Feet big," she affirmed.

Stan chuckled, "Yes, they are." He held out one enormous, shaggy paw. "Will you come with me?"

After a moment's consideration, she said confidently, "Ailish come with Stan Big Feet," and climbed onto his hand.

The two of them disappeared into the kitchen. "Take good care of her, Aunt Fiona," I said. "Ellis tells me Connor adores her."

"I can see why" Fiona said. "How are you holding up, honey?"

"Okay," I said. "Worried."

"Of course you are," she said. "Does your mother know yet?"

I shook my head. "No. Before we go through the portal, I'm going to ask Barnaby to use Moira's mirror and place a call to Briar Hollow."

My aunt put her arms around me and held me tight. "It's going to be okay, Jinx," she said. "The story isn't going to end like this. I just know it."

I had hoped to talk to Tori directly, but she was upstairs when we connected with the lair. The news about Pete's death shocked me, and I wasn't thrilled with Greer's theory that the Strigoi Sisters had a hand in his demise.

I would have liked to be able to say something comforting to Chase, but there just wasn't time, and Lucas was standing right beside me.

"I'm sorry," I said, catching his eye, "but you all are just going to have to deal with this on your own. I trust you to get to the bottom of what happened to Pete and take care of it. I couldn't come back to Briar Hollow even if I wanted to because of the weather up here. And I have to go after Connor."

Chase nodded, looking like he wanted to say something more personal to me as well. What he settled for was a firm assurance that I was doing the right thing, which helped me—a lot.

"What you're doing is the most important thing right now," he said. "You have to put your family first. Find Connor. Greer and I can handle this."

"Absolutely," Greer agreed. "Do not concern yourself worrying about this. Chase and I have the matter in hand. I will give Tori your message regarding your parents."

Lucas stepped up beside me. "It may take us a bit to get back there," he warned Greer. "I had to use the last of Plan B."

"Ah," Greer grinned, "and how was the landing, laddie?"

Looking a little sheepish, he said, "The base of the Mother Tree stopped us from rolling into the street."

Greer sighed with resignation. "If you cannot use my dried blood properly, I am not going to continue opening a vein for you."

"Hey!" Lucas cried. "It was in the middle of a blizzard. Give a guy a break."

"We will take this matter up later," Greer said. "Is there a specific rescue plan afoot or is this a more spontaneous operation?"

Lucas moved aside and let Barnaby come full-frame into the call. "There are two GNATS drones left in Shevington," he said. "The rest are either in Briar Hollow, watching Tori's father, or caught on the other side of the storm near Brown Mountain. The pilots will take the craft through the portal with Lucas and Jinx, who will communicate with them over a closed channel. The drones will search the area where we believe the portal would have ejected Connor. The dolphin who accompanied him will, most likely, help the boy to reach land, probably on the chain of barrier islands known as the Outer Banks."

Over Greer's shoulder, I saw Beau spread a map across the work table. He briefly studied the sheet and then said, "That is a large area to reconnoiter."

"I know," I agreed grimly, "but we have to do something. Take care of my parents and Tori for me, Beau. I don't think anything will go wrong but . . . "

The Colonel held up his hand. "Do not invite bad fortune," he counseled. "Complete your mission and fear not for the safety of those whom you love. We will all guard them with our lives."

I knew that already. I count on it every single day, but it still made me feel better to hear the stalwart old soldier say the words. Beau told me once that bravery is equal parts fear and resolution. If that was true, I was good to go on both counts.

TWENTY-FIVE

From his vantage point in a shadowed alley, Chase surveyed the local funeral home. The baobhan sith stood beside him, melting into the night. The vampire didn't need dark clothes to appear invisible. The blackness he felt radiating from her came from within.

"You're not breathing," he whispered quietly.

Greer chuckled lightly. "Cat's ears," she said. "Almost as good as mine. I have no need of respiration. "I only draw air into my lungs and expel it in the presence of humans. It makes them feel better. If you wish, I can breathe."

"It's fine," Chase said. "I just never noticed before. My father has told me stories about you, by the way."

Clicking her tongue, Greer said, "Well-edited stories, I would hope."

"With Dad *well-embellished* might be more like it," Chase said. "How did the two of you meet?"

"There are some bits of information sons do not require about their fathers," Greer replied sagely. "Shall we just say Festus and I had wild times in his youth, all of which stopped when he met your mother, God rest her soul."

Gesturing toward the mortuary, Chase said, "The last time I saw her was in a place like that. Lying in a damned box. I hate funeral homes."

"Would you rather I go in alone?" Greer offered.

"No, but thank you. If they had a body on display, the front porch lights would be turned on. They wouldn't do that for a non-paying customer. Pete's family hasn't claimed him for burial—or paid a deposit."

Greer sighed. "Render unto Caesar," she muttered. "Some things never change, regardless of the century."

"Oh," Chase said, "Caesar gets his cut alright, or at least he used to. Until just a few years ago, funerals in this state were taxed. Then the law changed, so the mortuaries just raised their rates instead."

"If you detest funeral homes," Greer said, "why are you so knowledgeable about their practices?"

"Because of Jinx's Aunt Fiona," Chase replied. "You know she faked her death in the human realm to live in Shevington full time?"

"I do."

"Well, she researched everything first," he said. "I helped plan the service when we all believed she was dead. She left a newspaper clipping about the changed tax law stapled to the burial instructions."

Beside him, in the darkness, he saw the vampire's teeth flash in a grin. "Oh, I do look forward to meeting her. The lady would appear to have style."

"You'll love Fiona," Chase said. "It's impossible not to." Then he added sadly, "And you'd have liked Pete. He was a good guy no matter what Jinx says."

"Do not fault Jinx for her vigilance," Greer advised. "That should be as much a part of the nature of the *Quercus de Pythonissam* as blood hunger is my own birthright."

Chase set his jaw stubbornly. "I still say Pete was a victim. If the Strigoi did kill him, I don't want him to become what they are."

"An understandable and justified sentiment," Greer said. "My vampiric state comes naturally, therefore choices are available to me, but the *Strigoi mort blasfematoare* live enslaved to their hunger. I would not wish such an existence on any friend of mine."

"Exactly," Chase said. "If they've turned Pete, I'll behead him myself."

"Let us hope we can accomplish that deed long before he awakens," Greer said. "Shall we engage in the crime Tori calls 'breaking and entering?'"

"Hold on," Chase said. "Maybe I can make the job a little easier for us."

The air around him shimmered and his form sank toward the ground. Now, looking up with the glowing green eyes of a cat, Chase could clearly discern Greer's outline in the darkness.

"You, sir," she said, "are a handsome fellow in fur. You remind me of your father in his prime."

Chase's whiskers pulled back in a smile. "Don't let the old man hear you say that. He thinks he's still in his prime. Would you stash my clothes for me? I'll need them before we head back."

"My pleasure," Greer said, "but what are you planning to do?"

"I'm going to see if I can get us inside and skip the whole breaking and entering part," he said. "Wait here. Will you hear me if I call to you?"

"I will, and you won't even have to raise your voice."

Glancing left and right to make sure the street was deserted, Chase darted across to the funeral home lawn and disappeared down the driveway. To Greer's surprise, only two or three minutes passed before her keen ears heard, "Follow me. Down the drive."

She found Chase at the rear of the building staring at an open back door.

"Did you find it like this?" Greer asked.

The cat nodded. "Not a good sign, eh?"

"I should think not. Let's have a look."

They entered a long hallway paneled in dark, cheap wood. Fake LED candles flickered in brass sconces on the wall. Stick-on black letters marked the third door: Embalming Room.

Greer opened the door just enough for Chase to dart inside. When he scratched on the door signaling the all clear, she followed him inside. Sinister silver equipment filled the sterile room, which smelled of death and chemicals.

They found the answer they sought on the back wall where a four-door morgue cooling unit hummed quietly. One of the stainless steel doors stood open, hanging at a crazy angle on bent hinges. The tray for the body was pulled out, and a green sheet lay crumpled on the floor. Nearby, a discarded dry cleaner's bag and hanger had been tossed atop the wreckage of an overturned clothing rack.

"What do we do now?" Chase asked.

"We look for a reanimated corpse dressed in a dead man's suit," Greer said drily, "and two pieces of Transylvanian trash."

⸺⸻⸺

Irenaeus Chesterfield materialized inside the pizzeria. On a Wednesday evening, the restaurant should have been filled with people. Instead, the room was dark and silent. Seraphina and Ioana stood waiting for him with cheeks and eyes no longer sunken and hollow from hunger.

"You are looking quite restored," he said pleasantly. "Shall we discuss . . . "

Out of the corner of his eye, Chesterfield sensed a sudden motion. He reacted instantly, disappearing in a rush of pale smoke only to materialize several feet away. He was no longer smiling. Pete stood in the spot the wizard had just vacated. Dressed in a suit at least two sizes too small, the risen man flailed wildly, his hands contorted into claws, jaws snapping.

"I am deeply disappointed, ladies," Chesterfield said. "I specifically forbade you to create an acolyte. Did you really think your puppet could destroy me?"

Seraphina hissed, curling back her lips to reveal sharp fangs. "Kill him," she ordered.

Pete launched himself toward Chesterfield, who casually sliced through the air with the flat of his hand. The shambling corpse stopped, his hands reaching for his neck. A thin line of blood appeared across Pete's throat before his head separated neatly from his body and fell, end over end toward the floor, landing with a sickening thud. The eyes rolled toward the Strigoi, the mouth struggling to voice a silent plea. The headless corpse fell first to its knees, then slumped forward, coming to rest alongside the head. At the same instant, both turned to dust.

With a sweeping motion, Chesterfield raised the remains from the floor and funneled them into a waiting flask. The vessel stoppered itself and levitated toward the wizard's outstretched hand. Sliding the bottle into his breast pocket, he returned his attention to the Strigoi.

"That was a very bad idea," he said. "I have one question for you. Take care how you answer it. How did Peter break into your temporal cage?"

"He was our servant," Seraphina said haughtily. "We had complete power over him. He strained and strained against that which he could not see until the force of his loyalty overcame your barrier, and he joined us."

"Thank you," Chesterfield said. "I should have wondered about that most interesting detail. Now, as *I* have complete power over *you*, payment will be rendered for your treachery."

"Wait . . ." Ioana cried, but the entreaty died in her throat. Where the Strigoi had stood there now rested two black caskets wrapped in silver chains.

Crossing to them, Chesterfield removed his watch, adjusted the dials, and clicked the crown. He disappeared, taking the trapped Strigoi with him.

Festus slapped at the collar he wore with his hind leg activating the RABIES beam. "This better be good," he muttered. "You woke me up out of a sound sleep."

He moved the light around the deserted pizzeria dining room, halting when it illuminated a gray image of Pete dressed awkwardly in a black suit clawing at the air before him.

"Damn," Festus said. "There he is. What is he doing?"

Greer walked closer to the image. "Look," she said, "his fingers are striking something solid."

"I don't see anything there," Chase said. "What is he hitting?"

"An invisible barrier of some sort," Greer said. "Ah, there it is. Look."

Pete's arm disappeared through the air in front of him as if he'd punched through a hole. On the other side, they could just make out a dim echo of his hand and fist.

"Why is it flickering like that?" Festus asked.

As they watched, Pete used both hands to push the edges of the hole open, wiggling and straining to get his body inside. The air began to reform and smooth over, but before it finished, Seraphina and Ioana appeared, and Pete fell to his knees before them.

"What did we just see?" Chase asked.

"I believe," Greer said, "that we watched Pete break into some kind of temporal holding cell to reach the Strigoi Sisters. Only Chesterfield could have put them there. I do not think, however, that the young ladies are willingly assisting the Creavit wizard."

Festus slapped the silver disk and shut off the beam. "Why do you say that?"

"Because had they been allowed to turn Pete," Greer said, "he would not have had to fight to get to them."

"But how is that even possible?" Chase said. "He just ripped a hole in time and stepped through?"

When Greer looked at him, Chase saw the stirring of green fire in her eyes. "You cannot imagine the power of the blood hunger," she said. "When first turned, the human must return to his maker and drink first from his master's veins. I believe the Strigoi counted on that hunger to help them escape from Chesterfield."

"What's up with your eyes?" Festus asked.

"There is blood in this place," Greer said, "and death magic. I do not know what happened here, but I do not believe your friend Pete still walks the earth in any form."

"And the Strigoi?" Pete asked.

The fire in Greer's eyes danced again. "You cannot hear it, can you?" she asked.

Chase frowned. "Hear what?"

"The screaming," she said softly. "The cries of the damned."

TWENTY-SIX

Connor allowed the weightless sensation of floating to lull him into a complacent state. Everywhere he looked, something new and intriguing caught his attention—iridescent creatures on the seafloor, the kelpies dragging construction materials to the city, and the playful dolphins emerging from the open portal.

Nothing that he'd imagined matched the true appearance of the underwater gateway. The circular channel, at least 30 feet in circumference, created a steady influx of fresh ocean water. Because he'd never worked with aquatic lifeforms, Connor's job was to monitor the salinity meter in his hand. If the needle edged into the red, he was supposed to alert the head of the work crew.

Completely aware of the importance of maintaining a proper environment for sensitive creatures, Connor paid close attention to his assignment, but he couldn't keep his eyes from flicking back and forth from the screen to the scene around him. As the last of the dolphins passed into the Sea of Qynn, the chief signaled the workers that the portal was about to close.

No longer concerned about salinity, Connor allowed his attention to linger too long on the shimmering water that receded and changed directions before his eyes. When he felt the pull of the suction against his body, it was already too late. He was being pulled into the portal.

Fighting to remain calm, Connor struggled against the force, his heart pounding wildly in his chest. He saw the other workers gesturing frantically to him. The message was clear. "Get out of there!" Connor would have liked nothing better than to do just that, but already fatigue threatened to claim his remaining strength.

Then, in the distance, he saw a gray speck rushing toward him growing larger and larger. A single dolphin rode the current, swimming toward Connor at full speed. As the creature approached, it called to him in a high-pitched voice. "Grab my fin and don't let go!"

The dolphin sped past. Connor reached out and caught hold of its dorsal fin, pulling himself into alignment with his rescuer's streamlined body. The dolphin swam straight for the center of the portal, matching the speed of the rushing water. The pair broke through a membrane of resistance, angling sharply upward as the dolphin leaped out of the water.

The instant Connor saw blue sky, he let go and found himself bobbing on the surface of the ocean. Land masses lay on either side of him, but neither was within easy reach.

To his left, the dolphin's snout popped up out of the water, breaking into a toothy grin. "Hi! That sure was a wild ride, wasn't it? I'm Capensis, by the way."

"You saved my life!" Connor blurted out. "Thank you!"

Cackling happily, Capensis said, "Oh, sure. No problem, but we're not quite done with the saving part. We need to get you to dry land."

"That would be great," Connor agreed, "but which land?"

"The island over there," the dolphin replied. "Fewer people. You're in the human realm now. It will be hours before the portal opens again. By then, your breathing potion will have worn off. You won't be able to breathe underwater anymore, so you can't just dive back through."

"Will I be safe on the island all by myself?" Connor asked.

"Oh," Capensis said, "you won't be by yourself. There are some lovely wild horses over there. They'll keep you company."

For the first time since he felt the current tugging at him, Connor relaxed. "Horses?" he said. "That sounds perfect."

"Grab hold, I'll get you as close to the beach as I can."

Reclaiming his grip on the dolphin's dorsal fin, Connor allowed himself to be pulled through the water until they reached the shallows and he was able to stand on wobbly legs.

"Get ashore and stay hidden," Capensis said. "When I can get back to Qynn, I'll send someone for you as quickly as I can."

"Thank you again," Connor said as he waded toward the beach. "Maybe we'll see each other in Qynn?"

"You bet," the dolphin chirped happily. "Looking forward to it!" With that, he jumped playfully and disappeared under the surface.

Connor emerged from the water and stood on the beach wringing out his clothes as best he could. In the distance, the sound of pounding hooves made him look up, only to stand rooted in place by the majestic sight that rushed toward him.

The wild horses ran just at the edge of the surf, their nostrils flaring in the salt air, manes flying behind them. Connor never thought to move out of their way until a pair of strong hands landed on his arms and jerked him backward.

The herd thundered past without breaking stride leaving Connor in the company of a glaring, bushy-bearded old man wearing a sailor's cap. "Were you just going to stand there and let them run you down?" the man demanded. "What's wrong with you? Are you touched in the head?"

Connor blinked in confusion. "Touched by what?" he asked. "And why would the horses run over me? We haven't even been introduced."

The man shook his head. "That's what I thought, touched. What your name, young'un?"

"Connor, sir. Connor Endicott."

"Well, young Master Endicott, folks around here call me Captain Mack," the man said. "Any particular reason you were swimming around in the ocean with all your clothes on?"

"I, uh, fell in," Connor said uncertainly. "What are you a captain of?"

"My own destiny," Mack said jovially. "Come on before you get into any more trouble. My place is just over there. Let's get you out of those wet duds."

"Duds?"

Shaking his head, the captain said more slowly, "Clothes. We need to get you out of those wet clothes."

"Oh," Connor said, "thank you. That would be nice."

He fell in step behind Captain Mack who led him to a rundown cottage just above the dunes. Odd pieces of drift-wood littered the yard along with colorful glass bottles, fishing buoys, and tattered nets.

"Are you a fisherman?" Connor asked.

"Hmm?" the old man said, following Connor's gaze. "Oh. No. The guy who lived here before me had all this stuff. I just left it where it was. Come on in."

"But I'm wet," Connor protested.

"The bathroom is right inside the door," Mack said. "Have yourself a nice shower, and I'll find some clothes for you. Lean into the hot water handle. It sticks."

Not anxious to appear that he had no idea what his

host was talking about, Connor went into the tiny room and closed the door. A curtain on a rod covered the interior of what appeared to be an open tank. Experimentally twisting one of the silver handles on the wall, Connor was rewarded with a stream of cold water issuing from a spigot near the ceiling. When he twisted the second handle, the water warmed.

Ah! A system for bathing!

Stripping out of his soggy clothing, Connor stepped into the tank and drew the curtain around him. He picked up a bar of green soap sitting in a small recess and lathered his hair and body, rinsing away the salt, and warming himself in the process.

When he finished and drew back the curtain, Connor found a pair of pants and a shirt waiting for him, both made of a faded blue fabric he didn't recognize. The clothes were a little big, but they were soft, clean, and above all, dry.

In the main room, the old man stood in a makeshift kitchen heating something on a stove that leaned precariously to one side. As soon as Connor smelled the food, he realized he was starving.

"Well, hello there!" Mack said. "Thought you might like some of this leftover beef stew."

"Uh, thank you," Connor said, "but I don't eat meat."

"No worries, lots of nice vegetables in here. You're not squeamish about potatoes are you?"

"No, sir."

Mack ladled a steaming portion of stew into a bowl and set it in front of Connor with a plate of bright yellow squares. "Help yourself to the cornbread," he said.

"Bread made from corn?" Connor said. "I've never had that."

"You've never had cornbread?" Mack said. "Then you haven't lived. Here, let me show you. Take your knife and cut the piece like this, so you've got two layers, top, and bottom. Slap a bunch of this sweet butter on the bottom and put the two back together. Try some."

Connor carefully raised the buttered cornbread to his mouth and took a bite. "Oh my!" he said, as melted butter dribbled down his chin. "This is good! Can you teach me how to make this?"

"It's from a mix," Mack said.

"What's a mix?" Connor asked.

Leaning back in his chair, the captain said, "Son, where are you from anyways?"

Not wanting to lie, but realizing the absolute truth would be a bad idea, Connor said, "A valley a long way from here."

"Tell me again how you wound up in the ocean?"

"I was helping some friends, and I fell overboard. I got caught in the current before they could help me."

"Current's not that strong between here and the mainland," Mack observed mildly.

Hesitating, Connor said, "It wasn't a normal current."

"Did you get caught in the place where the ocean boils?" Mack asked. "I've seen it happen more than once these past weeks. Everybody around these parts thinks I'm seeing things, but I'm not. It happens."

The old man didn't seem to want to hurt him, and the portal did create turbulence on the water's surface. "Yes, sir," Connor said. "That's exactly what happened."

"Do you need to get back in the water when the ocean boils again?" Mack asked, watching him carefully.

"Yes, sir," Connor said, "I think I do. You won't tell anyone, will you?"

Mack chewed at his lip thoughtfully. "Oh, what the hell," he said, seeming to have come to a decision. "Everyone thinks I'm crazy, so they wouldn't believe me anyway. Who am I to tell you where you can and can't go? Have some more cornbread. We'll pass the time together until you get back in the ocean. You know anything about UFOs son? Because I've got me some theories on that subject."

❧

In his cavern, Chesterfield positioned the identical chained caskets upright between two of his book cases. Standing back to inspect his handiwork, the wizard admired the way the polished silver chains reflected the firelight. A faint sound from inside one of the boxes made him lean forward and listen.

Taking a silk handkerchief from his pocket, the wizard carefully polished the chains. "It will do you no good," he said softly as he buffed the metal to a high shine. "I warned you not to defy me and you did not listen. Scream all you like, there's nobody here but me to hear you and I do not care about your suffering. In fact, I rather relish it."

Behind him, a brass bell sitting on the desk, levitated a few inches and rang softly drawing Chesterfield's attention away from the caskets.

"Well," he said, crossing to the desk, "what do we have here?"

Addressing the bell, the wizard commanded, "Silence."

The ringing stopped, but the bell remained suspended in mid-air. Chesterfield reached into the top drawer of the desk and took out a thin, black ledger. He flipped through the pages until he found a single entry glowing red on the page. Tapping the words with his index finger, Chesterfield watched a holographic map rise off the page.

Over the past few weeks, he had made note of reported disturbances of "boiling water" in the Atlantic Ocean off the coast of North Carolina. The human news channels, which he monitored for useful information, made mention of the phenomenon, but so far no one had determined the cause.

Intrigued, Chesterfield placed several beacons up and down the coast, and one of them had just been triggered.

Making note of the time and coordinates, he left the desk—dismissing the bell to float back in place as an after-thought—and went to his workbench. This was a perfect opportunity to test his latest project in temporal chronography.

Sitting down on the high stool, the wizard ran his fingers lovingly over the French Art Deco case of a table clock still under construction. The block of green marble decorated with gold accents lent an air of elegance to the newly constructed interior. Carefully setting the instrument, the wizard activated the mechanism, and instantly, a second, larger hologram projected amid the reclining cherubs topping the timepiece.

At first Chesterfield thought he was looking at nothing but an expanse of open water lying between the coast and the barrier islands, but then he noticed a single dolphin swimming in the center of the image. Rotating another dial, the wizard magnified the scene until he could make out the figure of a young man holding fast to the sea creature. Something about the face seemed familiar. Then it struck him.

No!

Could he be that fortunate?

The swimmer was the Hamilton woman's long lost brother. Connor Endicott.

As Chesterfield watched, the dolphin led the castaway to the shore where he emerged from the surf only to be nearly trampled by a herd of wild horses. Fortuitously, a grizzled old man with a white beard and a nautical cap pulled the fool out of harm's way and led him away to a ramshackle beach cottage. There, the recording ended.

Examining the time codes, Chesterfield calculated the passage of approximately two and a half hours since the events in the hologram occurred. If the boiling water phenomenon stayed on the rough schedule he'd discerned from the reported sightings, it would be at least three hours before the next incident. Perfect. For a bargaining chip of this magnitude, the inconvenience of a field trip was more than in order.

Rummaging among the bottles on the table, Chesterfield selected one and slipped it in the pocket of his suit coat. Then, removing his pocket watch and consulting his notes, he set the coordinates. No sooner had he depressed the winding crown than Chesterfield found himself standing on the stretch of beach from the recording.

As he approached the ramshackle cottage, a voice called out, "Something I can do for you, mister?"

"Good afternoon," Chesterfield said, taking out a wallet and extracting a creamy business card. "I'm Dr. Elliott Mansfield of the Mansfield Mental Health Institute. One of my patients was spotted in the vicinity of your cottage. A young fellow. Rather dark hair, strong jaw. He would appear rather innocent and disoriented. His name is Connor Endicott."

The old man examined the card. "Guess I should have figured him for a nut case," he said. "The feller you're looking for is in there on my couch sound asleep. You want me to wake him?"

"Yes," Chesterfield said, "but only to serve him some sort of drink with three drops of this medicine mixed in."

He held out the bottle, now bearing a prescription label and dosing directions. "I assure you, this is nothing more than a mild sedative. It will not harm the lad in any way, only make him somewhat more compliant. I'm afraid he has something of a tendency to become agitated when he feels threatened. Post-traumatic stress disorder. I'm sure you understand."

"Yep," the man said. "I was in Vietnam. I've seen guys get 'agitated.' Wait out here. I'll take care of it, Doc."

TWENTY-SEVEN

Barnaby went with us to the portal at the edge of the woods east of the city. He wore a heavy woolen coat caped at the shoulders. Every wind gust made the fabric flare dramatically.

"You look like a character out of one of those Bronte sisters' novels we were talking about," I said as we trudged through deepening snow.

My literary joke made him laugh. "So long as you are not casting me as Heathcliff, I will take that as a compliment," he said. "We are here."

He stopped in front of two weathered, gray stones. There was no red arrow pointing "portal here," but I would have known we'd reached our destination even without Barnaby's announcement. The gateway's presence crawled over my skin like prickling ants.

"This isn't like the portal in the lower valley," I said. "It feels different."

Barnaby seemed pleased by my heightened awareness. "Your magical perception is growing more finely honed," he said, "and you are correct. This portal is much older. It was one of the first we forged when we came to this land."

"You make it sound like digging a mine shaft," I said.

"After a fashion, it was," Barnaby agreed. "The local Cherokee were aware of the Otherworld, but visited it only in visions. Moira and I 'dug' this entrance through the In Between with our magic. It was from this spot that I first saw the valley that has come to bear my name. When you emerge on the other side, in the human realm, you will not be far from Roanoke Island."

"You know, Grandad," I said, "people are still trying to figure out what happened to the 'lost' Roanoke Colony. There are films about it."

Even in the middle of the current crisis I saw the curiosity of the inveterate researcher come into his eyes. "Are there really?" he asked. "Perhaps you can show one to me. I quite like motion pictures. I think it would be amusing to learn the causes to which the humans have attributed our disappearance."

Lucas cleared his throat. "Uh, guys? Freezing my fedora off here. Can we get the portal open, please?"

Remembering himself, Barnaby said, "Yes, of course. My apologies." He turned toward the stones and began to recite the words of the opening spell. Slowly the air rippled like a calm pond when a stone skips over the surface. Then a shaft of sunlight broke through, and we could see what looked like a swamp on the other side.

"Ironweed tells me we may experience sporadic video reception due to the great distance," Barnaby said. "Once you are through the portal, you will be passed over to the Brown Mountain remote command. Two of their best pilots will assume operation of the drones. I can do nothing more now but wish you good fortune. Please send a report as soon as you can."

Impulsively, I hugged him. "Thank you, Granddad," I said. "I love you."

Barnaby returned my embrace. "And I love you," he said. Then looking toward Lucas, he added. "Take care of my granddaughter, Mr. Grayson."

There was just a hint of threat in the words, like a father

warning a teenage boy to get a girl home on time. Lucas heard it, too. "I will, Lord High Mayor," he said formally. "I will guard her with my life."

"Geez," I groaned, "could you two be bigger drama queens if you tried?"

I don't think Barnaby knew the exact meaning of the phrase "drama queen," but he picked up on the humor of the remark and laughed anyway. "Are we being unduly male?" he asked with a self-deprecating smile.

"Yes," I replied, "and unduly paternalistic, but in a kind of sweet way, so you're off the hook."

Lucas made a show of wiping non-existent sweat from his brow. "Whew!" he said. "We dodged a bullet on that one, Barnaby."

From the look on my grandfather's face, I could tell he wasn't used to people teasing him, but I think he liked it. He was smiling when I looked back just before the portal closed. It was a good image to take with me.

From our point of view, the temperature spiked 30 degrees in the human realm, but I still needed a coat against the dank autumn air. At least two dozen snapping turtles served as our welcoming committee, their knobby black heads sticking out of the layer of green slime covering the nearby water.

The GNATS drones took up position on either side of us, waiting for instructions. I swatted some kind of flying insect roughly the size of a golf ball, only to duck in astonishment when a small beam of purple light shot out of the nearest drone and vaporized the offending insect.

"What the heck was that?" I exclaimed.

Lucas took a small tablet out of the pocket of his duster and stared at the screen. "The pilot says it's a 'defensive systems modification currently undergoing field testing.'"

"Fine," I said, "just tell the pilot to make sure they aim for the bugs and not us."

Lucas tapped commands on the screen.

"He says to tell you 'duly noted, ma'am.'"

Groaning at the ridiculous level of military officiousness, I said, "So how are they planning to tackle the search?"

Reading from the tablet again, Lucas said, "The pilots are telling us to get comfortable and wait. They're dividing the search area into quadrants. They'll ping us if they see anything."

"'Ping' us?" I said. "What the heck is a 'ping?'"

The words were barely out of my mouth before I heard a tone that I swear should have been followed with the words, "Attention KMart Shoppers."

"I'm guessing *that* was a ping," Lucas said. As we watched, the drones broke off in opposite directions and disappeared from sight.

I looked around at the marshy patch of ground on which we were standing. "How are we supposed to get comfortable in a place like this?" I asked.

"Oh," Lucas grinned, "never fear, the DGI is here! I am in possession of cool toys. First order of business, shelter and camouflage."

He removed a small tube from his pocket and flicked a switch on the barrel. A mild electrical charge passed through me as a translucent dome formed around us.

"Personal force field," Lucas explained when I gave him a questioning look. "It has the dual effect of keeping the bugs and the elements out and ensuring that no one sees us. Now, how about a fire?"

I shook my head. "Won't work," I said. "Your force field doesn't have a chimney."

"Oh ye of little faith," he said. "The force field will filter and disperse the smoke. Nothing for any curious parties to see and no choking for us. Would you mind conjuring up a nice stack of wood?"

I decided not to tell him that my conjuring skills were still a work in progress. Surely I could manage a few simple logs. Reaching into my mind, I found the spark of my magic, allowing it to paint a detailed picture of a warm, crackling fire. Visualizing a space in the center of the clearing to receive the image, I said, "*Incendium*."

We got our fire alright, in a perfectly circular stone firepit complete with a grate, a steaming pot of coffee, and two cups.

"Show off," Lucas said.

I shrugged and grinned, acting like I did the whole thing on purpose.

Not. Even. Close.

Lucas Grayson had just witnessed a grand, albeit successful, accident. But any accident involving coffee is no mistake at all in my book.

Not to be outdone, Lucas took two small squares of canvas out of the bag at his waist and snapped them open. Now, we not only had a fire and coffee but two camp chairs.

"This swamp is starting to get pretty swank," I said. "Would you mind telling me how you managed to get all of this stuff in your pockets and bag?"

"The DGI is big into miniaturization," he said. "We believe in traveling light, but that's no excuse to compromise on the creature comforts."

I sat down gingerly in one of the chairs, half afraid it would collapse. Instead, it conformed perfectly to my body. A sudden wave of fatigue washed over me. I couldn't even remember the last time I'd slept. I didn't realize I'd closed my eyes, but when I opened them, Lucas had squatted down beside my chair and was holding out one of the cups.

"Take some time to unwind," he said. "I don't think you've taken a good breath since you heard your brother went through the Atlantic portal."

Accepting the cup, I said, "I don't think I have either. Think about it Lucas. When we dove down to the city, we must have gone right by where they were working."

Lucas pulled the other chair closer and filled the second cup for himself. "Don't think like that," he said. "There was no way you could have known Connor was there, much less stop what was about to happen. You're a witch, not a soothsayer."

"Do you know any of those?" I asked. "Soothsayers?"

"Yes," Lucas said, "and I do my best to stay away from them. We weren't meant to know the future, Jinx. That would take all the fun out of living."

That was when I really understood the difference between Chase and Lucas. One of them made room for fun in his life, not as an afterthought, but as an important part of being. Chase saw living as a much more serious business.

We couldn't do anything to help the GNATS drones and talking about Connor would only make me worry about him more. Lucas seemed to understand that, so for the next two hours, he regaled me with one story after another about exotic ports of call and hilarious DGI operations with Rube as his wingman.

When the ping did sound, I'd forgotten what it meant, so I jumped half out of my skin. Lucas reacted a little more efficiently. He activated the tablet, and moved to show me the screen.

The drones had something concrete for us alright, as in a ton of bricks falling right on top of my head.

As Lucas and I watched, the video showed Irenaeus Chesterfield leading my brother away from a dilapidated beach house. Connor walked slowly, dragging his feet through the soft sand as if he'd been drugged.

"We have to get to them," I said desperately. "We can't let Chesterfield get Connor."

But it was already too late.

The wizard took out his pocket watch, clicked the crown, and disappeared, taking Connor with him.

"Is there anything you haven't told us?" Kelly asked.

"No," Tori said. "That's everything Jinx told us. She and Lucas are going through a portal that will get them close to where Connor should have surfaced in the Atlantic."

Jeff leaned forward, resting his elbows on his knees. He stared down at the floor in Jinx's tiny kitchen and didn't look up when he said, "But you're sure he's alive?"

Beau drew his chair closer and replicated Jeff's posture. "There is no reason to believe that he is not," the Colonel said. "May I suggest that you hold fast to that?"

Still staring at the carpet under his feet, Jeff said, "We had to give him up once, Beau. Damn it, this is not fair."

"No, sir," Beau said, "it is not, but I know with all my soul that if your boy is out there, Jinx will find him."

Kelly scooted closer to her husband, resting her head against his shoulder. "He's right, honey," she whispered. "We owe both of our children our faith in them."

"So we just wait?" Jeff asked helplessly.

"I'm afraid so," Tori said. "Since Jinx and Lucas aren't here, Beau and I have to go to Anton Ionescu's funeral this afternoon with Chase and Festus. Jinx felt like she would know something by the time we get back."

"Kelly and I are coming with you," Jeff declared, clenching his fists into tight balls. "If Chesterfield or the Strigoi show up, I want a piece of them."

Tori winced. She hadn't been looking forward to this part of the conversation, which Jinx had predicted perfectly.

"I can't let you do that," she said. "Jinx specifically told me not to let you get anywhere near the funeral."

Before Jeff could protest, Darby materialized in the middle of the room.

"Damn it, Shorty!" Jeff snapped. "I told you to warn us before you just show up like that."

Looking a little startled by the vehemence of Jeff's reaction, the brownie said contritely, "I am sorry, Master Jeff. The red-headed vampire says you must come to the lair immediately."

❦

Connor awakened slowly, struggling to focus on his surroundings. After several foggy seconds, he realized he was lying on the floor staring up at sharp stalagmites hanging from a high, domed cavern roof. Around him, several imposing pieces of furniture created a makeshift "room."

Then he realized he wasn't alone. A tall man stared at him from the depths of a heavy, ornate chair that seemed oddly throne-like in its current setting.

Behind the man, standing upright between two bookcases, rested a pair of black caskets wrapped in shining silver chains. As Connor watched, one of the boxes vibrated as if whoever or whatever was inside was beating against the lid with clenched fists.

"Where am I?" Connor asked, sitting up and fighting back a sudden wave of vertigo. "Who are you? What did you give me?"

"My, my. Such a barrage of questions. You are in my temporary home, a cavern lying under the range near Brown Mountain. I am Irenaeus Chesterfield. You are suffering the mild after effects of a compliance potion. It ensured that you would come with me amiably rather than staging some kind of useless, enervating fight."

"What do you want?" Connor asked.

"And more questions," Chesterfield sighed. "How

tedious. For the present, I want nothing but to talk with you about your parents."

The statement appeared to confuse Connor even more. "They're dead," he said. "They died when I was just a baby. I don't know anything about them."

"I have no doubt about the veracity of the second half of your statement," Chesterfield said. "But your parents are not dead. Their names are Jeff and Kelly Hamilton. The witch, Jinx Hamilton, is your sister."

Connor pushed himself upright. "Wh . . wh . . . what are you talking about?" he stammered.

"Let me indulge you in a little family history lesson," Chesterfield purred. "Your parents abandoned you in Shevington. You have no magic, you see, so you were quite useless to them. They gave you to Endora Endicott to raise while they tried again to have a normal baby."

"That's not true," Connor said hotly. "Nobody would mistreat a baby just because the child had no magic."

Chesterfield's eyes darkened ominously. "I assure you, that is far, far from the truth. You and I suffer from the same birth defect. I, however, found a way to awaken my magic, and with my help, you will do the same. Together, we will exact revenge from those who have wronged us."

"I'm not going to help you do anything," Connor said resolutely. "I may not have magic, but I know evil when I see it. I won't help you."

Casually, Chesterfield motioned as if to reach forward. When he did, Connor's hands went to his throat as his face contorted in pain.

"Air is rather a valuable commodity taken for granted until it is no longer in abundance," Chesterfield observed mildly. "You think you will not help me now, but you will, once you realize that in your current state you are nothing but a helpless, defenseless mortal."

As Connor struggled to speak, Chesterfield rose and

walked toward him. "I'm sorry," he said, "are you trying to tell me something? Perhaps that you long to fill your lungs with fresh, life-sustaining oxygen? Very well. Breathe."

Collapsing on his hands and knees, Connor gasped raggedly.

"Think over my proposal carefully," Chesterfield said. "I must attend a funeral now. When I return, I will ask you again. If your answer is not to my liking, I will arrange a second persuasive experience for your consideration."

Still fighting not to pass out, Connor didn't look up until a different voice said, "Psst! Psst! You there. On the floor. He's gone. Come over here to the chessboard."

Greer held a cream-colored envelope out to Tori. The red sealing wax was broken, but when reunited, the two sides revealed an ornate family crest. "What is it?" Tori asked.

"Chesterfield's signet," she said. "Take a look at what's inside."

Dreading what she would find, Tori took out a single photograph. It showed Connor Endicott on his hands and knees between two caskets wrapped in silver chains. He appeared to be choking. Silently, Tori passed the picture to Kelly, who in turn handed it to Jeff.

"What does it mean?" Kelly asked, her voice breaking. "What's wrong with him?"

Although Greer's eyes conveyed the sympathy she felt for Kelly, she stayed focused. "Look at what's written on the back," she said.

Flipping the print over, Jeff read, "I will be in touch."

"How in the hell did Irenaeus Chesterfield get my boy?" Jeff demanded. "And what are we going to do to get him back?"

From the full-length mirror to his left, Jinx's voice said, "We have to find him first, Dad."

Twenty-Eight

We had no way to follow Chesterfield. Going back to Shevington seemed like our best and only option. When we came through the portal, I was relieved to discover that the wind had at least died down. Since my grandfather saw everything we saw over the drone feed, a horse-drawn sleigh waited to take us to my grandfather's house.

When I came through the front door, I didn't even bother with a greeting. "Tell me you have a way we can find him," I said.

From the look of uncomfortable indecision on his face, I knew Barnaby did have a possible solution, but it wasn't one he liked.

"Come sit by the fire," he said. "There is something I need to tell you."

I'm going to try to spare you all the complications and just focus on the vitals. You should already understand that the Daughters of Knasgowa are a matrilineal magical line. Knasgowa's second husband was a Scotsman named Alexander Skea, but that was his adopted name only.

Alexander's great-grandparents were the Creavit sorceress Brenna Sinclair and a castaway named Hamish Crawford. When the hapless man came to understand the true nature of the woman who carried his child, he colluded with a local Druid to imprison her in a cave after

251

the birth of the baby. The Druid, who was a Skea, took the child to raise as his own.

For three generations, the sons of the Crawford line were raised alongside their adopted brothers. A few years after Alexander came to the United States in 1786, his "brother" Duncan Skea the Younger followed him.

When Duncan arrived in the New World, Alexander insisted they have no association with one another because Brenna wanted to use Alexander to help her found her own magical line and she had a habit of killing the the real Skeas when they got in her way.

Duncan refused to leave the area, however, arguing that since the two men had no real blood relation and didn't resemble one another, Brenna would not come after him. He took a Lowland Scot name—Hamilton.

Yep, that's right. My truck-driving, dedicated fisherman father was descended from a pack of Druids on the Orkney Islands. The Hamiltons remained around Briar Hollow, but with each generation, grew farther and farther from their Druidic roots, with one exception. All of them worked with wood or had an affinity for animals.

Eight generations down the line, Jeff Hamilton married Kelly Ryan, uniting the Daughters of Knasgowas with the patrilineal magic of the Skea Druids, which meant my dad and my brother probably possessed untapped magical abilities.

"There is a significant risk involved," Barnaby said, "but if you were to work blood magic with your father, I believe you could awaken Connor's powers."

Stunned by what I was hearing, I said, "And what good would that do? Connor wouldn't have any idea what was happening or how to use his magic to get away from Chesterfield."

"That is true," Barnaby agreed. "But once his magic has been awakened, you can use Myrtle's tsavorite amulet to scry for his presence."

"You've lost me," I said. "I can't keep up with all this magical jewelry."

"It would be a long, translucent green stone hanging from a silver chain," he said. "The stone is a means for communicating with the spirit realms and has a deep affinity for blood."

Oh. That thing. Myrtle used it to test Tori's loyalty to me since Tori and Gemma are, technically, Brenna's descendants as well through the child Alexander Skea fathered by Knasgowa.

Now I understood Barnaby's plan. "Okay," I said, "let's do it."

"This will mean breaking the news to your father that he may have magic," Barnaby said. "How will he take that revelation?"

"Honestly?" I said. "I think he'll be relieved. He doesn't like it when he can't keep up with us."

While we'd been talking, Lucas had been poring over Barnaby's map of the portal system figuring out a route to get us back to Briar Hollow. He kept up a low running conversation with himself as he worked that sounded like a round of play from that old TV game show *Name That Tune.*

I kept hearing things like "that would take seven jumps" or "we can do it this way in five." Finally, he slapped his knee triumphantly and declared, "I can get us there in three jumps."

It took all my self-control not to shoot back, "I can do it in two." Both men would have taken me seriously, and the explanation would just have taken too long.

So, as absurd as this is going to sound, that is how I returned to Briar Hollow via Two Egg, Florida, with a layover in Dime Box, Texas before taking the portal to Nowata, Oklahoma, which allowed us to pop into the woods outside Briar Hollow where Tori picked us up in my cherry red Prius.

We filled her in on the way to the shop. All things considered, Dad took the news pretty well until I produced a dagger and asked him to roll up his sleeve.

"What for?" he asked suspiciously.

Tori piped in cheerfully. "Don't worry, Jeff," she said. "I've done this with Jinksy before. You won't have to actually open a vein."

"Good to know," Dad said, starting to unbutton his right shirt cuff.

"Has to be the left," I said, stopping him. "That's a more direct line to the heart."

Dad switched sleeves and sat in one of the chairs. I asked him to sit one of the corners of the work table in the lair. I positioned myself so we would be able to co-mingle our blood over the map Beau had spread out.

Tori held the tsavorite amulet, which had already begun to pulsate quietly.

"Why is it doing that?" I asked.

"There's a lot of power in this room," Greer said. "The stone senses all of you. The pulsations bode well for the success of this effort."

Meeting Dad's eyes, I said, "You ready?"

He nodded and never looked away as I made a long cut across his forearm, repeating the same cut on my own skin.

"Take my hand," I said, "like we were going to arm wrestle."

My hand disappeared into my father's, and instantly his flowing blood stood away from the skin, snaking across the space between us to mingle with mine.

As Barnaby instructed, I whispered, "*Quaerere*."
Search.

The bloody tendril moved toward the tsavorite in Tori's hand. She allowed the chain to uncoil until the stone hung over the map. Mom laid her fingers over the back of Tori's, and then Gemma joined them. As we watched, the blood wrapped itself around their joined hands, and the silver chain began to sway.

"Are we supposed to do anything other than sit here and bleed?" Dad whispered.

I shook my head, and he fell silent again as the chain's arc extended before coming to an abrupt halt. It quivered, suspended at a 90-degree angle, before plunging toward the map with such force the tip of the stone impaled itself at a location in the mountains of the Pisgah National Forest.

It would sound cool if I told you that Chase took out some kind of magical navigational thingy and figured out the coordinates, but truthfully? He used Google Maps and dispatched every drone at our disposal to search the area.

"Tell me again what they're using?" I asked, as Moira quietly healed first my cut and then Dad's with a wave of her hand and a few whispered words.

"Do you know what ground penetrating radar is?" Chase asked.

"Kind of," I said. "Isn't that what the police use to hunt for buried bodies."

"Yes," he said, "but not just bodies. Anything under the surface. The drones are using the magical equivalent. They're searching for Fae power signatures where there shouldn't be any."

Half an hour later, we had a hit. I'll give the drone pilots credit. They don't give up. As we watched, the lead drone began to look for a way into what seemed to be an impenetrable rock face. He tried cracks and crevices, following wind currents, scanning with minuscule searchlights, probing deeper, backing out of tight places. An eternity had passed before we were looking into the very chamber pictured in the photo of my brother.

Amid the static and interference, we could barely make out Connor, sitting with the musical chessboard.

"I knew we should have smashed that damned thing," Tori muttered. "He looks like he's talking to it."

"Have the pilots found any way for us to get in there to him?"

Chase shook his head. "None," he said. "Ironweed and his team at the command center have been studying the scans. The cavern is completely sealed off from the outside world. We're looking in through a crack that's no more than a millimeter in width."

Just then the video cut out altogether.

"What happened?" I asked.

"The drone smashed into the rock," Chase said. "The pilot says there just isn't enough room to navigate in there. They'll try to come up with a fix, but it won't be fast."

"Okay," I said, "so that's it. At least we know Connor is alive. Chesterfield said he'd be in touch. Now we wait to see what he wants."

⸺◦◦◦⸺

Connor looked down at the face of the alchemist trapped in the White King. "If we try this," he said, "and fail, Chesterfield will kill us."

"I fear he will kill us anyway," Gareth answered. "All of the ingredients we need are on his workbench. Carry me there, and I will tell you how to mix the Bilocation Potion."

"First," Connor said. "I want to hear again how this is supposed to work."

"You will drink the potion and dip me in the remainder of the liquid," Gareth explained. "So long as you do not let me go, we will not be separated. For a few hours, it will appear that we are still here in the cavern, but I will use the same spell that put me here in the White King to transport us into Chesterfield's fountain pen.

Connor chewed at his lip thoughtfully. "Because he always takes the pen with him?" he asked.

"Correct," Gareth said. "The pen is covered in a decorative lattice of copper. The metal will prevent Chesterfield from detecting our hiding place. When he carries us into the outside world, we will escape at the first opportunity that presents itself."

"How are we going to do that?"

"You will combine your powers with my own to eject us from the pen," Gareth replied.

"That's where your plan falls apart," Connor said bitterly. "Didn't you hear what Chesterfield said? I don't have magic. I'm not normal."

Smiling up through the wood grain Gareth said, "Do not be so sure, Connor. The Creavit wizard has badly misjudged you. Every night before he retires for the evening, Chesterfield writes in his notebook. He leaves the pen lying beside the book on the table. Mix the potion now, and tonight we will enter the pen. If Chesterfield hears anything, he will see our doppelgangers. It will be morning before he realizes we are gone, and by then, like the Greeks, we will be safely within our Trojan horse."

TWENTY-NINE

Would it be incredibly disrespectful of me to say Anton's funeral was kind of a letdown? The Strigoi Sisters didn't show up and so far as we knew at the time, neither did Chesterfield. At the end of the service, as we filed past the grieving Ionescus, Cezar leaned toward me and whispered, "It will be done before the sun sets."

When we returned to the shop, however, Mom met us in the back alley with the news that a second message had arrived from Chesterfield. In exchange for my brother's safe return, he wanted a living branch of the Mother Oak.

"Where the *heck* did that come from?" Tori asked.

No one—Barnaby and Moira included—could answer her, but all agreed on one thing. If Chesterfield could threaten the integrity of the grid with amber amulets, what could he do with living sap? Even in the absence of a concrete answer, it seemed clear Chesterfield was upping his game.

However, we had no intention of just slicing off a limb from the sacred tree and handing it over to a traitorous wizard. We agreed to table the 'why" for now and jump to the "how"—as in how could we use this new demand to our favor?

If we weren't going to pay the "ransom," we had to at

258

least make it look like we were in compliance. Moira returned to the Valley immediately to work on a solution.

Thanks to a concerted effort, the drifts in the lower valley had been cleared, and the road to Shevington was open again as well. The weather no longer stood in the way of our movements, which in itself was a blessing.

The elegantly penned note from Chesterfield ended with, "Tell Barnaby we will meet in Adeline's garden. I so look forward to seeing it again."

Speaking from the polished silver surface of the mirror in the lair, Barnaby explained the reference. "He is talking about my old home in Kent in the south of England. He has picked that location to taunt me."

"He's taunting all of us," Festus grumbled. "That's what the Creavit do."

"Agreed," Barnaby said. "Moira and I will be ready when the rest of you arrive."

After he broke the connection, the rest of us dissolved into a bickering argument about who would go to England and who would stay in Briar Hollow and wait.

Both of my parents wanted in on the rescue mission, which was absolutely out of the question. Dad's magic had started to awaken and let's just say he was being a "erratic." So far, he'd blown out every light bulb in the lair twice, inadvertently put Rodney in a clown suit, and levitated Beau's rolltop desk six inches in the air.

Thankfully, Mom agreed with me. "You're a loose cannon, Jeff," she said, before rushing to add, "and don't think about cannons, or anything else gun related. Think about something harmless, like M&Ms."

No sooner had she said the words than a 5 lb. sack of M&Ms appeared in the center of the coffee table.

Reaching for the bag, Tori said, "Good thinking, Jeff. Keep at it."

We also nixed any idea of Beau coming along since we

couldn't risk Chesterfield getting possession of the Amulet of the Phoenix. Festus pulled rank on Chase.

"I've got old business with that Creavit scum," Festus said as a wave of glittering energy passed over his form leaving a massive mountain lion, graying at the muzzle, reclining on our hearth. "Don't even think about telling me I can't go, which means you have to stay here and guard Kelly. No arguments."

Chase wisely chose not to offer any.

In the end, we decided our group would include me, Lucas, Greer, Barnaby, and Moira. Gemma didn't want to leave Mom, and Tori didn't want to leave Gemma, so that settled that.

Greer flew us all to the portal, and then from the portal into Shevington proper. At Barnaby's house, Moira showed us a highly believable facsimile of a branch of the Mother Oak. The counterfeit even emanated a degree of power that felt like the great tree herself.

"When we emerge in Kent," Barnaby said. "We won't have long. Irenaeus may be fooled by this ruse at a distance, but once he touches the fake branch, he will know it does not come from the body of the Mother Oak."

"Don't you worry about the Creavit," Festus said. "I took him down once, and I can do it again. Just get the kid clear and leave the wizard to me."

Greer spoke up. "Lucas and I will remove Connor out of the line of fire. I will use the flight of the baobhan sith to carry him to safety."

Barnaby nodded, "An excellent plan. That leaves me, Moira, and Jinx to bind Irenaeus."

It *was* a good plan—or it should have been.

We made a series of portal jumps that brought us out in the fallen ruin of an ancient home. The portal opened in the remains of an enclosed garden filled with rose bushes.

Chesterfield was waiting for us, holding the end of a rope tethered to a hooded figure. "Hello Barnaby," he said pleasantly. "Pity how Adeline's garden has gone to ruin."

"Do not speak her name," Barnaby said coldly. "It was you, wasn't it, brother? You killed my wife."

The Creavit's laughter floated across the distance between us. "Has it truly taken you all these centuries to come to that conclusion?" Chesterfield asked. "I thought I was supposed to be the magically defective in the family."

"For as much as I might relish trading insults with you," Barnaby said, "we are here for the boy. Hand him over."

Chesterfield made a clucking sound. "Tsk, tsk," he said. "Mother would not appreciate the disintegration of your manners, but very well. I will send the boy forward, and you will instruct the witch to do the same with the ransom I have requested. She will place the branch on the ground and back away with her brother. If any of you so much as moves, I will kill them both."

It was a classic hostage exchange. One that created no advantages for us, but it was all we had. I took the oak branch from Moira and started walking. Chesterfield gave the hooded figure a shove, and he moved as well. When we came even with one another, I said, "It's okay, Connor. I'm your sister, Jinx Hamilton. You're safe with us. I'm going to take hold of you and lead you the rest of the way. Don't be afraid."

The only response was a frightened whimper that almost broke my heart. We began the slow walk back to Barnaby and Moira. I kept my eyes on my grandfather. When we were within ten feet of reaching his position, he yelled, "Now!"

I pushed Connor to the ground and shielded him with my body, which is why I saw little of what happened next.

Twin streams of energy from Moira and Barnaby's out-stretched hands shot over us, and Festus charged past me, covering the ground in bounding, three-legged leaps.

They were all fast, but Chesterfield was faster, leaving the old werecat to close his claws around open air. Although his physical form was gone, Chesterfield's fading voice lingered. "You will live to regret this day."

I rolled away and hastily removed the hood only to find that the boy I had shielded was not my brother at all. He was just a confused, frightened human with wide, terrified eyes. He knew nothing about Chesterfield or Connor and after Moira had mumbled the kind words of a Forgetfulness Incantation, the events of the last few minutes disappeared from his mind as well.

We had gambled with Connor's life and lost. I had no idea if my brother was alive or dead, and I dreaded returning to Briar Hollow to give my parents that news, but I had no choice.

Irenaeus Chesterfield checked into a small, private hotel in Raleigh under an assumed name. He still burned with irritation. First, that idiot alchemist in the White King facilitated some type of escape for himself and the Endicott boy, and then Barnaby Shevington had the gall to attempt an ambush.

If his meeting with the good Mr. Smythe went well, Chesterfield would soon be in possession of the Amulet of Carorunn and all the insufferable fools would pay for their perfidy. Preoccupied with his thoughts of revenge, Chesterfield forgot to return his fountain pen to its habitual spot in the breast pocket of his coat when he changed clothes for dinner.

He remembered when he reached the lobby, but there was no time to return to his room. The business he planned to transact with Smythe would not involve the signing of contracts or the issuing of receipts. Confident that he had no need of the writing instrument, he stepped into the crisp evening air and strode down the sidewalk.

Back in his room, the pen on the desk began to vibrate slightly. The intricate spiderweb of copper glowed briefly, and then Connor Endicott found himself standing in a bedroom with a short, graying man in something like a monk's habit at his side.

"We did it!" Gareth cried. "We're free."

"No," Connor said, "we're not. We're just out of the pen. Chesterfield will be back. Come on."

Cautiously opening the door, Connor surveyed the empty hallway. When he felt certain they would not be seen, he slipped out, with Gareth following behind. At a doorway marked "Stairs," they nodded to one another and started down, ducking through the lobby and out into the street.

"Now what?" Gareth asked. "I have not been in the human realm in more than 200 years, and you have never been here."

Scanning the signs up and down the street, one stood out for Connor.

"Look!" he said. "The shop of a soothsayer. Miss Shania Moonbeam's Divinatory Emporium. We must consult her for the best course of action."

"Do you have coin to pay her?" Gareth asked as they began walking again.

"No," Connor said, "but perhaps she will take pity on us."

⸙

"Is this Mr. Chase McGregor?"

"It is," Chase said. "Who's calling, please?"

"Miss Shania Moonbeam, Glory's friend. We talked in

Raleigh a few days ago. You left me your card. You remember?"

"I do, Miss Shania," Chase said, purposefully using her name so the others in the lair would know the identity of the caller. "What can I do for you?"

In her Divinatory Emporium, Miss Shania turned partially away from her visitors and lowered her voice. "You remember how you told me to call you if anyone came in here talking about Mr. Chesterfield?"

"Yes," Chase said. "Is someone asking about Chesterfield?"

At the wizard's name, Jinx and Tori both sat up, and Jeff took his eyes away from the fire for the first time in hours. Gemma put her hand over Kelly's. Chase quietly switched the phone on speaker.

"Two someones," Miss Shania said. "Odd ducks. One of them is dressed like some kind of monk, and the other one looks like an escapee from a Renaissance faire. Says his name is Connor something or other. They claim Mr. Chesterfield was holding them prisoner. Just between you and me, I don't think either one of them is right in the head."

At the sound of Connor's name, Kelly gasped, her eyes instantly filling with tears. Jeff reached for her free hand.

"Thank you, Miss Shania," Chase said. "We know both of them, and you're right, they are a little simple so don't pay attention to anything they say. Can you keep them entertained? I'm not far away. A friend and I can get to you in an hour or so."

"Oh, sure," Miss Shania said cheerfully. "I just took a bunch of cookies out of the oven. Both of them are sniffing the air like hungry hound dogs. I can keep them busy for you, Mr. McGregor."

Chase thanked her and broke the connection.

With tears now streaming down her face, Kelly turned to her daughter. "Norma Jean?"

"Yes, ma'am?" Jinx said

"Please go bring your brother home."

EPILOGUE

Introducing my brother to our parents was one of the most incredible moments of my life—well, that and the way Connor looked at me shyly in Miss Shania's shop and said, "I have a sister? I always wanted a sister."

We all cried oceans of happy tears, and we haven't stopped talking in days. Connor is everything I thought he would be and more—a sweet combination of both of our parents. When our mother asked his forgiveness for giving him away, he asked, with perfect innocence, "Why would I forgive you for saving my life? I'm just sorry about how you and my father have suffered."

Every time Connor says "Father" dad's chest swells a size larger. I suppose I should be jealous, but I'm not. More and more it feels like the four of us have never been apart, and we're all anticipating spending the holidays together.

Of course, there was a lot of other leftover business to get settled, starting with Gemma's divorce. She and Mom took care of putting a spell on Scrap by themselves.

Gemma said she didn't feel right asking Tori to work magic on her own father. I think she was secretly afraid Tori might get a little carried away. My bestie isn't very happy with her dad, and may not be for a long time.

As for Scrap, he's the soul of cooperation, and Gemma has already signed a contract on the old hardware store.

The news about my folks moving over to Briar Hollow and Gemma coming along came as a surprise, but a welcome one. If I have my way, my family will never be separated again.

After Connor and Gareth told us the whole story about their escape, the GNATS drones went back into the cavern with improved navigational software. The pilot couldn't get any closer, but he didn't crash, and he was able to see that Chesterfield cleaned the place out with one exception. The chained caskets.

Awful as they are, none of us like to think about Seraphina and Ioana chained up for eternity, but we have no way to reach them and put them out of their misery.

When I finally got around to asking Tori and Beau about the baseball ghosts, I could not believe their response.

"Hold on, hold on, hold *ON!*" I said. "Was I not clear? I asked you two to make this baseball thing go *away*, and now you're helping organize something called the Dead Majors?"

Tori already had her counter argument formulated. "Jinksy," she said, "things have a tendency to get pretty serious around here. The baseball thing will be fun. You remember something called 'fun,' right?"

"This is November!" I protested. "Baseball is a *spring* sport."

Yeah, I know. It wasn't much of a retort, but I was running on empty, and Tori knew it.

"It never snows around here," she said reasonably, "and all the players are dead, so you know, not really caring much about the cold? And then there's the contingency clause."

"What contingency clause?" I asked suspiciously.

"We've made it very clear that Briar Hollow has been rebranded as a paranormal location and all apparitions will be strictly regulated," she said.

My eyebrows went up. "We have regulations?" I asked.

"We will," she said, waving her hand dismissively. "That's beside the point for right now. The big thing is that this is a 'pay to play' scheme. We let the ghosts organize the league, and in exchange, they're our eyes and ears around Briar Hollow or anywhere else we need them to go. Think about it, Jinksy, we have our own spectral secret service!"

As much as I might have liked to shoot that one down, the idea had merit—a lot of merit. If we were going to be spending our time amulet hunting—which would seem to be the agenda for the new year—more metaphysical boots on the ground sounded pretty good.

In the end, they won me over. For one thing, we could pass Mindy, Nick, and Kyle, our intrepid ghost hunters, over to the ghosts themselves for management. Tori and I have already agreed we'd keep Mindy through the holidays and then let her go. Having a non-magical person on the premises cramps our style too much for anyone's tastes.

But for right now? We are declaring Briar Hollow a crisis-free zone. Unfortunately, we've already agreed to spend Thanksgiving at Uncle Raymond's with the extended family. Since everyone thinks Connor died in infancy, we can't take him along. We'll have a second dinner in the lair later in the day, but Christmas?

We're all going to be together in Shevington. Our first Christmas in the Valley. I can't wait.

ABOUT THE AUTHOR

Juliette Harper is the pen name used by the writing team of Patricia Pauletti and Rana K. Williamson. As a writer, Juliette's goal is to create strong female characters facing interesting, challenging, painful, and at times comical situations. Refusing to be bound by genre, her primary interest lies in telling good stories.

Six of Juliette's series are currently available. *The Jinx Hamilton Mysteries* opens with *Witch at Heart*, a lighter paranormal tale featuring a heroine who possesses powers she never dreamed existed. Jinx has been minding her own business working as a waitress at Tom's Cafe and keeping up with her four cats. Then she inherits her Aunt Fiona's store in neighboring Briar Hollow, North Carolina *and* learns that her aunt has willed her special "powers" to Jinx as well. They say admitting you have a problem is the first step and Jinx has a major problem. She's a new witch and she has no earthly clue what that means—until she's given the opportunity to use her magic to do a good thing.

In Book 2, *Witch at Odds*, Jinx accepts her new life as a witch and is determined to make a success of both that and her new business. However, she has a great deal to learn. As the story unfolds, Jinx sets out to both study her craft and to get a real direction for her aunt's haphazard approach to inventory. Although Jinx can call on Aunt

Fiona's ghost for help, the old lady is far too busy living a jet set afterlife to be worried about her niece's learning curve. That sets Jinx up to make a major mistake and to figure out how to set things right again.

By Book 3, *Witch at Last*, A lot has changed for Jinx in just a few months. After the mishaps that befell her in *Witch At Odds*, she just wants to enjoy the rest of the summer, but she's not going to be that lucky. As she's poised to tell her friends she's a witch, secrets start popping out all over the place. Between old foes and new locations, Jinx isn't going to get her peaceful summer, but she may just get an entirely different world.

Book 4, *Witch on First*, has Jinx walk out the front door of her store in Briar Hollow on a Sunday morning only to find her werecat neighbor and boyfriend, Chase McGregor, staring at a dead man. Under the best of circumstances, a corpse complicates things, but Jinx has other problems. Is her trusted mentor lying to her? Have dangerous magical artifacts been placed inside the shop? Join Jinx and Tori as they race to catch a killer and find out what's going on literally under their noses.

Book 5, *Witch on Second*, opens just a week before Halloween. Jinx and Tori have their hands full helping to organize Briar Hollow's first ever paranormal festival. Beau and the ghosts at the cemetery are eager to help make the event a success, but tensions remain high after the recent killings. Without a mentor to lean on, Jinx must become a stronger, more independent leader. Is she up to the task in the face of ongoing threats? Still mourning the loss of Myrtle and her breakup with Chase, Jinx finds herself confronting new and unexpected foes.

Six volumes of the best-selling *Lockwood Legacy* are currently available. The story chronicles the lives of three sisters who inherit a ranch in Central Texas following their father's suicide. The titles include: *Langston's Daughters*,

Baxter's Draw, *Alice's Portrait*, *Mandy's Father*, *Irene's Gift*, and *Jenny's Choice*. The seventh, *Kate's Journey*, will appear in 2017.

Descendants of the Rose is the first installment of the Selby Jensen Paranormal Mysteries. The second book, *Lost in Room 636*, will also be available in 2017. Selby's business card reads "Private Investigator," but to say the least, that downplays her real occupation where business as usual is anything but normal.

And don't miss the hilariously funny "cozy" *Study Club Mysteries*, a light-hearted spin off of *The Lockwood Legacy*. Set in the 1960s, this series takes on the often-absurd eccentricities of small town life with good-natured, droll humor. The first book, *You Can't Get Blood Out of Shag Carpet*, is already listed in the Amazon store with *You Can't Put a Corpse in a Parade* will be coming in 2017.

Juliette has also made forays into the arena of short fiction arena with *Before Marriage*, a light, sweet romance and Langston's Ghost, a short-story companion to *The Lockwood Legacy* books.

Fermata: The Winter is the first in a four-novella post-apocalyptic survival series. Five years after an unknown virus divided the world into the living and the dead, four survivors stumble into a winter sanctuary. Brought together by circumstance, but bound by the will to stay alive, a concert pianist and a girl from South Boston forge a friendship and a purpose to cope with their new reality.

*Want to know more about
author Juliette Harper?*

*Visit Juliette Harper's home on the web at
http://www.julietteharper.com*

66116621R00169

Made in the USA
Lexington, KY
04 August 2017